Wildest

A Demon Hunter Romance #2

Carrie Thorne

Published by Thorny Books

Carrie Thorne

https://carriethorne.com/

Also by Carrie Thorne

A Demon Hunter Romance

Six

Wildest

Changed

Echo

Fury (TBD)

Foothills

All the Days After

The Next Day

A Day Late

A New Day

About Yesterday

280 Days (2025)

Day Dreaming (2026)

Again Tomorrow (TBD)

Days of Summer (TBD)

A Beachside Romance Series

Chasing Forever

Running Home

Hiding Away

Standalones

The Christmas Bet: A Double Feature Christmas Standalone.

Enjoy free books, first looks,

review team access,

and occasional hellos from Carrie?

Let's do this: carriethorne.com/newsletter

For my daughter. Too young to read it herself, but a diehard werewolf fan and budding little author herself.

1

Thanks to their distinctive odor of sweaty socks, sporting patchy fur like bedraggled gorillas, and attired in disintegrating scraps of grimy fabric, hand-to-hand combat with werewolves was nauseating.

How had she been suckered into leading the recon? No doubt her team's idea of a hilarious joke at her expense. And not only was her contact officially late, but now she had work to do.

Astrid Edmonds endeavored to banish the stench from her nares with short, sharp exhales, but her lungs burned from the fruitless effort Stalking down the alley, she ducked behind a dumpster that smelled nearly as rotten as the monsters atop the building.

If the god-awful stench weren't enough to convince her, eerie howls from above crushed any hope that the lead had been a case of mistaken identity. It could have been some other hairy monster ravaging Montana. Humans loved werewolf tales, and she and her team had been sent on enough wild goose chases. Werewolves were generally uncommon, solitary bullies, which was why she had hoped this was another hoax.

In the shadows of downtown Kalispell, Astrid took one last look to ensure she was alone. Matched short-swords strapped to her thighs, she jumped atop the dumpster and leaped to the second-floor windowsill. She pulled herself higher and ensured the room was empty, then climbed onto the concrete ledge. Fingertips wedged into the bricks above, she scaled the weathered building.

Another howl. And another. Damn full moons. Werewolves didn't care if it was day or night, cloudy or clear, to wreak havoc. Yet on a full moon, they were particularly excitable.

According to their contact—the one who was now seven minutes late—there was a pack encamped in the mountains consisting of thirty werewolves, maybe more. Their bloody trail stained the earth from Calgary to Salt Lake City. Tales of peculiar howls in the night were multiplying. In all of her research, she had found no evidence of werewolves behaving this way.

Bound to her inherited role of demon hunter, she fought vampires, regularly, in fact. Sirens. Sphinxes. Creatures that had no names. Hell, a few weeks ago, she and her team had taken out the sister of the demon king. That had been intense.

Yet werewolves freaked her out. They were like a human had mated with a wolf and got high on meth and steroids, but there was no coming down from the belligerent trip. Unlike the myth, werewolves didn't shift between human and monster, and were never more than the gnarly humanoid brutes. Of all the legends that the passage of time and oral tradition had muddled, werewolf history didn't make any sense.

Fingernails frayed from the chipped mortar, Astrid drew closer to the roof. Three points of contact at all times, grip steady. Peeking over the ledge, she discovered a trio of the monsters in question chewing on the mangled remains of a human.

Shirts in shreds over their torsos, pants stretched tight over their burly legs, shoes absent—presumably lost in the change from human form. Somewhere between wolf and man and beast, down to the elongated furry face, clawed fingers, and humanoid shape, they emanated restless aggression.

Withholding the bile that rose in her esophagus at the grotesque sight of the human remains, Astrid accepted that she would be no help to the poor soul they feasted on. But she could prevent these creeps from dining on anyone else tonight.

With a growl, she hurled herself over the side and drew her swords. Perfectly well balanced, the matched pair cut smoothly through the air.

Dinner interrupted, blood dripping from their jaws, the trio drew back their lips and rose to their feet, their feral snarls rattling the night. The nearest two hurtled toward her while the other waited, watching.

A patient werewolf? That was odd.

Patiently waiting herself, she held back. Just out of reach, she dove into a slide tackle between the snarling duo. Swords swinging as extensions of her long arms, she sliced into the hamstrings of the nearest two.

As soon as her swords were occupied and her position seemingly compromised, the third pounced toward her. Ratcheting her body from the ground, she swerved and spun from his reach as he neared.

Fuming at her wily dodge, he started back for her. Raising an eyebrow at him, she taunted him to try again.

He didn't get the chance.

From the darkness, a gray wolf dove into the fray.

A natural, normal, genuine wolf of the animal kingdom?

Teeth sinking into the monster, the wolf tore a gash in its side, expelling the flesh with a disgusted spit, before going in for another strike. Pure power in its haunches, the wolf was unstoppable.

Shaking off the surprise of seeing a wild animal join the fight, Astrid returned her attention to the two that were recovering from her blades. Beckoning one closer, she cricked her finger.

Foolish as she'd hoped, it pounced at her.

Spinning out of its range, she drove her swords into its abdomen.

The other dove into the fray.

Fuck. Did they...?

No, werewolves don't set traps. They don't strategize. These were not ordinary werewolves.

She wrenched her swords from the first and tried to spin before the other got behind her.

Too late.

Clawed fingers wrapped around her waist and pulled her close, its teeth aimed straight for her neck. She whipped her head back and knocked into its wet nose. A histrionic whine echoed across the rooftops as it released her.

Snarling, a mucousy mix of drool and blood dripped from its canines. Slashing wildly, it swung at her with its grimy claws.

The gray wolf dove at it. Its gleaming white teeth gnashed, and it tore into the creature's neck. The werewolf crumpled to the ground, landing atop its dead friend in a gruesome heap.

The wolf sniffed the area, confirming the fight was over. As the life drained from the three werewolves, the full moon illuminated the gory scene.

Unable to pull her attention from the striking wolf—a creature as ordinary as the clever, teamed-up werewolves they'd just killed were extraordinary—Astrid didn't attack, despite her raging instincts to go after it as well. Demon hunters were inherently violent, but with a shred of common sense, she had no difficulty suppressing the impulse.

Shiny and clean, its fur was a magnificent pattern of light and dark, silver blended with an earthy brown undercoat. Meticulously, the wolf licked the blood from its lips, then preened its paws.

Was it wearing a... backpack? Had someone trained a wolf to fight?

Its limbs were long and muscular, its movements graceful. Clearly deeming itself tidy, the wolf gazed up at the moon, inhaled deeply, then turned to face her. Eyes as intensely blue as the sunny Montana sky she'd savored this afternoon, it gazed at her with an awareness she couldn't place. Standing proudly before her, the moon framing his silhouette behind him, the image could easily win National Geographic's photograph of the year.

The wolf smiled at her with an unmistakable amusement.

Her mouth opened to say something, somehow knowing the animal would understand.

She shook her head, knowing it was a stupid thought. Just a wolf, right? Okay, fine. Astrid Edmonds was stumped. Not a common occurrence, and, quite frankly, she didn't care for it.

As she berated herself for becoming distracted by her own ego, the wolf winked at her and slipped out of his backpack.

Within a fraction of a second, the wolf became a man.

Astrid's limbs froze, her feet pinned to the ground as she mentally sifted through every text in her library to explain what was happening. If it weren't for the unchanged eyes, she would have thought the transition a clever magic trick, the wolf disappearing and the man appearing in its place. Shifters were lost to ancient legends, and there was no record of human or wolf having the ability.

A blush flooded her cheeks as she scanned the man standing before her. Astrid lost her voice, and all thought, really, as she accepted this was a man. A very naked, ridiculously attractive man. From the strong angle of his jaw that was accented by a roguish hint of a beard, to the chiseled abs, to the... unapologetically... completely uncovered... penis.

Air refused to pass in and out of her lungs, and she struggled to find something, anything to say in light of the bizarre change in circumstances. To demand an explanation.

Instead, she blatantly checked him out.

Yet another lesson learned tonight, perhaps the most important of them all: don't go so long without seeing an attractive man naked.

Get a grip, Astrid... She strained to avert her eyes from, well, his amazing body. Demon hunters were inherently fit, active types, and apparently shifters, or this shifter at least, were deliciously stacked. *Wow, he was really...*

GRINNING AT THE APPRECIATIVE reception, Bodie rubbed his hand over the back of his neck as he decided whether to get dressed or claim he had nothing to wear, so he could enjoy her blushing ogle a bit longer. Grammy had made the arrangements, but said she'd spoken to a male demon hunter, Vann, who'd promised to send one of his team. Werewolves held their secrets close, especially from demon hunters, but Grammy seemed to trust this team.

Bodie hadn't expected the willowy bombshell. Who knew those terms could play together so nicely? Yeah, small tits and narrow hips, but something about those lush lips and honey-brown eyes sealed the deal.

"I, uh... who are you?" Sweet voice, too. Not like benevolent sweet, but a husky soprano, if that were possible. Sweet more like honey on a sore throat.

"Sorry I'm late. Boden Connery. Everyone calls me Bodie." He extended his hand. Late was a bit of a lie. He'd wanted to get a feel for the hunter before revealing himself. Demon hunters weren't exactly a werewolf's best friend.

Then, wouldn't you know it, but a trio of baddies decided to ruin both of their nights. Nice timing though. He had been worried about how to convince the demon hunters that not only was he a werewolf, but also a good guy. Revealing himself was a risky move, but worth it, and not just for the flattering eye-fuck.

He waited for her to respond.

A fiery red blush heated her cheeks further. Damn, he liked it. Stubbornly polished, she averted her eyes from his package and silently declined stepping close enough to shake his hand. As she avoided looking at him now that she'd recovered, her gaze now roamed *anywhere else*.

Okay, he needed to leave the ranch more often. His libido was usually a bit easier to tame. But, damn, she was not at all what he had expected.

Keeping busy, she cleaned her swords and sheathed them. "Astrid Edmonds. I... you can't be who Vann spoke with on the phone. I don't understand."

Figures. Demon hunters and their narrow minds. Thought they were the only decent demon-human hybrids out there. There were enough feral werewolves, like tonight's odorous trio, to blow it for the rest of them. Every werewolf had the potential to go feral, and a long fucking time ago, enough proactive hunters had decided to eliminate the potential before it happened. Hence the secrecy.

"I'm not. My grandmother set up the meeting." Turning, he knelt down and pulled his clothes from the backpack. He'd wound up naked enough on vigilante ventures like this one. Grammy finally modified a backpack for him so he could wear it as the wolf. Policing their own was a hell of a lot safer than letting hunters get close.

Demon hunter chick was a curious thing, observing him like a scientist. Well, a horny scientist. It had been getting a bit cool in the June evening anyway, and shrinkage would quickly ruin her first impression of him. Once he felt a bit more presentable in his jeans, black tee, and dusty old hiking boots, he turned to her and shrugged. "Better?"

Nodding, she relaxed her stiff posture, her hands pushing into her pockets, and a genuine, fricking dynamic smile blossomed. Damn, that was worth waiting for. The subtle expression lit her up like a beacon on a foggy day. How would she look, lit up from laughing out loud with an unrepressed grin... or crying out in exhilarated orgasm?

Down boy, he threatened himself. *Don't let the demon hunter chick catch you fantasizing about her.* Without her team, his pack was toast.

"Never seen a real werewolf before?" He smiled, but found his hand rubbing the back of his neck nervously.

"I have seen a lot of werewolves. The first demon I slayed was a werewolf. You're not a werewolf."

"Figures. Come on."

"What?"

"I'll walk you back to your hotel. We'll leave in the morning. You staying at West Montana Inn?"

She loosened the ponytail and ran her fingers through the silky locks. Glossy as the woman, the hair was just as enticing. "No, I'm at Glacier Resort."

"Nice digs. Let's go." No cheap hotel for a demon hunter. Not that his pack wasn't well off, but they didn't flaunt it. Well, they might, if they ever left the ranch.

Suffocating compound was more like it. Content to live their entire lives within a hundred-mile radius, the pack didn't need the money.

Their investments were primarily intended to fight off the tycoons that continually tried to buy them out. The land bordered Glacier National Park and was stunning—albeit excessively isolated.

"In a moment. I need to call the coroner first." She pulled out her phone and started dialing.

"Coroner?"

"Yes. We can't just leave these bodies up here for humans to find."

"I was thinking dumpster..." *Coroner?*

She stared at him like he was daft. Well, he felt like it at the moment. Staring right back, he raised his eyebrows in confusion.

Rather than saying more, she did exactly as she'd said. With a few quick beeps, she connected with the local coroner's office and notified them of the human victim, and then asked for a special pick up requiring their expertise with an "odorous species."

Satisfied, she pushed the end key and slid the phone back into her pocket.

"Uh, wow," he said stupidly. "That's a handy one."

A light, almost smug smile grew on her lips.

Realizing she wasn't saying more, he hopped over the side of the roof. They could have broken in and taken the stairs, but she'd gotten herself up here, surely she could get herself back down.

She didn't disappoint. All proper on the outside, but fearless slayer throughout. She was incredibly agile, lowering from ledge to ledge with a few leaps. Those long limbs were made for climbing.

What else would she climb so well? *Stop it.*

They remained quiet over the half mile walk up the slope to her hotel. She didn't question as he followed her to one of the cabins on the far side of the property. She unlocked the door and headed straight through the unit and out the sliding glass door.

She gestured for him to join her on the secluded patio with a nod. At home in the classy, yet unassuming cabin, she lit the propane fireplace and parked in one of the cushioned outdoor chairs.

Not taking her bait, Bodie hung in the doorway and scoped out the patio, then turned back into the cabin. Opening the fridge in the kitchenette, he found the six-pack he'd been hoping she had. Not quite the priss she wanted him to think. Local beer from one of his favorite microbreweries. At least she had good taste.

Looks like she'd been here a week or more from the state of the fridge. Good head on her shoulders. He figured she, or whoever Vann sent, would arrive early, and get a feel for the area before meeting the mysterious "werewolf expert" with an at-risk ranch. An incautious demon hunter wouldn't have been reassuring.

He popped the tops off of a pair of bottles and sauntered out to the patio. Casually, he set one of the beers on the ledge of the tiled fireplace in front of her and dropped into the chair next to her. He gazed up at the full moon and soaked up the invigorating glow.

Legs stretched out long, he sank into the chair and savored the silence.

After an impressively long bout of impatient waiting, Astrid scrunched her brow and scowled at him. "You're not a werewolf." The words were certain, but her tone was lilted with uncertainty.

The corner of his mouth quirked up. His eyes didn't stray from the sky. Nights like this, he could almost taste the cool blue of the moon. He took an easy sip of his beer. "Sure about that?"

An exasperated sigh passed those delicious lips. "Those things on the roof were werewolves."

"Yep."

With a growl, she grabbed the beer and curled into the chair as the formality melted away. After a hell of a gulp, big enough to make Grammy nod in appreciation, Astrid scowled at him. "Speak."

He bit his lip in amusement. "Not a were*dog*. Were*wolf*. Less trainable."

This time, a hint of humor flourished on her watermelon-pink lips.

He sat up and grinned, then turned in the plush patio chair toward her. "Astrid?"

Her lips blossomed into an almost-full smile in response to his own.

"You don't like being wrong, do you?"

Ah, there it was. Gorgeous fucking smile that blazed warm as the sun. "No, I confess, I hate being wrong. It doesn't happen very often." One eyebrow raised in adorable arrogance.

"Well, then, I apologize for being the one to lower your stats. I am a werewolf, born and raised. Don't sweat it. We're a secretive breed."

"Born and raised? Is that possible? You're different from the guys on the roof."

"I *could* be like the guys on the roof. I'd rather not, however."

She paused, honey eyes searching his with a thirst for knowledge. First time in his life he didn't mind being studied. Kinda liked it, actually, how she soaked up every word, watching his lips as he spoke. Werewolves generally avoided study. Easy to end up some genius's thesis. Better to stay under the radar, especially considering what they could turn into with enough provocation.

Not pushy, Astrid was open, keen to drink up his words.

"As the wolf, I am a wolf, with a man flowing through my veins. As the man, I am a man, with the heart of a wolf. The space between is chaos, anger, as the man and wolf battle for a dominance that neither will win. The remnants of the beast from our demon ancestor. Some crave the power of it, the endless adrenaline rush."

"You don't?"

"Hell no. That's a power no one can control. Anyone who tries can't pull out of it, and goes feral. That's why you don't see many, but when you do, they're wild, ruthless, and tough to kill."

"How do you avoid it?"

He took a long pull of his beer and looked at her, unsure.

"Being both, the man and wolf, I mean. The beast. That's all I've ever seen. Is that because they did not have time to adjust, after being bitten?"

His eyebrows scrunched together as he realized just how much the outside world was clueless about werewolves, even demon hunters. Maybe they should scale back on the secrecy a bit. "Lycanthropy isn't contagious. We are all born from a demon-human hybrid and a human parent, just like you."

"Wait a moment. You... I'm sorry. I'm just trying to comprehend what you're telling me. No one bit you?"

"Not lately, but I'm open if you're interested." He flashed her a wink and bit his lip impishly.

"Ha ha." She surprised him by smiling rather than shifting her posture uncomfortably like a stereotypical priss would. There was hope for her yet.

"Seriously though, I shouldn't be surprised you don't know much about werewolves. We're incredibly secretive, or we'd end up at the end of your blade, hanging from a noose, whatever. I'll spare you the history lesson. It's not flattering to your kind."

Her expression darkened, but she kept her eyes on him.

"The nasties on the roof? You call those werewolves because that's what you know. And they are werewolves, but we call them ferals, as they're beyond saving. It takes a hell of a lot of untamable rage to reach that point. So, part of a werewolf's rearing includes meditation, martial arts, and education to balance the mind and body to prevent them from letting their anger turn them into a monster."

"Like Hulk?" Honey eyes glowing with amusement, she curled up into her chair and watched for his reaction.

Bursting from deep in his chest, surprised laughter vibrated through him. "Sort of. Less green. More fur and teeth. But equally violent and brainless."

Chuckling with him, Astrid didn't take her eyes off of him. Now he felt like the shy one, hiding behind his beer. Clearing his throat, he sat up in the cushy patio chair. "Anyway. You can find out all about normal werewolves once we get home."

Raising that eyebrow at him again, she said, "After a good night's rest."

"Thought you demon hunters don't need much sleep."

"Need and want are two very different things. Sleep is quite restorative. One of those nasties from the roof struck me hard enough to wrench my neck, so I could use the sleep to heal." She sat up in her chair and looked at him expectantly. "Where are you staying?"

"Here." He shrugged and looked around the patio.

"In the main building?"

"I can sleep on your patio as the wolf, but I might scare the landscaper in the morning. Or, I can crash on your couch." He smiled hopefully. He slept outside a lot as the wolf and didn't mind it, as he had the last few nights, but that was a comfy looking couch.

Clicking the switch for the fire, she drained her beer with a final swig. "I'm not letting a strange demon crash on my couch." She moved to the doorway and blocked it with her body, assessing his every movement.

He took a final gulp of his own. "Strange, yeah, I'll give you that. Demon, sure, I guess, but no more than you. Don't trust me yet?"

"Why would I?"

"Astrid, if I wanted you dead, or even maimed, I would have joined my estranged brethren on the rooftop tonight." As his father had warned him, demon hunters liked to pretend they weren't half demon like the other hybrids. Sure, they'd been created to keep the world safe from demons, but they had the potential to be just as dangerous.

With a haughty flip of her hair, she sighed. "I was doing just fine against those three. I most certainly could have taken you, too."

Stalking closer, he paused inches in front of her, so she had to look up to meet his gaze. In the light, he was surprised to see a delicate dappling of freckles over her nose and cheeks. She'd probably sock him if he commented on it. "Sure about that?" He bit the edge of his lower lip as he gauged her reaction.

"I am not intimidated by you." Her eyes searched his in confusion, but her words were firm.

Catching her scent with a subtle sniff, he could tell she meant it. The corner of his mouth quirking up, he shook his head with curiosity. "Then you won't mind me sleeping on your couch. For all I know, you're like a lot of other hunters, and you're going to call in your team to take me out, before I have a chance to go feral. No offense, but I'd rather keep an eye on you."

"Likewise," she admitted, but didn't blink from studying his face, as if memorizing each detail.

"Tomorrow, I'll be taking you miles away from civilization, and you'll be crashing at my place. Just you and me in the middle of nowhere."

Her breath caught in her throat. Chest rising slowly up and down, she nodded her head in acceptance.

He quickly added, "And Grammy. And my parents and little sister live next door. So does the rest of my pack."

"You are relentless." She smiled softly, her nose turned up in bewildered amusement. She backed up and waved him in.

2

As the moon disappeared on one side of the horizon, rays of the summer sun glimpsed over the opposite. Not a peep from the main room. Astrid wasn't afraid of Bodie. Still, she didn't trust him.

No, that wasn't true. She didn't trust how much she *wanted* to trust him. Some hunters might say something about souls and mystical connections, as those with demon realm felt these things more strongly than humans. Others might claim her demon hunter instincts were guiding her.

Her dreams last night said it was something else entirely. Lust, for sure. But who the hell was he?

Charming: Yes.

Rough around the edges: Absolutely.

Trouble: No doubt about it.

Sexy: Hell yes.

She had no need for any of the above in her life. Outside of her demon hunting team, there were few she trusted, and certainly fewer—well, none actually, with whom she socialized. Her parents were disinterested at best. With three older siblings, she had more immediate family than most demon hunters. Most of her team had no siblings at all. Hers were... somewhere.

Across the globe. Living their own lives. Left the nest on their eighteenth birthdays, when they accepted the demon hunter gift of strength, long life, and healing, in exchange for dedicating their lives to protecting humanity from the monsters that literature is fond of embellishing.

To have a stranger in such close proximity while she slept was downright odd. Not that she'd slept much. Through the thin wall, she hadn't been able to drown out the subtle sound of him stripping out of his clothes and sliding into the sheets of the sofa bed. Far too easy to visualize—in detail—after the show he'd given her on the roof. Tossing and turning on the spring-loaded sofa bed all night, he sounded to have slept as poorly as she had.

By four that morning, his groan echoed through the wall, mirroring the insomniac misery she was drowning in. Little was worse than a sleepless night. He was right, they may as well have left last night.

Smiling to herself, she imagined him lying in bed, staring up at the ceiling like she was. Wolves were cute. Aside from the predatorial killing instinct, they were adorable and potentially snuggly.

Giving up on any hope of sleeping in, she rose from the bed and pulled on the hotel bathrobe to cover her satin nightgown. Wouldn't that be a pleasant good-morning to her sofa-crasher? She'd seen all of him last night after his change. Perhaps he would appreciate the returned favor.

Sadly, no. Dammit. Lana would dare her to flash him.

While she laid out her clothes for the day, she heard the shower switch on. Closing her eyes, she savored the image, a surprising warmth brewing deep in her belly. He seemed to have enjoyed her reaction to him last night. The view had been pretty spectacular. She hadn't been tempted like that in a long time.

Which was part of the problem. Astrid's life plan was very simple.

1. Leave home. Check. Freedom tasted so much better than she'd even hoped.

2. College. Check. Maybe she'd do more of that in the next few years.

3. Find a team. Check. They were a pretty great team at that, better than she had expected.

4. Invest in a home she loved. Check. It had taken years of searching, but she'd just bought a house in Seattle. Amazing view, modern yet cozy, and easy distance to her teammates.

5. Fall in love.

Shit, when had she made it all the way through the first four steps? There were supposed to be years between steps four and five. Not a matter of weeks. She wasn't ready.

Dammit, look at what happened to Quinn. Her teammate and one of her best friends, although jealousy-inducing-deliriously-happy-in-love, was pregnant and married well before she had intended. At thirty-three, Astrid had a few hundred years of demon hunting ahead of her. She still had so much to learn about herself. And about demon hunting, apparently, as one of her most common enemies was, evidently, not so evil at all.

Not to mention, and well, probably top-tiered honorable mention, she sucked at romance. Or even dating. Or hookups.

Dumbass, she chided herself. A few steamy looks shared with a sexy-as-sin werewolf, who was the paranormal equivalent of a rough-edged cowboy, did *not* equate to love. He was absolutely *not* her type. She was getting the L-words mixed up. Hence, she needed some time to build up those dating skills with people that didn't set her hair on fire and make her toes curl in… among other physical manifestations she refused to acknowledge just yet.

The scent of coffee emanating across the cabin tickled her nose. A welcome distraction. *Mmm.*

Opening the bedroom door, she peered down the hall. No sign of him. She tiptoed toward coffee.

The bathroom door opened just as she was passing. Jumping like a foolish ninny, she pasted a subtle smile on her face and stepped back politely.

Bodie stood lickably wet from head to toe, wearing nothing but a plush white towel slung low over his hips. He bit his lower lip and grinned. "Mornin'." Rather than releasing her to her task like any normal person would, he leaned against the bathroom doorway, his penetrating blue eyes taking full measure of her.

"Good morning." She exaggerated the phony smile. Since when did she think of a man's skin as lickable? He must be rubbing off on her already… closing her eyes, she tried to shake the visual *that* stirred.

As he clearly missed the hint, she stepped back further and waved her hand to show him the way out of the bathroom.

Irritating man. Bodie didn't budge. "Didn't sleep so well, huh? Terrifying monster in your living room keep you up all night?"

"I slept fine," she said through gritted teeth, the lie dripping from her words. Chin held high, she refused to let her gaze drift lower so she could savor the view of those amazing abs. Certainly, she was *not* hoping the towel would spontaneously slip off and reveal the rest of the delicious image that had kept her from getting a good night's rest.

Flashing her a devious wink, he stood tall. In all his not-quite-naked glory, he stepped closer, his body only inches from hers. How hot of a shower had he taken? Her body temperature rose a solid two degrees from the close proximity. "Have you tried the rain setting on the showerhead? It's like standing naked in the field during a Montana summer storm."

And the damn blush flooded her cheeks again. Lips forming a hasty smile, she brushed past him and locked the bathroom door with an assertive click. Coffee could wait.

Closing her eyes as the torrential spray trailed down her skin, she absolutely did not picture his wet skin sliding over hers—in the field during a Montana summer storm. She did *not* imagine his mouth on hers, his hands gripping her hips and pulling her tight against him. Naked.

Who was she kidding? He was *hot*. Besides, a creative imagination was a natural, healthy part of life.

"WHAT'S WRONG WITH MY car?" Hands decisively gripped on her hips, she fired eye-daggers at him. Decked out in an expensive looking pink plaid shirt over a slim white tank, artfully distressed skinny jeans, and expensive hiking boots–very REI, she looked like a geologist posing for a sexy-nerd magazine cover.

So many things were wrong with the high-priced all-wheel drive, but Bodie didn't think she'd enjoy hearing his criticism. "First, we have a long-ass drive ahead. We'll probably be gone for weeks, and I don't want you to get stuck with the bill for having the rental for so long."

"I'm not worried about the—"

"Second, parts of the road washed out in the storm a few weeks ago and aren't passable without some serious four-wheel drive with high ground clearance. And someone who knows which mudholes to avoid. With all the recent rains, even my truck's going to have trouble getting in. It makes no sense to take two cars, and mine is going to handle the trip a hell of a lot better than yours."

Her foot tapping in an impressively rapid rhythm, Astrid's rebellious, jaw-clenched indecision was no laughing matter. No matter how much he enjoyed her ferocity. "Fine. But when I'm ready to go, you take me back immediately."

Sneering, he crossed his arms over his chest. "What kind of guy do you think I am? Not exactly going to hold you hostage."

"Fine." She said again. "You haven't exactly proven yourself to be a gentleman." At least she muttered the last bit under her breath, but he heard it all the same. What the fuck was that all about? One minute she'd been gaping at him over a cup of coffee—that he'd made her—the next she looked ready to tear his face off. She was a real piece of work.

She stepped closer so she had to look up at him, but he didn't uncross his arms. "Maybe not a gentleman, but I'm not an asshole either."

Honey-eyed scowl softening an inch, he didn't wait for her to come up with another reason to not ride with him. Excuse after excuse. Bodie was beginning to think she was afraid of him after all.

"Come on. I'll follow you back to return the rental." He hid the smile that teased at the corners of his lips as she held her ground, he relaxed and put his hands on his hips, but couldn't step away. He'd already learned her prissiness was a façade. How many more times would she try the tactic on him?

"Fine," she hissed again, clicking open the back hatch of the fancy SUV and pulling out her well-stocked backpack.

He held his hand out to take the bag from her. She nearly shoved it at him, but he saw her swallow her pride and hand it over nonviolently.

His hand brushed against hers as he took the handle. Radiating through his arm like a thousand volts of pure energy, his skin meeting hers for the first time, power, life, longing, ignited at the connection. He blinked as he tried to recover his bearings, but he couldn't pull away.

Staring at the light physical connection, Astrid's breath quickened.

He shifted his gaze, desperate to see if she was as dazed as he was. Gooey honey, her eyes locked onto his.

Flashes of something, *everything*, ricocheted through his brain. *Full grin, delighted laugh, like an apparition she strode toward him through a field of pink lupins. Cradling his jaw in her hands, she rose up on her toes, her glorious lips meeting his.*

Eyes fluttering closed, he tried to grasp hold of the vision before it slipped away. But, as with all good things, it floated away with the breeze.

What the fuck was that? She was attractive, but not at all his type. Not that he had a type. Either way, a snooty demon hunter was not his idea of a summer fling, and absolutely not a potential life partner.

Still, that touch was off-the-charts electric. Grammy would have a lot to say about it, but... fuck. No. Not a demon hunter.

Clearing his throat, he nodded to the backpack. Her brow was still scrunched together in confusion, but she released the bag and backed away. Movements forced, or he'd stand there like an idiot all day, he tossed her gear onto the backseat of his truck.

"Astrid?" he asked, afraid to say more for the confounding something that threatened to boil over.

She inhaled forcefully and slammed the back hatch shut. "Meet you there."

Brain well and truly muddled, he turned and climbed in his Toyota Hilux. Snob that she was, she must realize that his truck was a hell of a lot more kitted out than her rental, imported and maxed out in upgrades. Besides, he didn't want to be trapped at the ranch any more than she did. If she wanted to leave, he wouldn't hesitate.

He fired up the engine and slammed his forehead against the steering wheel. His Bluetooth connected and Imagine Dragons blasted from the speakers, reminding him to do *Whatever it Takes*. He shook off the shock of the last few moments and focused on his mission. Bodie turned up the music and shifted into reverse.

After a short drive to the airport, Bodie waited out front of the rental car office for Astrid. Within a few minutes, in all her lithe glory, she strode out with a secretive smile on her face. What made her smile to herself? Whatever it was, the subtle expression fired right into his chest and triggered a disarming flip-flopping sensation.

Typical. By the time she opened the passenger door and climbed into the truck, the smile was gone. In its place, her nose was turned up in that snooty expression she pasted on.

He shifted into gear and headed toward home. She was quiet on the drive. As they passed through Whitefish and increasingly tiny towns, he pointed out interesting landmarks along the way. While nodding politely, she was in a different world.

By the time they turned off the main road, her brow was drawn in a tight scowl, and she wouldn't even look his direction. Wow, yeah, she was hot, but priss might be too kind of a word.

3

GAZE FOCUSING OUT THE window, Astrid took in her surroundings. Fortunately, Bodie stayed quiet for the first hour of the drive. Not that she could talk, anyway. First demon hunter in history to get carsick, she was lucky to be holding down her breakfast.

As they left civilization, she let herself get lost in the rocky outcrops, crystal-clear lakes, raging rivers, and pink and white blooms that blanketed the expansive fields all around. The view almost made up for the nausea. And the surprisingly pleasant company.

So far, this recon mission wasn't at all what she had expected. As with any op, from the initial tip to recon to the big push, she analyzed every outcome, and studied every ancient text in her library. Not in her fifteen years of demon hunting had she ever heard of werewolves like Bodie. Yet, if he was to be believed, he was more of the norm. If werewolves were truly nothing like she had been taught, did this oversimplification and demonization extend to other monsters?

With Ryan, the newest member of their team, they'd learned so much of their own history, as well as how brutal other demon hunters could be. The child of a different demon-sire, he'd been the victim of violent bigotry. His experiences put so much of her outlook in check.

Not that she considered herself to be one of the bloodthirsty sorts, out to annihilate all monsters mindlessly. She knew a handful of vampires that could be trusted. There was a scattering of peaceable monsters that had become lost on this side and found they enjoyed the tranquility in their private corners of the globe. Still, she'd never met a werewolf that wasn't blinded by an enraged hunger, smelly, and covered in mangy fur.

"You okay? I know you're pissed I made you return the rental, but trust me, in a few miles, you'll see why." One hand loose on the wheel, his other in his lap, Bodie asked nonchalantly, but his tone was thick with concern—or guilt.

Dammit. She inhaled slowly through her nose and held back the disequilibrium that had taken over. *Please, please don't puke in front of the werewolf.* Only her team knew her unpleasant weakness. She really didn't want her overbearing host to think her weak.

"Really, you sure you're okay?"

"Fine," she hissed through gritted teeth.

"I'm getting that," he muttered under his breath, then quickly tried to lighten the mood again. "Enjoying the view? Ever been to Glacier?"

Watching out the windshield, she was astonished at the stark contrast between the rugged peaks and fields in full bloom that graced the western edge of the national park. Hand supporting her gut, she ignored each wave of nausea that was more pronounced than the last. "Yes, it's pretty, and no, I haven't." She inhaled in through her nose, exhaled through pursed lips. "Looks like part of the Swiss Alps," she said, forcing a smile.

"I've never been." His eyes scanned the horizon without focus, but he didn't say more.

"Did you grow up here?" she asked as the road straightened out.

"Born and raised."

"Beautiful," she said as they seemed to be free from steep cliffs and twisty roads for the moment. The view widened as they descended into a colorful valley.

Resting one hand on the top of the wheel, he pointed to the far side of the basin. "We'll turn there and wrap around the side of that ridge. Road gets a bit rough, but the scenery can't be beat."

And it wasn't already rough? Her stomach wasn't going to last much longer.

As promised, they entered a canopied forest where sunlight dappled through the trees. The paved road veered left, but they turned right onto an unmarked dirt road. For a mile or so, gravel crunched under their tires as they climbed the hill, then the road turned downward again.

Nausea washed over Astrid. Rushed up her belly and into her throat. Her lips slackened as they grew numb in preparation for the inevitable. She felt her cheeks drain of color.

Shit. Not good timing. Rolling down the window, she breathed in the fresh air desperately.

"Seriously, Astrid. You okay?"

Nodding tersely, she latched onto every oxygen molecule she could breathe in.

Stopping the truck, he turned toward her. "Are you... carsick?"

Without answering, she dove out of the truck and dashed behind the nearest tree. With a painful heave, her breakfast rushed out and splattered onto the ground in front of her. Wiping the corner of her mouth with the base of her thumb, she closed her eyes.

A warm hand splayed across the small of her back. "Easy there. Can I get you anything?"

Astrid shook her head and turned. Bodie's hand shifted from her back but stayed rested on her side, soothing, but she suspected he was actually preparing to catch her if she passed out. "I just get carsick. I should be good for a bit."

"Uh, no offense or anything, but I didn't think demon hunters got sick?"

"We don't. I'm special, I guess."

"Sucks. Let's walk it off."

Astrid stopped back at the truck and took a sip from her water bottle, swished and spit out a few sips before daring to swallow any. Bodie stood back, and when she was ready, he passed no judgment, and simply strolled with her down the shady dirt road.

"Dammit." Bodie crossed his arms and glared at the bottom of the hill.

"Problem?" Astrid blocked the sun from her eyes and followed his gaze to the cluster of boulders that rendered the road impassable. Her mouth formed an *Oh* as she realized the extent of the damage.

At the base of the hill, the road was completely washed out. A muddy riverbed held evidence of a debris flow that had wiped out a stretch of road. Boulders and broken trees were strewn within its destructive path.

"Guess that storm the other night was bigger than I'd thought. This road wasn't looking too good when I left, but it was functional. Give me a hand with these boulders?"

Nodding, Astrid pulled her hair back into a secure ponytail and joined him. Standing side by side, they pushed against the seven-foot boulder. "Wow, that's heavy." Astrid laughed. Demon hunting came with a number of perks, but superhuman strength was her favorite.

Chuckling, he nodded. "Solid granite. Come on, on three."

A soft growl passed her lips when they got to three. Pushing with even more force, they got it off the road.

"Stronger than you look." Bodie wiped the sticky mud onto his jeans.

Realizing she'd have to do the same, Astrid brushed as much off her hands as she could before finishing the job on her jeans. "You too."

As much as she kept her gifts secret, she'd enjoyed surprising the occasional asshole that assumed her skinny arms meant she was weak.

"You're the first demon hunter I've met. Wonder how many of the stories are true?" He smiled as he tossed one of the smaller boulders off of the road.

"What have you heard?" Astrid helped him clear their path, tossing a leafy branch out of the way.

"Dad always said I should keep clear of violent sorts like you demon hunters. Judge, jury, and executioners."

Scowling, Astrid caught herself before she ran a muddy hand over her hair. "I'd like to argue, but I've met more than a few of those. Things are changing. At least, I hope so."

"Guess things ought to change for us, too."

"How many werewolves do you think there are, like you, in existence?"

Grunting as he lifted one end of a log and nodded for her to take the other, he said, "Don't know. It's not like werewolves make great pen pals. Maybe a few thousand across the globe? I know of a few other packs we check in with now and again. There are at least a few hundred of us in the states that I'm aware of."

Astrid took the other end and pivoted as they heaved it into the woods. "I suppose an interpolative statistician could configure the population based on feral appearances and geographic clusters." She fruitlessly brushed off another layer of mud before throwing another log off the path. "What does your pack think of you bringing home a demon hunter?"

Chuckling, he nearly rubbed his hand on the back of his neck, but stopped when he saw his mud-caked palm. "I, uh, haven't told any of them yet. Grammy and I were sort of waiting to see if you'd even agree to help before we risked it. Let's just say it's not going to go over well. We won't stop for introductions. We'll pack up and head out to scope out the feral camp before anyone knows I brought you home with me."

"Good. I want to see what we're up against before we make a plan of attack, anyway."

"Agreed. Hopefully you and I can collect enough info on the ferals to convince them that we need your team. And, to ensure they can accept that you aren't out to kill us or give up our secrets." With his feet planted firm, he rammed at another boulder twice his size, then glanced over at her with a pleading smile for assistance.

She moved next to him and shoved at the rock. "From what it sounds like, I'm not sure we'll be welcome no matter how we approach this."

"Grammy's the one that makes the official calls. She's alpha, and it's her decision. Although, I agree with her and would have called myself, if I'd known of any halfway decent demon hunters. I'm not going to stand on ceremony when we need help, and the rest of the pack better get in line."

Shit, she hoped she hadn't offended him. Why was it so difficult to articulate her thoughts without offending anyone? "Don't get me wrong, I'm glad you called. My whole team is. This is what we do. Even if you changed your mind now, there is a danger to your pack and any humans nearby, so we would still work the case. If we'd discovered them on our own, we'd handle it." They paired up to take care of the next fallen tree.

Heaving on the count of three, they tossed it off the road. Turning toward her, he put his muddy hands on his hips. "And if we asked you to stay out of it?"

"Well, I suppose if we knew you could handle it, we'd back off. Still, this is what we do. What if I were to ask you to never change to the wolf again, citing that it was unnatural?"

His brow scrunched in irritation. Okay, she'd really pissed him off now. Back-pedaling, she tried to correct it.

He shook his head. "No, you're not wrong. You can't ask someone to go against their purpose. I couldn't ask you to back off any more than you could expect me to suppress the wolf. Think I'd go nuts if I had to ignore my heritage. To turn my back on my pack." He moved closer and stopped a few feet away. "Thank you, really, for responding. Doesn't matter what my pack thinks of demon hunters. We're alone out here. They'll accept help because we don't have another choice," he said, but trailed off and subtly sniffed the breeze.

Turning toward the stimulus that was clearly bothering him, a deep crease forming between his eyebrows, Astrid stepped closer. "What is it?"

He shook his head. "Not sure."

As if in a trance, Bodie walked up the cluttered riverbed. He climbed atop the tallest boulder and stared into the distance, shaking his head as if he couldn't quite see what he was looking for. Waiting back on the road, Astrid rested her hands on her hips. There was nothing unusual in the air that she could sense. Even in human form, he seemed to have wolf-like senses.

Changing to the wolf, he leapt off the boulder and sprinted upriver.

Dammit, a little warning would have been appreciated

Astrid tore off after him. Could be a trap. Still, curiosity was a persuasive bitch.

Vaulting over fallen branches, weaving through boulders and trees, she didn't want to lose his trail.

A hairy arm launched out from behind a tree, aimed straight at her neck in a sloppy attempt to clothesline her.

Ducking, she spun in place and rammed the mangy werewolf with a straight-legged kick to the chest. *Feral. Not werewolf.* Change wasn't easy, but vital to the future of werewolf and demon hunter relations.

The air huffed from its chest. It recoiled for half a second before snarling with yellowed fangs.

Breath held in caution, she waved the foul stench from the air.

It swung its muddy claws as if offended.

Grabbing one of its fists before it reached her face, she yanked the creature closer and jammed it in the nose with the base of her palm. Still holding it tight, she spun him around and tossed him across the riverbed.

Pissed off and raring for more, he hurtled over the rubble toward her.

A few feet from her, the gray wolf launched over the nearest boulder and flattened the feral. With a few well-placed strikes, Bodie finished it.

As he turned toward Astrid, he shifted into the man. He wiped the back of his thumb over his mouth. Out of breath, he put his hands on his hips and looked upstream again. His eyes, an unnatural electric blue, seemed to spark, but he blinked away the distraction.

Shifting his gaze back to her, he seemed to return to the present. The corner of his mouth turned up in a mysterious smile. "Hey."

"Hey." Focusing anywhere except on naked Bodie, Astrid tried to get her brain in check. She was furious with him, but damn he was nice to look at. The perplexing man was crossing all her wires.

"I'm so sorry about that." The smile morphed into a guilt-laden grimace.

"What was that? Don't do that. If we're going to work together, you can't just take off like that."

"Really, it won't happen again. I'm used to working alone." He rubbed his hand over the back of his neck, his eyes searching hers for forgiveness.

"Well, you're going to have to get over that. We need to work together if we're going to win this."

"You've got a pretty great right hook. I'll keep that in mind next time I run off on my own."

She rolled her eyes. "You looked spooked."

"Something's weird. Couldn't say for sure." Or wouldn't. He still seemed shaken despite his joking facade, but he wasn't sharing. Not that she should be surprised. As openminded as he seemed, he'd been raised to think her kind the enemy.

"That feral, it was waiting for us, wasn't it?"

"Pretty sure. It wasn't alone. I smelled at least three others, but they took off."

"Feral werewolves don't typically get scared. They attack. They don't run away when threatened."

"Yeah. More than a little weird. Maybe watching the road for a lucky lunch, but not many drive through here." He started walking back down the riverbed.

Well, Astrid Edmonds was in entirely new territory. She wanted to clock him for being cagey about whatever was bothering him. For not expounding on his theory about why no less than four ferals were in the area, and why they ran. There was something he wasn't telling her, but the threat was real, and at least he didn't diminish it.

For now, she let it go and followed him back to his clothes and the truck. At least the view was nice. That was one very, very fine ass.

CLIMBING BACK INTO THE truck, Bodie fired up the engine. *Couldn't say* what bothered him was not exactly honest. *Wouldn't* was more like it. Whatever that scent was on the air, he knew that smell.

Against his upbringing, and his dad's frequent warnings about demon hunters, Bodie trusted Astrid wholeheartedly. Maybe foolish of him, but he trusted his gut. It hadn't led him astray so far. Still, he wasn't ready to share a weak speculation. He needed to chew on it awhile.

She was pretty spectacular to watch in action. Graceful in her movements, with sword or fist, yet she was lethal. Despite her pristine appearance, Astrid didn't shy away from dirty work either.

She tugged the tie from her hair and ran her fingers through the sleek locks. Did she do it on purpose? Like in a trance, he watched as she worked out the nonexistent tangles. Satisfied, she pulled the seatbelt across her and clicked it into place.

Realizing he'd been staring, her watermelon-pink lips turned up in an amused smile that knocked him flat on his metaphorical ass. Working his lower lip between his teeth, he laughed it off.

Neither spoke for the next few miles. Not that conversation would have been easy, thanks to the road noise. She'd grabbed the oh-shit handles through some of the deeper ruts that tossed the Hilux about, gone clammy with nausea, but washed it away with fresh air. When she couldn't, he'd pull over again until it passed.

He was pleasantly surprised to discover she hadn't been lying about being unafraid before. She was fearless. Which wasn't always a good thing.

These ferals that had settled so close to his pack were worth fearing. What he couldn't figure out, was whether they had intentionally settled so close to Connery Ranch, or if the proximity was coincidental. It was pretty fucking close to just be a coincidence. A few days hike away, they were far enough that they couldn't smell each other, so they may not even realize the Connerys were so close.

Wishful thinking. They were watching the road. His road. They were either tracking him for their own security, or they wanted something. Death or recruitment?

After an ancient aspen grove, illuminated by the sun's final shimmer before setting, they crested one final hill. Across the truck, Astrid's breath caught as she took in the wide-open space ahead, sheltered by mountains in the distance and cedar-hemlock forests encompassing the valley.

"It is nice to look at." He leaned back in his seat, one hand on the wheel while he watched her reaction to seeing the heart of his pack's land.

Those honey eyes were scanning every detail. He didn't think she even realized she smiled openly, her curiosity unshrouded. When she wasn't being all snooty, she was stunning. Not that she wasn't fucking hot when she was looking down her nose at him.

"Like something that belongs on a postcard. Or was created for a Hallmark movie."

Log and cedar cabins, both old and new, dappled across the valley. No fencing and no horses, as neither were wolf-friendly. They had cows and pigs now and again, but not since he was a kid. Four little ones played tag in the near field. He waved to his Aunts Eliza and Lilith who rocked on Eliza's front porch.

Yikes, she might be right. It was like something out of a cheesy movie.

"Where are you from?" he asked, glancing over at her.

"Georgetown. Have you ever been to DC?" Her answer wasn't exactly upbeat, and he doubted it was only carsickness causing the disgruntled tone.

"I've never been out of Montana. Well, I mean, I've crossed a few borders tracking ferals, but not for fun."

As the road narrowed, he turned onto the last driveway at the far end of the valley. Lined with blossoming fruit trees that were older than his father, the drive opened to the house that had been his home long before he had moved in, the final half mile the best part of the trek. Standing two stories high, the deeply weathered, majestic log cabin was nestled happily amongst the shrubbery, a handful of fir trees, and overlooked the ranch. One of the earliest structures in the region, built by his great-grandfather, it remained the heart of the family.

After he'd had a blowout fight with his dad a few years back, Grammy had insisted Bodie come live with her. Gramp had passed a few months prior, so she'd claimed the house was too quiet. Aside from the constant coming and going of neighborhood kids. Raulf had been mollified, as Bodie was at least still in the valley.

Parking in the garage at the side of the house, Bodie tossed his backpack over his shoulder and grabbed Astrid's bag by the strap before she had the chance to argue.

Hobbling down the front steps with her gnarled-wood cane, Grammy came out to meet them.

4

HUMBLE YET GRAND IN character, the house stood a proud pillar amidst the mature landscape. An expansive covered porch was framed with weathered beams. Bright windows hinted at an inviting interior, and functional blue shutters adorned either side of each. The two-story structure told of high ceilings and clever architecture that defied the changing styles of the last few centuries. Cheerful annuals brightened every open nook and cranny of the porch.

Astrid hung back and watched as Bodie shifted their bags on his shoulder and wrapped his free arm around a petite, ancient woman, her feet kicking in the air as he swung her in a circle.

Her riotous laugh danced through the air. "Boden Connery, one of these days you're going to make me break a hip," she hooted as he lowered her to the ground.

"As if. You may be nearly three and a half centuries, but you're still strong as an ox." Bodie turned toward Astrid and motioned for her to join them. "Grammy, this is Astrid."

Voice strong and steady considering the wrinkled face and limping gait, Grammy smiled and extended her hand. "You must be Vann's friend. Thanks so much for coming. I just hope you and your team are able to help."

"I'm Astrid," she said, accepting a firm handshake. "You must be Molly. We'll certainly try." She breathed in through her nose and looked around at the cheerful setting. "You have a wonderful home. I've never seen such a welcoming entry."

"The house is nearly as old as I am but will stand strong twice as long. Bodie's been helping to spruce things up around here. Keeps saying we should add solar panels and update the kitchen."

Hands on his hips, Bodie grinned. "Hey, you've kept the house updated beautifully, but the 1920s are done. I risk life and limb every time I bake anything. And, they invented this fancy machine that washes your dishes for you."

"I'm not arguing. Next time you're in town you can pick one up."

"And a contractor." Bodie dashed up the porch steps two at a time.

Molly linked arms with Astrid, her other gripping her gnarled walking stick, and they walked into the house together. Astrid had anticipated something between a musty old lady's place, an odorous bachelor pad, and wet dog. Pleasantly surprised, she inhaled deeply, savoring the scent of the summer breeze and chocolate chip cookies.

Astrid gazed down the hall, eager to scope out the unusual place. Psychic or something, Molly nodded for her to explore. Not leaving the wide hall, Astrid took a quick perusal.

The layout was unique. The foyer was wide and long, a sort of hallway that was open to the entire bottom floor. To the right as she walked in, was a massive reclaimed wooden door, louvered with iron hinges. She'd expected to see a formal parlor or a dining room, but the thick doors gave no indication as to what lie behind it.

The plank floors were smoothed and dark from at least a century of foot traffic. Cream colored area rugs led the way to a wide staircase ahead. To the right of the stairs at the back of the house, the hall opened to a cozy family room. To the left, a guest bathroom, laundry, and extra bedrooms were eclectically decorated, as she imagined a beloved grandmother's home should be.

Surrounded by foreign coziness, Astrid ended her self-guided tour and found Molly in the kitchen. As homey as an old movie, the kitchen beckoned her in. Nothing fancy, but clearly the heart of the home. An empty cast iron pan sat on the wide, claw-footed stove, ready for skillet-sized pancakes. A red rooster-shaped trivet sat in the center of the large table, and each of the six chairs around it was from a different era. A pair of sunny yellow curtains dressed the window. Her stomach rumbled as she breathed in the scent of seasoned meat, carrots, and potatoes that wafted from a crockpot, its lid wobbling as steam escaped around its edges.

At Molly's nod, Astrid took a seat at the table while Molly set the kettle on the stove to boil. "How far are the ferals from here?" she asked.

"Bodie?" Molly hollered across the house. "You've ventured closer than the rest of us. How far would you say the den is?"

Bodie dashed down the stairs swiftly but without rushing, the depth and height of the stairs memorized, and the jog down was habit more than expediency. He rubbed a hand on the back of his neck, the short hair at the base of his head spiking up under his fingertips, then dropped down onto an ornate wooden chair across the table. "A day or two on the quad, then a few days hike on human feet, give or take. And it's not a den, but an old mineshaft." Turning to Astrid, he said, "We'd been watching the news, and noted a rise in the number of deaths that appeared to be feral related, but it was so widespread, it had to be more than one. Anyway, while I was out exploring a few weeks ago, I caught the scent of death and ferals. Lots of them."

"Werewolves—I mean ferals, don't typically run in packs. Well, I guess, I hadn't ever seen any that did. After meeting you, I'm realizing my werewolf knowledge is rather paltry."

Bodie rose and pulled a trio of plates from the cupboard, glanced at Molly, and raised an eyebrow in question.

She subtly shook her head and responded, "I already ate."

He returned one of the plates, then dished up two generous portions from the crockpot. He tossed a fork to Astrid and slid one plate in front of her, taking the other for himself. A few bites, and he'd practically annihilated his meal.

The meat was so tender, she didn't need a knife. Astrid nibbled a small, testing bite. She'd expected salty mush, but it was surprisingly juicy and flavorful. Swallowing, she looked to Molly and said, "This is delicious. What is it?"

Chortling, Molly leaned back in her chair and slapped her knee in amusement. "You've never had pot roast?"

Astrid laughed and shook her head with equal surprise. "No, sadly. Crockpots were not acceptable by my parents' standards—I mean no disrespect, rather, to describe their snobbishly picky habits. Everything must be fresh from the market, and handmade from scratch, of course, by the cook. Don't get me wrong, the food was excellent, but it was so artfully curated... anyway, once I learned what comfort food was from my team, I took a few cooking classes for fun."

His food nearly gone, Bodie swallowed his massive bite of potato, carrot, and meat from one forkful. "You've been missing out."

She found herself chuckling and scooping a combination bite for herself. "I may have to invest in a slow cooker. Coming home to a hot meal after a long day of slaying sounds amazing."

For the rest of dinner, Astrid eagerly learned the marvels of baking, casseroles, and window herb gardens. She should have taken notes.

Once she'd scraped the last of the potatoes from her plate, Bodie hopped off his chair and set their plates in the sink, returning with the tray of cookies she'd been trying not to stare at.

Handing one to Astrid, he ate another in two bites and sat back down. As he swallowed, he nodded. "So, feral werewolves. You're not wrong. They're too wired to live in packs. Or to have any sort of normal life. Generally, they're too restless to be anything but nomadic and too short-tempered to tolerate others for long. No way they could even trust each other, pretty damn fickle creatures that will attack one of their own without needing a reason. Actually, that's part of why everyone thinks lycanthropy transfers via bite wound. They do like to sink their teeth into anything they can. There is also some confusion with vampire mythology as well, as paranormal history has been shared via oral tradition for a lot longer than via written or videographic stories."

Biting into the gooey cookie with a hint of crispy on the edges, Astrid managed to avoid groaning. "These are excellent, thank you." She paused, considering what he'd said. "Some of the earliest records I could find on werewolves tell of a demon hunter watching a human and a feral fighting. The feral attacked, biting the human, and the human changed. Now I wonder if it wasn't a human at all, but a werewolf that was driven into a rage by the feral."

Molly said with a nod, "That sounds more likely. Most ferals run off after the change. We're pack-oriented and stick together, but ferals are too mindless to remember who they were, or even recognize who they cared about. It wouldn't be a leap to imagine one going after a family member that tried to calm it down, enraging the well-meaning werewolf enough to turn them feral."

"Any theories on how such a large population are living together?"

After stuffing another cookie in his mouth, Bodie brushed the crumbs off his hands. "Couldn't say. I didn't dare get close enough to get an accurate count. Well." He chuckled under his breath. "Gotta admit. It scared the shit out of me. I've never seen, or smelled, anything like it. Must be fifty or more. I could hear their howling from a few miles off. The scent of death was suffocating. Smellier even than the ferals themselves. Human, animal. I don't think they're picky about what they eat."

"What could make them change their patterns so severely? Could there remain enough pack instinct, that a high enough density of ferals would group together like that?"

Molly rose from the table and poured boiling water into a teapot she'd prepared with dried chamomile leaves. After lining up their cups on the table and setting the pot on the rooster trivet, she joined them at the table again. "Every century or so, some feral werewolf has enough control over the chaos of the unnatural form to create a pack. Brains on top of that untamed power is a dangerous combination. Still, at this scale, something isn't adding up."

"In my research, I have seen stories of small packs of werewolves, albeit rarely, and never more than five or ten together. An average demon hunting team can handle those, with difficulty. If this pack's numbers are five or ten times that?" She crossed her arms over her chest and leaned back in the creaky chair. "I'm not being immodest when I say, my team is stronger and smarter than most. Part experience, and part a gift imparted on us during our last mission. But I have my doubts that we will be enough. We'll need a cunning plan, rather than relying on brute force."

Bodie poured three steaming cups of tea and passed them around.

Molly took a thoughtful sip. "Did Bodie tell you how I tracked down your team?"

Astrid shook her head. Bodie sat back in his chair, watching quietly.

"A century or so back, I ran into a powerful man. Kind, fierce. Leapt in front of a vampire to save me. He asked me why I was out alone, so late at night, with the reports of murders in the area." She grinned, raising her eyebrows, as if seeing the scene in her mind as clearly today as she had a hundred years ago. "Two more vampires came out of the darkness after him. I returned the favor and fought at his side. He didn't ask who or what I was, as he must have realized I wouldn't say. But he's been a good friend ever since. When I reached out for help, he was sorry to say he and his team were out of the country on a hunt, but he informed me his son's team was unbeatable, and trustworthy."

"Vann's father."

Molly nodded. "I keep my ear to the ground. I know what you and your team are capable of. I wouldn't have called if I didn't think you could handle this."

Astrid dared a sip of her steaming tea, not trusting herself to speak. Their last big mission had been harrowing. Demon hunters were hard to kill, and a single monster had nearly crushed them. All because they had gone in with egos blasting.

Bodie nudged his foot against hers, rescuing her from the barrage of memories. "What do you think. You and I can leave at first light tomorrow, take the quad until we can't. Hike along the river, then upland. We'll check things out. Once we're back here, we'll get your team heading this way. My dad, Uncle Angus, Auntie Lilith, Stevie, and my cousins Nash and Rain are good warriors, and they've already agreed to join the fight. Not that they'd say no, but good to have them on board."

Jaw set firmly, his eyes fixed on hers as he laid out the plan. He had no intention of letting any harm come to his pack. Losing was not an option. For the lives at risk, for Bodie's pack.

Astrid leaned back in the creaky wooden chair and held the delicate porcelain cup close to her lips, letting the heat radiate through her. As he finished laying out the plan, his glowing, sky-blue eyes met her gaze across the table. The corners of his mouth quirked up when he caught her staring. For the life of her, Astrid couldn't look away.

She hardly noticed as Molly excused herself and limped out of the room, teacup in one hand and her walking stick in the other. Astrid managed to mutter, "Goodnight," but something clicked in the way Bodie was looking at her. Like the unexpected electricity of his hand on hers that morning, the air was charged with kinetic energy.

He seemed to be enjoying it. "Didn't see me coming, did you?" he asked, biting his lower lip in a devilish smile.

Drawing in a testing sip of tea, she felt the blush heating her cheeks. "Honestly? I'm surprised I didn't smell you coming."

"Nothin' but Oars and Alps deodorant and clean laundry." His grin grew deeper, eyes twinkling with amusement. "See? Not what you expected." He wasn't even close to what she was expecting, and he continued to challenge every rapidly changing preconceived notion about him. That playful ego didn't seem to be going anywhere, however.

"You're enjoying this, flipping demon hunter knowledge upside down."

"Maybe," he said, his smile twitching in satisfaction. "Gotta say, you're not at all what I was expecting either."

"No?" Her eyebrow quirked up in challenge. "What did you think, you'd be meeting up with a hard-hearted killer?"

"Well, yeah. Some guy with ratty hair. Dressed in head to toe studded leather. Maybe a few teeth knocked out, a chainsaw for a hand." He grinned at her, shifting in his chair, but his shockingly blue eyes didn't leave hers.

"I've got a black leather miniskirt. Not that I ever wear it, but I could give it a try if it would satisfy your image of demon hunter."

Coughing as he choked on her words, he said, "Yeah, that would satisfy... a lot."

Okay, so the skirt wasn't her idea. Lana, the most fashion-daring of their team, had convinced her to buy it a few years back. For the first time since she'd bought it, she was actually tempted to wear it, just to see Bodie's jaw drop. "If I was a stereotypical demon hunter, what would you have done with me? Would you have left me on the roof alone, or driven me back here to your Grammy's house?"

"Hell no. I'd have ditched you to the ferals and wonder if Grammy was demented. Instead? I find this gorgeous badass with a haughty air about her that would happily kick my ass, if she didn't find me so charming."

"Charming? I wouldn't go that far."

"Okay, so maybe not charming, but don't deny you haven't at least enjoyed the view." He waggled his eyebrows suggestively, leaning back in his chair. Oh my. He was ridiculous. And she was a sucker for that adorable grin.

"Maybe more egotistical rake than charmer." Before he could continue on his contagious flirtation, she leaned back in her chair and changed the subject. "Is there water along the way or should I pack enough for the whole trip?"

Downing the last of his tea in a subtle gulp, Bodie began to clear the table. "We'll cross a few rivers. Your shoes good for a lot of walking?"

He glanced down at her feet, lingering on her calves before nodding in approval. "Those should do."

"Glad I have your stamp of approval."

"Just saying. I usually camp out as the wolf, alone, and we're intentionally getting close to a massive pack of feral werewolves. Little nervous." He raised his eyebrows synchronously with a shoulder shrug.

"Three months ago, I nearly lost my team on a recon op. I'm not risking them, nor will I ever underestimate my enemy again." Draining the last of her tea, Astrid stood and helped Bodie wash and dry the dishes. Side by side, they finished the job in minutes. After drying the crockpot and returning it to its nook on the countertop, she leaned against the counter.

Shutting off the water, he folded his arms over his chest and stood next to her. "My pack's lives are at stake. I'm scared for good reason. Whatever this looks like, I'm not risking you, your team, and certainly not my pack."

Astrid caught what he didn't say. What was implied. The fear, the courage, the dark look. He might not risk anyone else, but he would go all-in, alone, if that's what it came down to.

Dusk settled over the quiet valley. Scouting the area before settling in for the night, Bodie made his usual circle of the ranch. Well, compound was more like it. His family, a few others, banded together for privacy. He loved his home, but he was suffocating in captivity.

A tease of moisture hung in the air, hinting at rain later in the week. The breeze brushed through his fur as he trotted back toward the house, cooling his muscles that he'd pushed to the limit.

In the distance, he could just make out Astrid on the deck off of her bedroom, looking out over the river in the distance. Long, ash-blond hair ruffled by the wind, she didn't tame it.

He'd surprised the hell out of her, but the feeling was mutual. Yeah, he knew a bit about demon hunters, significantly less than he'd realized, but she'd so quickly accepted him.

Raulf had always insisted demon hunters would slay a werewolf without question. Their entire pack was at risk if they were ever discovered. Despite the anticipated resistance from the rest of the pack, Grammy was alpha, and made the call—but Bodie wasn't about to tell the rest of the pack yet. Not until they had a plan.

Practically a hermit these days, yet Grammy knew this team had faced the worst of the worst and come out stronger for it. Had known that they wouldn't attack first. If she wanted him to take over as alpha someday, she could at least let him in on a few of her secrets.

Despite the late hour, Astrid had immediately reorganized her gear, now that she knew the timing and terrain to expect. No excess, but nothing missed. She hadn't complained once so far, just went with the crazy plan. Like him, she wanted to know what they were getting into before risking her team.

He knew she watched as he strolled back to the house. At his wolfy wink, shot him a flirty grin that struck him like an arrow to the chest. While he stood there dumbfounded, she sweetly rolled her eyes and went back inside.

At the back door, he shifted back into the man and headed inside. He grabbed his jeans from the shelf and tossed them on before heading upstairs to hit the hay.

SUDDENLY THIRSTY FROM HER stomach tying up in knots, unsure what to make of her host, Astrid tossed a flannel shirt over her nightgown before heading downstairs. A bathrobe would have been a good idea, but she packed light for a remote trip. At the top of the stairs, she stopped fast.

Jeans slung low over his hips, having not even bothered with the top button, Bodie strolled up the stairs. When he caught sight of her, he slowed his pace, stalking toward her in measured steps. Eyes never leaving hers, the corner of his mouth turned up.

He paused on the front step, standing inches away. Pulling her gaze away from some damn good abs, Astrid met his sky-blue eyes. Pulse quickening under her skin, heat licked through her, threatening to engulf her if he so much as touched her.

This is the precise moment in which her teammate, Lana, would make a move. Might step closer, tracing her fingers along those corded arms, perhaps slide those jeans down over his hips. Astrid inhaled sharpy, off-kilter as she experienced the entirely novel sensation of raw lust. If only she were just a little more… something.

Remembering what she was doing at the top of the stairs to begin with, Astrid inhaled deeply to catch her breath. Not helpful. As promised, no wet dog smell, only the fresh mountain air coating his inherently clean scent, although a bit sweaty from recent exertion—but in a sexy way. Odd. It must be a werewolf thing, a lickable scent.

"Astrid?" he asked, his head tilted as if about to kiss her.

"Yes?" she said, forgetting how to breathe entirely.

"See you at dawn." With that, he stepped to the side and strolled into his bedroom.

Frozen at the top of the stairs, Astrid ran her fingers through her hair and audibly sighed. Smarter than the average bear, Astrid didn't play dumb. She acknowledged that she was absurdly attracted to the werewolf. More, she knew it was entirely mutual.

How could she make clear decisions when she was distracted by constant daydreams? And lusty ones at that?

Thirstier than ever, she focused on her mission. Heading downstairs, she allowed her brain to wander while it was safe to do so, knowing her thoughts wouldn't easily be redirected this evening. When Quinn had disappeared all those months ago, only to return head-over-heels in love with a constant dreamy look in her eyes, Astrid now accepted that the ongoing knot in her gut since, was envy.

Demon hunters mated for life. Not an ordinary life, either. It was a multi-century commitment lasting the long life of the demon hunter, their human partner taking on their longevity and healing abilities when they wed. Her parents were a perfect example of where that went wrong.

Mr. and Mrs. Edmonds didn't hate each other. Nor did they like each other. It was more of a mutual tolerance. They'd had four children together, so there must be something compatible about them. Thus, Astrid had grown up in an indifferent, stilted environment in which hugs were paltry, kisses unheard of, and genuine PDAs were nonexistent.

One look from Bodie, and she wanted to tear off his clothes—when he wore them, and taste every inch of his magnificent skin. PDA all day and all night.

Gulping down a liter of water, Astrid placed the glass in the sink and turned back toward the stairs. A throat-clearing stopped her in her tracks.

Molly appeared from her bedroom that lie off the family room. Long white hair tucked behind her ears, she hobbled across the hallway. "Glad I caught you alone." She glanced around conspiratorially.

Astrid paused at the foot of the stairs.

"Take care of my Bodie. It wasn't easy to convince him to accept help. He's already so broken up about his brother. And I think his promise to me is the only reason he hasn't gone tearing in there already." Molly's wrinkled blue eyes were heavy with worry.

"His brother?" Astrid didn't know he had a brother. Not that they knew much about each other, but she hated that she didn't know that he was grieving.

"Don't let him do anything rash."

"That's why you called Vann, isn't it?"

A blush flooded Molly's cheeks. "Yes. I don't want him to try going in alone. Not that Noah would have been any easier to rein in, but at least they'd have had each other."

Astrid moved closer and rested her hand on the papery skin of Molly's forearm. "Don't feel bad. This is what we do. What we were born for. To fight the monsters that threaten our world."

"We like to take care of our own."

"That's what I'm gathering from Bodie. We will never understand each other if we don't work together. Not twenty-four hours ago, I had no idea that werewolves weren't mindless killing machines."

"I like you, girl. You've nailed exactly what I've been telling my kind for centuries. Bodie's dad, Raulf, is about the hardest-headed of them. Stubborn ass would rather we all never left the ranch. Safer and saner in our secluded neck of the world. With this feral pack so close, his oldest son gone, he's lashing out like a cornered wild dog."

"Aren't you the alpha?"

Molly grimaced and steadied herself on her cane. Astrid braced her at the elbow. Molly refused the help as she righted herself, her eyes glowing blue like Bodie's. "Thanks. I'll be all right. Some things are beyond this tired old body's ability to heal. Bodie doesn't like to think on it, but my time in this world is winding down. I'm ready to join his late grandfather. As much as Bodie's always itching to get out of here, he is dedicated to his family. To the pack." A bit steadier now, Molly reached up and rested her free hand on Astrid's shoulder. "Raulf has good reason for fearing the outside world, as many of us do. This feral pack has us all scared. Our sanctuary isn't as isolated as we'd like to think."

"Things are changing for demon hunters as well. Not everything is as black and white as we have been raised to believe."

"You're a good match for Bodie. Don't let him take himself too seriously."

Astrid resisted the ironic snort about that one. How many times had her team pulled her out of her own head? Bodie didn't seem to take anything seriously, but Molly knew him better. Astrid freely admitted that her own exterior was a curated and convenient mask. Quiet superiority was much safer than depth, so she didn't try to change people's first impressions of her.

"You've got an early morning. Bodie's usually awake before the sun and won't want to wait around." Molly gently pushed Astrid toward the stairs, not-so-subtly telling her to go to bed. Astrid's own grandmother had passed a few decades before she was born. Her parents hadn't been involved enough to be bossy. Warm and fuzzy inside, Astrid said goodnight and headed upstairs.

Sliding into the surprisingly luxurious Egyptian cotton sheets over a pillow-top mattress, Astrid snuggled under the quilt. Everything about the ranch was homey and old-fashioned, but the werewolves were quietly luxurious. Fabrics were soft and inviting, furniture was sturdy and handmade. Inhaling the mountain air, basking in the serene glow of the moon filtering through the gauzy white curtains, Astrid's limbs grew heavy.

Unintimidated by her own imagination, she indulged in the thoughts of naked Bodie that her conscious brain had been sidestepping all day.

5

HEART THUNDERING AGAINST HIS ribs, cool moisture on his forehead, blankets in erratic disarray on the floor around the bed, Bodie knew the nightmares had haunted him. Again.

At least he couldn't remember the terror this time, but he didn't doubt that his brother had been at the forefront.

He rubbed a hand over his face, wiping away the nightmare, and dragged his ass out of bed. Something ensnared his foot. He nearly panicked, but quickly remembered he was safe in his own bed and kicked his foot free from the scrap of sheet that he was tangled in. He shook his head at himself and slid out of the wily sheets and sat on the edge of the bed.

Sunrise was coming, but the last traces of darkness held the room in a welcome stillness. He remembered his houseguest and pulled on the nearest pair of pants and sauntered to the bathroom.

After lingering in the shower a few minutes longer than necessary, he tossed on some hiking clothes and dashed downstairs. Just as he cleared the last step, he could hear the coffee pot announcing a successful brew with its pleasant chirp. He filled two mugs full and sipped his as he strode back up the stairs. Still dark, the house still, no one else was awake yet.

Mugs carefully balanced in one hand, he turned the nob to Astrid's bedroom. Amber rays of sun fingered across the room, casting a luminous glow that embraced her sleeping form. Blond hair fanning out over the pillow, she snuggled in the blue and white quilt. As he entered, she softly smiled.

He stalled, thinking she was awake. Her breathing still steady and slow, he realized she was actually smiling in sleep. Dreamland must have been a kinder place to her than it had been to him.

After setting their mugs on the bedside table, he lowered himself onto the side of the bed. Couldn't help himself. He brushed an unruly lock of hair out of her face.

Fists flying, she bolted up and she growled, nearly clocked him in the jaw.

Bodie caught her hand before she nailed him, and whispered her name gently, reassuring her that she was safe.

She blinked away the sleep and stilled as she seemed to realize she wasn't under attack.

He grinned at her and eventually released her hand. "Sorry about that. Didn't mean to scare you."

"No, I'm sorry. I, uh..."

"No need to explain. Demon hunter fast asleep. Demon waking her from what looked to have been a pleasant dream. And, I, uh... probably too friendly to come in and wake you like this, but, um... sorry." Hell, he should have knocked first.

"That about sums it up. Again, I'm sorry."

Rather than going back and forth in excessive apologies, he grabbed her coffee from the table for her. "No worries—" His breath caught in his throat.

As she sat up to accept the cup, the strap of her nightgown slipped off her shoulder. Pale pink, the silky fabric was light as air. Mesmerized, his eyes followed the lace edging downward. Barely hanging on, the delicate fabric graced the upper curve of her breast, tormenting him with the hope that the rest would slip further with her next breath.

To keep his hands busy, he gripped his coffee mug tighter, resisting the urge to slide the strap down further, to cup his hand around that petitely pert breast.

Astrid shifted her strap back up and cleared her throat. Eyes swiftly returning to her face, Bodie bit his tongue to hide his blatant appreciation. Calmer than he was, she accepted the offered coffee. The subtle shake of her head and blossoming smile said she wasn't offended by his blatant ogle.

Astrid took a testing sip from the steaming mug. At least she didn't shoo him out of her room right away. "Good morning," she said, starting over.

"Mornin'." He grinned and grabbed his own coffee. "Thought we'd head out as soon as you're ready."

"And I was taking too long, so you thought you'd bribe me with coffee?"

"Pretty much. Didn't mean to startle you, or act like an ass and stare at your tits."

Eyebrows forming a thoughtful scowl, she took another sip before responding. "I wasn't offended by the ogling, actually. My imagination has been similarly occupied. It's more the term *tits*."

Behind his coffee, Bodie floundered, at a complete loss for a decent defense. Her tone bordered on snooty, but the words were honest, and the teasing smile on her lips was fuckably hot. "Again, sorry. I spend way too much time on the ranch." He lifted a teasing grin, and tilted a daring look to mess with her. "Preferred term for the girls? Breasts, boobs, tatas, jugs?"

Head thrown back in laughter, Astrid surprised him yet again. She *should* be offended. He was trying to get a rise out of her, yet she kept surprising him. "I really couldn't say. Thanks for asking, I suppose. Tits is better than jugs I guess, especially to describe these wee things." She chuckled, eyes lively with merriment. He didn't think she even realized she did it, but she ran her fingers through her sleek hair, eyes closing and pink lips parting just slightly.

Stifling a groan, he got lost in the vision. At least his eyes were on hers when she met his gaze again, not wandering tactlessly south. "Trust me, they may not be jugs, but they're fucking spectacular. Although, I can't judge accurately, without seeing the rest..." He grinned mischievously.

"Nice try. And, again, thanks." The corner of her lush lips quirked up. Why wasn't she smacking him upside the head? Miraculously, she seemed almost amused by his antics. Maybe even enjoying his company.

Beyond mutual, he was floored by the enticing dizziness she spun inside him.

"Alright, no more messing around. Let's get moving." He rose from the bed and headed for the door.

"I can be ready in ten." Throwing off the covers, she stood from the bed.

Jaw dropping open, yet again, Bodie stared at her mile-long legs, her nightgown barely covering the good stuff. At her chuckle, he shook his head and smiled sheepishly. He was beginning to think she was torturing him on purpose.

AFTER A LAST-MINUTE PEE, Astrid sauntered outside. Glowing purple and orange in the distance, a scattering of sunlit clouds announced the sun was ready to start the day. Bodie was parked out front, leaned against a mud-splattered quad with their backpacks strapped to the cargo crate in the back.

The moment he saw her coming out, his eyes lit up, and he bit his lower lip with an adorable smile. There it was. The look she'd begun to crave more than the air she breathed.

Every logical neurotransmitter in her brain demanded that she fight it. She was working. He was a werewolf and most certainly didn't fit in with her timeline or lifestyle. And he was all wrong for her.

Was he? Molly seemed to think they were well matched, that she was what he needed. What if he was what she needed? In the last thirty-seven hours, she'd already discovered that much of her worldview was in question, but she'd also laughed more and, quite frankly, contemplated more creatively erotic thoughts than she'd imagined possible.

Demon hunters and demon myths had a lot to say about soulmates and related romantic notions. Demons and their fanciful lore. Ugh. There was no way she was fated for a werewolf. That would be as ridiculous as a demon hunter fated for a vampire. Although, werewolves weren't actually rageful killing machines...

Clearing her confusing musings—and pathetic excuses—she refocused her attention on the mission. Despite the thundering in her chest, the heat coursing through her veins as she drew closer... the mission came first.

Still, she couldn't manage to mask the blush and the smile that tugged at her lips. Stopping just out of arms reach, not trusting herself to get closer, she said, "Ready."

Rubbing the back of his neck, he said, "Great. I, uh, it's a bumpy trail. Think it'll help if you drive?" He stepped to the side and waved for her to climb on first.

Not helpful. His thoughtfulness, presented shyly, was not alleviating her crush. "Thanks. I do much better when I drive. I wasn't looking forward to the inevitable motion sickness."

"I should have thought of that yesterday, on the drive over."

"You didn't know me well enough then."

"A lot's changed since yesterday," he said, shaking his head as he laughed at the absurdity.

"It has, actually," she said, tilting a look before climbing on.

She turned the key and inspected the pedals, the controls, and collected the general idea of its mechanics. After giving her a moment to get comfortable, Bodie swung his leg over and settled behind her.

Okay, maybe this wasn't the best idea. She wouldn't get carsick if she drove, but Astrid wasn't sure she could concentrate with his legs straddling her, his body pressed against her backside. Wrapping around her, he rested his hands on her thighs. Every point of contact burned, yet she craved more.

Crush? More like... were there words for what he did to her? Spontaneous combustion?

The roughness of his whisper brushed over her like a caress. "Follow the trail as far as it will take us. Going to be a long drive."

Resisting the urge to melt into him, she revved the engine. As she eased off the brake, an engine roared from behind them and came to a gravel-crunching stop, inches behind their cargo rack.

"Shit," Bodie muttered under his breath. "Grammy must have fessed up." Pushing back, he climbed off the quad. Astrid shut off the engine and stood, but held back.

A man who looked remarkably like Bodie, plus a few gray hairs scattered in his beard, tore out of the truck. He couldn't be much past two, maybe three hundred, if werewolves aged similarly to demon hunters. The newcomer shot Astrid a canine-bearing sneer before turning to Bodie. "What the hell do you think you're doing?"

Fists balling at his sides, Bodie breathed in a calculated inhale before responding. Astrid could see the tension pulling taut the muscles across his back and shoulders. Despite his subtle signs of frustration, his voice was cool as a cowboy. "Taking care of things. Thought that's what you wanted me to do?"

"Not like this." Frank disappointment rolled off the man's tongue. This must be his father, Raulf. Astrid didn't recognize the parental tone from personal experience, but she understood the concept. Disappointment was undoubtedly more caring than the disinterest she was raised with, but exquisitely distressing.

"Not like what? We can't take the ferals alone." Despite the unmistakable defiance in his posture, Bodie's voice remained calm as the summer breeze. "They're growing. Recruiting more. Murdering humans, decimating wildlife as they go. They're smart. Organized."

"Bodie, come on. She'll turn on you as fast as a feral. Maybe not right away, but as soon as the job's done? Demon hunters aren't going to let werewolves walk free. We're too dangerous."

Tone cooling, Bodie grimaced but didn't growl back. "I'll take that chance. You want me to be alpha, then let me act like it. You can't handle that, then maybe *you* should be alpha."

Bodie's father's jaw ticked fast as he swallowed his retort, rubbing his hand on the back of his neck like Bodie when he was unsure of his next words.

Astrid smiled kindly. She considered the innocent look that worked wonderfully on unsuspecting demons, but she suspected that would fuel his ire. "Hi, Mr. Connery. My name is Astrid. I respect your concerns. Demon hunters can be a violent breed. I have met many myself that I wouldn't trust as far as I can throw them."

His expression remained suspicious, but he let her speak.

"Until I met Bodie, I had no idea that werewolves were gentle and family oriented. I was taught that werewolves were nothing more than the brutal ferals that demon hunters too often face."

Raulf's scowl didn't waver. Clearly, he didn't care that the false assumptions were not unilateral.

"One thing you may find unique about my team is that we ask questions. We consider before attacking. Molly chose well in calling us. I suspect you and I have similar goals. We intend to defend your pack and your secrecy—no other hunters will know that you exist. You're right, that some hunters would see you and see the potential you have to go feral. We're different. We were born to protect, and that extends beyond humans. Please, give us a chance."

Snorting, he pushed some dirt around with his toe. "Pretty fucking heroic of you." His sarcasm was... not refreshing. Still, Astrid couldn't fault him for it. He was distrustful for good reason.

She chuckled gently, rolling her eyes in agreement, capping it off with a heartening smile. "It does sound remarkably altruistic. Still, that is why we exist. Begat by the lover of the demon king to protect humanity from the monsters they released into this realm."

Raulf appeared unmoved, but maybe less acutely furious.

Bodie laced his fingers with hers and gently pulled her back toward the quad. The gesture, possessive and affectionate, was not lost on his father. Eyes nearly crossing with disbelief, Raulf turned abruptly and stormed back to his truck, slamming the door behind him. Rebelliously, the door bounced back open and refused to close again, the latch having broken from the force of his temper. He held the door closed and peeled back down the driveway.

Hand still linked with hers, Bodie exhaled like he'd been holding onto the oxygen since his father had arrived. "Sorry about my dad. He's..."

Astrid shook her head. "No worries. He's scared. I'll be happy to prove him wrong." Regretfully releasing his hand, she slid back onto the quad.

"You may want to consider avoiding words like 'begat' when you try to convince him that demon hunters are similar to werewolves."

She chuckled and fired up the engine. "And you may want to consider not touching me in front of him, when convincing him you've made a sound decision."

Throwing his leg over the quad behind her, Bodie wrapped his arms around her waist. "What can I say? I'm a glutton for punishment, and you, Astrid Edmonds, are hot as hell, you're fearless, and you are easy to joke around with."

"Likewise," she said, glancing back at him.

Nibbling his bottom lip, he reached around and looped a hand around her middle. Astrid slid rapidly backwards along the smooth seat as he pulled her against him. Wrapped securely in his arms, she let the inferno envelop her like a guilty pleasure.

Astrid shifted into gear and steered them along the muddy path. Funny, even wolves apparently enjoyed four-wheeling, as she could see a few track-heavy pullouts that explained the mud that was caked onto the wheel wells. They drove in silence, Bodie remaining pinned to her backside.

At some point—and she could recite the moment to the precise second—when the sun had cleared the horizon but had yet to warm the air, he'd slid his hands under her sweatshirt and brushed across the bare skin of her abdomen with his cool hands.

Glancing back, she raised an eyebrow.

With a grin, his whispered low and rich into her ear. "My hands are cold." They didn't stay cold for long. The connection heated them both to scorching in half a heartbeat.

Conversation limited thanks to the noisy engine, they didn't talk much on the ride. Astrid appreciated the drive for the delight of basking in the majestic scenery, but she also was stuck spending way too much time contemplating her situation. Her reaction to Bodie was... she wanted to say confusing. No, it was very, very clear what was going on. One's pulse didn't accelerate, breath didn't quicken, brain didn't muddle at the mere thought of someone unimportant. Lust: obviously. More, she knew it would take very little for her to fall flat on her face for him. And she knew she wasn't alone.

Ha, that would be a fantastic way to finally flash a little rebellion at her parents. Always the good girl, but damn, bringing home a werewolf?

Over-analyzing, as usual, Astrid couldn't help but explore the possibilities. They weren't good.

Physically: she knew they would be compatible. Although, would their children be more demon hunter or werewolf?

Mentally, emotionally: probably fine.

Geographically: outlook not so good.

Lifestyle: impossible. Demon hunting required a lot of travel, often last minute. Bodie lived hours outside of civilization and was the future alpha. He couldn't go anywhere.

Finally, acceptance: their joining would ruffle some Edmonds' feathers, but would tear the Connerys apart.

Astrid ignored the hunger pangs as lunchtime came and went. They had a lot of ground to cover. Climbing higher, curving around the hill, then descending again as the path led deeper into the Rockies, trees changed into subalpine firs, to spruce, then back again.

Why couldn't she be one of those people who could have a little fun, without wondering where things might lead? To act impulsively? To live for the moment? Lana would want to know how good werewolf stamina was in human form, and dive in headfirst. While clearing the road of boulders and fallen trees, Bodie had demonstrated demon-hunter like strength. Sex with another demon-human hybrid could be... mmm... satisfying and adventurous.

Reaching a raging river with no obvious crossing, the end of the trail, Astrid stopped and shut off the engine. Standing on solid ground, they both stretched and paced in silence. After sneaking away for a private refresh, Astrid returned to find Bodie crouched in front of the river while the final light of day filtered into night. Dipping his hands into the river, he splashed fresh water over his face, then ran his wet fingers through his hair.

Astrid's heart lurched when he rose to his feet. The quiet honesty, made adorable by his drippy hair standing on end, his expression a mix of worry about the mission and a desperation to succeed, tugged at something deep in her belly. As she approached, his gaze landed on her, and the depth of his expression didn't change, but the tone morphed into an unreserved longing that tugged deeper.

At least she wasn't the only one arguing with herself about the impossibility of the exhilarating lust. Well, she presumed that's what his look meant. The ache in it was almost palpable.

Realizing she'd been caught checking him out, yet again, her cheeks flushed red.

The corner of his mouth quirked up. Stalking closer, he paused just out of arm's reach. "There's a gorgeous spot to camp a few miles upriver. Should be plenty of light from the moon tonight, if you don't mind waiting on dinner a bit longer?"

Nodding, Astrid couldn't quite find the words to respond. Instead, she gulped from her freshly refilled water bottle and climbed back on the quad to drive along the wide beach, upriver. Bodie's arms wrapped around her again, like he belonged there. Electric yet comforting in startling harmony, his fingers grazed over the skin of her middle, sometimes tormenting her as he explored.

Hours later, the sun a distant memory, the river widened, and a waterfall rumbled nearby. As they entered a lush meadow, voice hoarse from a solid eighteen hours without speaking more than a few words, Bodie said, "We're here."

He'd been right, the glow of the moon over the river had provided plenty of light for the drive. A half-circle waterfall poured into a pool before the river narrowed again and flowed down the valley. A wide, sandy beach told of the centuries this pool had thrived here. Tucked just off the beach, a cozy meadow of low grass and wildflowers was surrounded by dense forest.

Astrid walked along the edge of the river and saw there was a brick firepit with a grate. Had they reached a campground? Scowling, she glanced around to be sure they were alone.

From behind her, Bodie stopped at her side. "I, uh, come here a lot."

While Bodie started a fire, Astrid unrolled the wool blanket from their gear and laid their sleeping bags atop it. The ground was still damp from the recent rain, but now there wasn't a cloud in the sky. They wouldn't need the tent tonight, and she wanted to sleep under the stars. It had been several years since she'd last been camping. Too many urban monsters these days, she supposed.

"I'm going to change and scope out the area." Bodie was already stripping off his clothes and tossing them on top of his sleeping bag.

Astrid glanced around, feeling amazingly secluded, but agreed. "I'll get some dinner going."

SOMETHING ABOUT THE BACKPACKER'S chili-mac-n-cheese for a late dinner that Astrid had shared was much more convenient and satisfying than the rabbit or deer he normally ate as the wolf while in the wilderness. Comfort food at its finest, after a long day of travel. Plus the cool glow of the moon and the rumbling thunder of the waterfall. It all filled Bodie's limbs with lead. In a good, sleepy way. Or maybe he was so zonked because it was past two in the morning, and he'd been pressed up against Astrid's backside on the quad for the last eighteen hours, struggling to keep things PG.

His situation was minimally improved now. Although his eyes had fluttered shut the moment he zipped himself into the sleeping bag, thoughts of Astrid danced in his brain. Correction, not *thoughts*, but vivid fantasies. What he'd like to be doing with the last few hours of darkness. Not one of those ideas included sleeping.

Her breathing evened out as she fell asleep, her shoulder only inches away from his. Were those watermelon-pink lips as lush and sweet as he imagined? He'd discovered that her hair was as silky as it looked, her skin was as smooth as he had imagined, and her subtle scent held a surprising lightness, like the air in the middle of a rain cloud. Demon hunters were tough to scent, as he'd quickly discovered, but now that he'd locked on to hers, he had no doubt it would be permanently imprinted in his mind.

Silently, he swallowed a groan before expressing his sexual frustration out loud. Apparently, it had been way, way too long since he'd been this close to a woman.

As the sandbags of sleep finally began to pour over his extremities, he was dragged into the typical nightmares. *Claws lashing at him, a growl demanding he follow. Sucking him in deeper, the nightmare imprisoned him in his nightly self-induced torment.*

Like an angel reaching for him, Astrid knelt over him. Her soothing whisper reassured him. The sweet honey of her eyes let him know that she wouldn't let any harm come to him. In the dream, he connected hands with her and let her pull him out from the pit he was buried in.

Gasping from the bizarre dream, Bodie's eyes slammed open, his heart thundered in his chest. Hand resting on his cheek, Astrid gazed down, her eyes melty with concern.

As quickly as it had sucked him under, the nightmare faded. In its place, a yearning washed over him.

Bodie buried his hand in her hair and rose to meet her, and pressed his lips to hers. Despite the clear sky above, brilliant lightning flashed in his vision, through his limbs and burrowing deep in his chest, more potent than the adrenaline of racing full speed across mountaintops.

Melding, penetrating, he caressed her tongue with his.

Moaning softly against his mouth, Astrid rolled to the side, pulling him with her.

Bodie shifted his leg moved to wrap around her, but the sleeping bag blocked him.

A splash of icy cold water couldn't have stopped him as abruptly as the damn barrier between them. Painful fucking reminder that they were on a mission and from different worlds. Fucking hell. Fantasizing about a demon hunter was one thing, even flirting with her was pushing it, but actually hooking up with the hunter would shatter his pack's trust in him—and her.

Dropping to his back again, his head hit the ground with a thud. Breath coming fast, he watched the mocking twinkle of the stars overhead. At his side, he heard Astrid's harsh sigh. The distance between them widened into a perilous crevasse, sending an aching chill that drilled into his bones as she rolled away.

She'd clearly been on board, kissing him back with equal fervor. Still, stupid things happened in the middle of the night, good intentions tossed right out the window. Emotionally, physically, they were pretty fucking inevitable. Mentally, he couldn't be so sure. It was clear she put work first, was dedicated to a fault. Which was part of her appeal.

He should say something. Anything. Acknowledge what happened. But he couldn't make himself. She would, and should, say this was a bad idea. Or, that she was as aroused as he was... and then he might just jump her.

Instead, he stared up at the stars until they blurred into nonsensical constellations. The next few hours were a montage of the many ways they could flesh things out, if things were different. A pleasant change from his dream before she'd rescued him.

Sunrise finally teased its pending ascent on the horizon. Chest rumbling as he chuckled silently, he thought about how many times he'd nearly come during the night and realized he'd been dreaming like a horny teenager.

Yep, he was totally losing it. Not two days ago, he had been worrying about how he was going to convince the demon hunting team to help them. Had been afraid Raulf was right, and they would be a danger to his pack.

Now... he was a walking erection, hoping the gorgeous demon hunter was as interested as he was. His poor brain was a muddled mess. Taking the feral pack was critical, but chances were, not all the good guys were going to make it out okay.

He needed a clear head, and that meant *not* thinking about Astrid twenty-four seven.

6

A WASH OF ORANGE and pink glowed over the treetops, dark blue fading on the opposite side of the sky. Purple clouds converged overhead. The waterfall rumbled nearby. Still cool, the dawn breeze brushed over Astrid's cheeks.

Smiling, Astrid decided this might be her new favorite way to wake up. Heart thundering in her chest, still ridiculously aroused from reliving that kiss in her dreams all night, plus thinking of where it could have gone, she was afraid she might jump him on sight. She sat upright and turned toward Bodie.

Gone.

His sleeping bag was laid out next to her, his backpack still on the quad. Smoke tickled across her nose as a stronger gust of wind blew through the meadow. Bodie must have started the fire before heading out.

He can't have been gone long. The pool at the base of the waterfall looked as warm as the golden sunrise, but Astrid knew it was sourced from snowmelt.

Still... she bit her lip in anticipation. A little cold never bothered demon hunters. And it might be days until she could shower. Bodie was probably on another long wolfy run, maybe scoping out the trail. Besides, she'd already seen him naked. Werewolves probably couldn't care less about nudity. It wasn't like they all ducked inside to undress, shift, open the doorknob with their wolfy teeth, then go for a stroll.

Pleased with her decision, she slipped out of her nightgown and tiptoed across the cool sand.

Yikes, not as warm as it looked. Oh well, Astrid decided to make the most of it. She grabbed the biodegradable soap she'd picked up in Kalispell. Ignoring the chill of the water, she washed efficiently, then enjoyed a few minutes of serenity.

Floating on her back, she gazed up at the brightening sky. Astrid worked and reworked every angle on what the hell was going on with her. That kiss last night had been one for the record books. Bodie's body pressed against her the day before, all day, had felt so *right*. She wanted to give in and let it happen.

But she knew she shouldn't. The night they'd met, she could have taken the three ferals as she'd boasted, but she couldn't have easily taken a fourth. Not with these ferals anyway, they were different. Tougher. Smarter.

Dammit, why did she always have to be the practical one? Why couldn't she dive in headfirst? To danger, or romance, or, well, anything.

From the corner of her eye, she saw a dark figure approaching at full speed. Swimming back, she looked up to the top of the ridge near the waterfall. As the wolf, Bodie ran with remarkable grace.

He leaped off the ledge, changing to the man in midair. He whooped and came splashing into the water a few feet away. Surfacing, he shook the excess water from his hair. With a few strokes, he reached her.

All of her good intentions were swept down river as a flash flood of *want* coursed through her.

Reaching, she wrapped her arms around his sculpted shoulders. Lips meeting fluidly, he looped his arms around her waist, anchoring her to him. Angling, she took him deeper as his tongue plundered. Heat licked through her body, suddenly burning up despite the cold water surrounding them.

Her legs encircled him, and he hardened against her. His mouth trailed over her jaw, her neck, her shoulders with a fevered urgency.

As the river danced around them, desire building, she rocked against him. His skin was slick, cool and burning. The rough of his beard rubbed across her cheek, her neck, before he shifted back and took her mouth deeply for a long, ravenous kiss.

Pressure and need rose between them as they plundered, everything else a distant memory.

Breath coming quickly as he held her, his length rigid against her core, they moved together. Instinct raged, no clothing to separate them, and she settled over him. Long and hard, he rubbed against her, and began to slip inside, the exquisite pleasure already taking her breath away... then he abruptly pulled back and cussed under his breath. "Sorry."

Lust firing hard, disappointment lurching over her, she tried to say something, but she couldn't find her voice to say anything. Intelligible thought was impossible. So, she swam away.

Avoiding eye contact, she walked out of the water and slipped on the navy-blue cargos and a white tank she'd laid out for herself.

Had "sorry" been an apology for stopping, or for taking it so far? She'd made her intentions pretty damn obvious.

She shook her head, refusing to let herself form a pity party of one.

No, it was mutual. She wouldn't attempt to convince herself that he hadn't wanted her as much as she wanted him. Or let herself over-complicate things. As usual.

At least one of them had enough brain power to stop things before they blew right past the point of no return. Hadn't she been telling herself how *that* shouldn't happen? If the others in his pack were even half as distrustful as his father… she couldn't be the wedge that drove them apart.

Lips turned down in a pitiful pout, she felt miserable doing the right thing. Always the good girl she was raised to be.

After packing up her gear and getting ready for the upcoming hike, she relented that she was going to have to not only look at Bodie at some point, but probably talk to him, too. She was about to turn around and pretend she wasn't upset, when he came up behind her. Reaching around her, he held a cup of coffee under her nose, the steam wafting out of the stainless-steel mug.

Grateful, she accepted the peace offering. She turned in his arms.

Now that he had both hands free, he cradled her face and brushed his lips over hers. "I can't seem to keep my hands… or, well, my mouth, off of you." He smiled sadly. "Sorry."

Astrid pulled in a controlled inhale before speaking, not trusting herself to articulate clearly. She stepped toward the fire and lowered herself to the ground, pouring him a cup and holding it out in invitation for him to join her. "Before… *that*, I had been telling myself all the reasons we shouldn't do *that*. I guess I'm glad you have more willpower than I do."

He accepted the coffee and sat next to her. "Willpower isn't the right word for it. Refusing to be *that guy* is more accurate. When we make love… I have no doubt, it's going to be spectacular." He waggled his eyebrows in a goofy seductive expression before continuing, serious on a long breath. "But, hell, typical, that I'm this distracted when there's so much at stake. We should probably, you know… not get distracted."

Her heart leapt into her throat at the sound of *when* instead of *if*. Perhaps just once, after this was over, she could indulge. It's not like sex equated to forever. Scowling, she didn't care for the sound of that, as if her heart was already breaking, when she hadn't even risked it yet.

Coffee cup inches from his mouth, Bodie stilled. "Okay, wait, weird question..." He trailed off, looking adorably awkward as he glared into his drink.

Astrid had little doubt that his brain was on the same track hers suddenly was. She didn't feel like taking it easy on him. Instead, she smiled innocently as if to say, *you may continue.*

"I'm just enjoying picturing when we do get to... be distracted, but I'm getting bogged down in the details. And, definitely one of those conversations that needs to happen *before* the good stuff. Werewolves, uh, when we... procreate... it's not always... I mean... I pretty much know when my landing team is going in hot and ready to strike."

Laughter bubbled up from her throat and erupted in a fit of giggles.

"Hey, it's a legit question."

Between giggles, she managed to say, "That wasn't a question."

He finally chuckled with her. "Semantics."

Calming the giggle fit, Astrid took a few sips before responding. "Demon hunters are similar. About once each year, one of the girls will venture down and try to catch herself a mate. And I can feel when it's happening." A few more giggles surfaced. "Actually, it won't happen if I'm on a mission, so we're in the clear if something, well, slips in." Like it almost did.

It counted as almost, not actually, right? When it wasn't any more than the tip? And now she was blushing like a horny virgin. Bogged down by sex semantics.

Laughter rumbled deep in his chest. "Double-edged sword, isn't it? A mission is a damn good reason to not get caught up in lust, yet apparently it has its perks."

"I must say... well, first, I'm really not one of those girls who writes our names together over and over in her journal because I have a crush on you... but while we're considering the nuances of our predicament, I think a demon-hunter-werewolf hybrid would be quite interesting. We are so much alike already from what I am finding, with at minimum, similar lifespans and strength."

"I've done some research on your kind. From what it sounds like, yeah, we have a lot in common. Different demon ancestor, but I gotta say, I'm a bit jealous of your healing abilities."

"You don't have accelerated healing?"

"We do, but nothing like yours. We have to eat healthy, and we can break bones and need medical care. Not easy to get a chronic disease or anything, but we have to work a bit harder at self-care than you do."

"Fitness and training are important, but we have an innate level of health that a lot of demon hunters rely on. Although, we can get cavities, so good dental health is necessary."

"Ha, got you beat there. Wolf teeth are resilient."

Joking around, one-upping each other with their abilities and then smoothing it over with a coating of self-effacing, they enjoyed their morning coffee and savored their gourmet breakfast of astronaut scrambled eggs for as long as they could draw out the relaxing morning.

"Speaking of focusing on the mission, we should get going." Bodie brushed the nonexistent crumbs from his hands and stood. They quickly cleaned their breakfast mess and double checked their gear.

Leaving the quad in the secluded meadow, they crossed a natural log bridge over the river and hiked northeast.

ANOTHER EIGHTEEN SOLID HOURS of travel, on foot this time, and Bodie was toast. It would have been easier alone, as the wolf. Still, werewolves and demon hunters were mile for mile in stamina. Well, almost. Astrid wasn't panting quite as heavily as he was, but they were both wiped out.

Admittedly, it was more spinning his mental tires than exertion that sapped his energy. He was already tied in knots before this thing going on between him and Astrid started. How was he going to convince Raulf to trust him, and to convince the rest of the pack that they needed help?

Dammit, Noah was supposed to be alpha, not him. Bodie had nearly convinced their dad to let him spread his wings—temporarily at least. To get an education, maybe travel for a few years. He had always planned to explore the world before settling back home again. Everything changed thanks to Noah.

What was wrong with werewolves, that they couldn't join the twenty-first century? Dynasties, monarchies. Bullshit. There were plenty in the pack who would gladly take on the alpha role and be damn good at it.

The whole Astrid thing complicated everything. He'd given himself mental vertigo trying to figure out what to do about his crush on her. Okay, so crush was an understatement. Pornographic lust was more accurate, live and in living color now, thanks to their swim. Yeah, maybe they'd get to fool around a bit when this whole thing was over. Then what?

Lust wasn't the half of it. That gorgeous smile. Tough to bring it out, but the more he got to know her, the more she let it show. That lithe body that was pure grace and strength. And that wicked sense of humor he suspected she shared with few others.

It would be hard enough to convince a human partner to move out to the middle of fucking nowhere with him, if she could even accept his bizarre heritage and demon ancestry. He didn't stand a chance at a future with a demon hunter. Feared and despised by his pack, his father in particular, she'd be an outcast. And she needed to be where the monsters were, far from the secluded ranch that he was bound to.

At the end of the ridge, they both paused to soak up the endless view, the big starry sky, before descending the final slope for the day. Fucking exhausted, he needed a break. The great outdoors provided too much time to think, which he normally enjoyed. But he normally didn't have so much to think about.

Wouldn't Raulf have a fit if he knocked up the demon hunter? Poor guy might spontaneously combust, knowing a demon hunter carried his grandchild.

Slow down, he shook his head and cleared those premature thoughts from his head. But he couldn't clear her from his mind. Something told him she'd still be bouncing around in his thick skull a couple hundred years from now.

Cautious as gravel rolled down the steep slope, he angled his feet perpendicular to the hill. Vegetation was sparse, and one wrong move could send them sliding hundreds of feet down.

If he had a future with Astrid or not, things were moving fast. Hell, his whole plan of holding off until the mission was done was going to be as ineffective as a horse and a donkey expecting grandkids.

Astrid kept pace as the slope began to level out. Not once did she rub her eyes or complain or say she needed a break. If all demon hunters were like her, no wonder Raulf feared them. Not threatening, but she was unstoppable. Grammy was right. They needed this team.

Tree trunks became longer and thicker as they lowered in altitude. The first eight hours, they'd joked around and talked about everything and nothing. The next ten hours had grown increasingly silent as they both sensed the eerie lack of life, thanks to the ferals.

"Let's set up camp," he said as the ground flattened and the forest became dense enough to provide good cover. They were only a few miles from the biggest damn feral pack in history. No fire tonight. No naked swim in the morning.

"Here?"

"Yeah. I'd guess they're another four hours' hike from here. We'll need to stay hidden in case any are out for an evening stroll."

Astrid dropped her backpack to the ground and gulped from her water bottle. She downed it by half, then took a deep breath. "I know they won't smell me. What about you?"

Bodie dropped his backpack. "Yeah, they'll smell me as an ordinary human. I shouldn't go any closer like this."

He'd immediately noticed how difficult it had been to get a scent off Astrid. He had to be inches away. Which, well, he preferred to be as close to her as possible, so he was getting to know her scent well. Made sense though. They wouldn't be useful hunters if a demon could easily pick up on their smell, and both werewolves and vampires had keen senses of smell.

"What about as the wolf?"

"They won't smell me as anything more than an ordinary wolf. We'll have to hope they don't have a taste for wolves."

After a quick dinner of protein bars and dried fruit, they curled up in their sleeping bags. Another rainless night, thank goodness. They didn't bother with the tent. This time, he'd behave himself. Sort of.

She'd clearly been on his same page, lying her sleeping bag next to his on the blanket, side by side again. Guess they were both gluttons for punishment. Once they'd zipped into their sleeping bags, he tucked his arm around her, snuggling tight. The restricting mummy bag was a helpful barrier, like a full body condom to keep his single-minded dick in check.

Maybe it was the exhaustion, maybe it was the close proximity to Astrid, who knows, but for the first time in months, Bodie slept soundly in dreamless sleep.

As the sun peeked through the trees, Astrid turned in his arms. Warm lips against his, she didn't linger, but pulled away and said, "Let's get moving."

Groaning, Bodie actually had a tough time waking up. That was rare. As soon as they got home, he was sleeping for twenty-four hours straight.

7

THEY'D LEFT THEIR GEAR behind in case they needed to make a quick exit. Nothing about the feral pack was reassuring. Organized ferals living on the dilapidated property of a ranch that dated back to the early 1870s? Not Astrid's typical fight. Apparently, the mine owner had built the ranch to hide his mining operation. Either a smart landowner, diversifying his holdings, or another foolish prospector that had found cattle to be more lucrative than gold.

They kept to the trees and crossed the valley before heading up the far ridge. With Bodie in wolf form, the walk was starkly quiet, although he was easy to be with no matter what form he was in. She didn't think he'd appreciate that it made her consider getting a dog when she got home. Or maybe he'd think it was funny. Or he might even be flattered.

As they neared the top of the narrow ridge, they dropped to the ground to stay out of sight. Lying on their abdomens, they crawled to the edge and watched for activity. A few ferals wandered around the desolate grounds. Peering through the binoculars, alternating with jotting down notes, Astrid started a detailed list of observations to bring back to the team.

Her stomach clenched as she watched a pair devouring a deer.

She snuggled closer to Bodie. He nuzzled under her chin and gave her a wolfy lick on the cheek. She turned her head and rolled her eyes at him. Mouth open in a gentle pant, he seemed to be smiling at her.

She scratched behind his ears before returning to the binoculars. It didn't look too bad, the snapshot moment, anyway. She counted five at the most.

They held their position as the sun rose toward midday. Bodie watched her routine with curiosity. She sketched the layout of the property, noting details of each structure, each cluster of trees, estimated dimensions. She set up a camera and recorded the property, highlighting feral activity. She wished they could have brought more permanent surveillance equipment, but it was risky even getting this close and staying for so long.

As a demon hunter, her scent was minimal, a beneficial safety trait. But anything they might leave behind could be sniffed out if the ferals patrolled the area. A remote monitoring system would be fantastic, but she didn't want to risk discovery and further endanger Bodie's pack. If these ferals were even half as intelligent as she feared, she didn't want them to have an inkling that they were being watched.

Five ferals in V-formation approached the main house, growling as they communicated with each other. Striding on their hind legs more smoothly than the average feral, dressed in ripped military fatigues over broad shoulders, these were like ferals juiced on steroids and testosterone. Similar to these, and markedly different from the others around the property, a feral in a sleeveless military jacket and ripped pants strode out with a purposeful gait and tidier appearance. He halted at the top of the front steps, the last of the day's sun casting him in an almost peaceful glow. At her side, Bodie growled under his breath, his body tensing from the tips of his ears to end of his tail.

Must be their leader. Molly was right. It had taken a powerful, self-aware feral to form such an organized group. More than one, as the V of five appeared to be remarkably more in control than any she had seen before.

Another group, this one numbering eight ferals, joined the formation. These weren't as rational, digging at their fur, snapping at each other. Yet even these were more coherent than was typical.

Nineteen ferals.

Ryan had requested an urgent shore leave from the Coast Guard to join the fight, and Quinn was hardly showing in her pregnancy. She had already made it very clear that she wasn't "sitting at home knitting" just because she was "knocked up." Vann, Lana, and Bennett were awaiting her call. Two to three each, doable even without Bodie's pack.

Shit, she calculated too prematurely.

The leader howled into the air as the moon rose, his voice rattling the air for miles in every direction, sending chills down her spine. From what must be the mineshaft across the property, the barn, another house, another dozen, no—fifteen, twenty-three, thirty-two...

Astrid's heart pounded rapidly. Blood leached from her face as she struggled to count their increasing numbers. Standing in a mass, pushing and shoving in front of the main house, nearly a hundred ferals began to howl in unison.

At her side, Bodie shifted his claws in the dirt, a low growl rumbling through his bared teeth.

Scratching their clawed feet on the ground, the ferals whooped and howled in unison. On command, they turned and sprinted to the south and east. Bodie had been right to take the long way around and watch from the steepest cliff. None were taking this route.

Astrid paled as she realized the significance of their paths. Major national park tourist centers were a few dozen miles east, and residential areas down the valley to the south. Not much to the north until they crossed the Canadian border, and they were surrounded by steep cliffs without proximity to civilization to the west. They weren't just pillaging for the benefit of their stomachs, they were acting with purpose.

Astrid stepped back from the ledge and put the binoculars in the case.

There was just no way.

They were hunters, a team, not a military battalion. She lay flat on her back, knees bent, crossing her arms over her chest, realizing just how much this situation was fucked.

Bodie snuggled closer and rested his head on her shoulder. Mindlessly, she brushed her hand in his fur.

ONCE THE HOWLS OF hungry ferals faded into the distance, Bodie slipped back from the edge of the cliff. Astrid packed up the rest of her surveillance gear and crawled out of site. Without pausing, she took off down the slope. Bodie ran along at her side.

Deep in the forest where they'd camped last night, Bodie shifted back to human form and threw on his clothes. After a quick hydration and protein bar dinner, they pulled on their packs and set off together at a boot-burning pace.

Neither said a word as they hiked through the night. The day's accumulating clouds were now a near-complete conglomerate of moisture. The threat of rain was heavy in the air.

The situation was so much worse than he'd anticipated. At least twice as many as he'd seen before. Either he simply hadn't seen them all when he'd scouted before, or they truly were actively recruiting.

He hadn't seen the leader last time. The militant organization. Even if their numbers weren't so high, the fight would be near impossible.

As the sun rose, Bodie uttered in a raspy voice, "I can't ask you and your team to take this on."

Voice tight with an edge of concerted control, Astrid pushed her shoulders back and kept walking. "I think I've made it clear. This is what we do. The reason we exist."

"You didn't sign on for certain death."

Flipping back, her hair loosened from its tight braid. "Actually, I did. That's my life. I made a choice when I turned eighteen and took on my demon hunter abilities. To dedicate my life to *this*." She inhaled forcefully before continuing. Bodie's jaw ticked rapidly with a fury that matched hers. "It won't be easy. I'll call in my team. We'll train. We'll research. We'll eliminate the threat because it must be done. I'm not walking away from this."

Stopping in front of her, Bodie growled as he said, "Not every problem can be solved by well-read, heavily armed demon hunters. Astrid, that—" He stopped abruptly, biting his tongue to prevent blurting out something he'd regret.

"Trust me, we know what we signed on for. Yes, it's worse than any of us could have imagined, but we'll deal."

"They have military training. Not some cluster of ferals out to play with their food."

"I noticed."

Matching stride for stride, neither slowed from their furious pace. Bodie ground his teeth together, pushing his emotions aside before they controlled him. "You and me, five more from your team, six more decent warriors from my pack. That leaves thirteen against a hundred."

"Raulf will fight with us? Will the others?"

He sneered. "They will, because they'll have to. You get some good footage?"

Astrid nodded. "We'll map it out. Analyze their strengths and weaknesses."

"It won't be enough."

"We'll figure it out."

He wished he shared her optimism. Not his first fight, but she'd been through some serious shit. Grammy had called this team for a reason. She'd better be right.

As HER FEET TRUDGED without any input from her conscious mind, Astrid wracked her brain to come up with a solution. The sky was glowing orange as the sun descended over the mountains. She couldn't find the will to stop and camp, her mind so preoccupied, she wouldn't catch a wink of sleep, anyway.

Taunting drips of rain dappled the ground as they entered a clearing, splattering on her cheeks and hair. Sniffing the air, Bodie groaned, "Not going to be a light sprinkle. We're almost back to the waterfall. Can you hike in the rain another hour or so?"

Nodding, Astrid strapped her backpack tighter and pushed on. They'd hiked without stopping at the punishing pace for nearly two days straight. Another few hours wouldn't hurt. Within minutes, fat drops fell from the sky and flooded down her cheeks, but she was too worn out to wipe them away. Legs of jelly, feet no more than numb appendages flopping at the end of her legs, Astrid knew she could keep hiking for a week if she had to, but her self-assurance was a ghost left at the hilltop overlooking the feral encampment.

She needed her team. She needed a dose of Quinn's snarky. Of Lana's energy. Vann's quiet fortitude. Bennett's doggedness. Ryan's thoughtfulness. They'd rally, boosting each other to keep going.

Despite the lead that filled her legs, she nearly did a cartwheel of relief when she finally heard the rumbling waterfall. They crossed over the log bridge and stumbled the last few feet to the secluded meadow.

Wordlessly, both dumped their backpacks on the grass that was bordering on soggy. Bodie had his tent up within minutes, and Astrid followed close behind with their sleeping bags and the rest of their gear to store in the dry tent. They'd brought two tents, but she didn't feel like setting hers up. Besides, she needed... him.

Platonically. Even if it killed her.

Sensation swiftly returned to her feet as she tugged off her muddy boots. Without glancing back, she crawled the rest of the way into the tent and started stripping before climbing into her sleeping bag.

"Be right back," Bodie murmured as he zipped up the tent against the rain.

Astrid immediately reopened the tent and watched him already starting his run around the perimeter as the wolf. She gathered his clothes and boots and tucked them neatly inside the door of the tent next to their backpacks, then laid out his sleeping bag alongside hers.

Curling up in her sleeping bag, she focused on the dull thumping of raindrops on the top of the tent, determined to keep her eyes open until he returned.

Bodie climbed into the tent a few minutes later. In the darkness, his eyes shone with a supernatural blue glint, and the cool glow of the moon accented every gorgeous feature on the well-built man. He slipped into his sleeping bag, leaving just enough unzipped to wrap his arm around her.

Astrid turned into him and buried her face against his neck, inhaling deeply. His unique scent, spiced with salt from the long day and washed clean with the rainy mountain air, was a potent aromatherapy.

"Bodie?" she asked, her voice so hoarse she didn't recognize it.

"Yeah?" His voice was even raspier.

"I... we..." Her brain was too tired to translate what her heart was demanding. "Never mind."

"I know. Me too." He opened his eyes and pulled back to look at her, the corners of his mouth forming a sleepy smile.

Her eyes drifted closed. Then open again. "Bodie?" she asked again.

"Yeah?" His crackly voice was laced with humor this time.

"What's your middle name?"

"Now you're chatty? We've been walking together for almost two days, and you hardly said a word."

She smiled against his neck as he laid his head back down. "I couldn't think of anything to say then. I was nearly asleep, and I realized I don't know your middle name. What if I accidentally have sex with you, and I don't know your full name?"

"Be careful, in case you trip and fall onto my dick." His hoarse laugh vibrated through them both. "Accidents happen."

"Shut up. You know what I mean."

"Ranger."

"What?"

"That's my middle name. Boden Ranger Connery."

"Seriously?"

His Adam's apple bobbed against her forehead as he chuckled. "What's wrong with Ranger?"

"You're a wolf named Ranger. May as well have gone with Fido."

"Hey, I like the name." As she snuggled close, he partially unzipped her sleeping bag and wrapped his arms around her.

"Me too. And I wouldn't have thought anything of it, if you hadn't been begging for treats and a scratch behind the ears earlier." Still nuzzled into his neck, she surrendered to a giggle.

"Fair point. Come on, what's yours?"

"Rosetta."

"Astrid Rosetta Edmonds. Oh my, you were destined for boarding school and limousines and posh brands, weren't you?" His hand traced along the bare skin of her back as he shifted her nightgown out of the way.

"I wish. Tutors only. Although I have ridden in many limousines. I was nineteen before I saw the inside of a department store."

"Who did you get into trouble with? I may have been home schooled the first seventeen years of my life, but I had the neighborhood kids to mess around with. Noah and I used to challenge Rain and Nash and Nash's older brother, Morrison, with fort building, foot races, sparring, hide and seek. Hide and seek is a hell of a lot of fun when you can sniff out your prey." His voice lilted in a dreamy pattern, the grit of fatigue coating it.

"Sounds like an amazing place to grow up."

"It really was. But Raulf doesn't seem to get that not everyone wants to spend their entire lives in the same place. We have about ten permanent werewolf families. A few more that travel, but this is their home base. Not many around my age though. Noah's gone. Rain's been back from college a few years now. Nash is the baby of our group and doesn't seem to have any interest in leaving the county. Morrison and his husband come to visit a few times a year, but for the most part, they're trying to lead a normal life together in Billings. Although

Morrison would come if I asked, he's a fire jumper and stays pretty busy this time of year."

"You miss them?" Until she'd found her team, Astrid had been desperate to find the sense of belonging Bodie described.

"Like a missing limb. Tell me about your team."

Her eyes grew heavier as she spoke. "You'll get to meet them soon. They're the best. Jovial and tenacious." She described each, their charms, their quirks. Demon hunters carefully selected their teams, and she'd been lucky to find such good people.

His palm splayed wide across her back like tree roots. "What's the dumbest monster you've faced?"

"Dumbest?" She was too tired to open her eyes, but she smiled against his skin. She couldn't seem to stop chatting, even though her voice was about to give out.

"Yeah. I heard about the toughest. Grammy heard rumors of that one across the Pacific. Besides, I'd rather hear you laugh again."

"Hmmm. Oh, I've got one."

His chin brushed against her head and his beard tangled in her hair as he laughed.

"I've met some friendly vampires, some vicious ones, and one exceedingly stupid one. I was twenty-two and had just moved into this adorable house in Denver. One of my first nights at my new place, I, of course, went on a detailed patrol to assess local demon activity. This vampire walked right up to me outside of a crowded bar, a drip of blood in the corner of her mouth already. She was wearing about the skimpiest outfit I'd ever seen, and it wasn't that kind of bar. Anyway, she asked me if I had some spare change she could borrow, as it was a few days before payday and she needed gas money."

"Borrow?"

"Yes, borrow. So, I said, 'I'm so sorry, that sounds so stressful. Here's fifty dollars, but I'll need you to pay me back. Can you show me where you live, so I can come by after you get paid?'"

"She didn't."

"She did. Clearly, blood was not her only drug of choice. As luck would have it, she lived with five other vampires. Lana was coming to check out my new place the next day, so we went back together and cleaned up my neighborhood."

The tent shook from his hearty laugh. "Thanks for that. Okay, I'm going to sleep now."

She nodded in agreement.

"Astrid?"

"I thought we were sleeping now."

"I like you."

"I like you, too."

"Okay, you can go to sleep now."

Sleep washed over her seconds later.

Morning came sooner than she would have liked. Before her eyes fluttered open, Astrid felt the loss of Bodie. Her skin was still salty from the interminable hike. At least it had stopped raining. One of Bodie's flannel shirts was on top of his backpack, so she grabbed it and pulled it around her.

Ignoring the wet ground under her bare feet, she stepped out and discovered Bodie had already started the fire and, best of all, the percolator was ready to brew. Her hero.

Before anything, she needed a hot shower. Since that wasn't happening, she stripped off the shirt and bathed in the icy pool. She was so grateful to wash away the grime of the last few days, she didn't care how cold it was.

Spending an extra few minutes arguing with herself about how likely it was that Bodie would dive in soon, hoping he would, but knowing she shouldn't want him to, she eventually both won and lost the mental debate simultaneously. Exiting the water with more disappointment than she ought to feel, she slipped back into his shirt and let the coffee percolate over the flame.

She laid the large wool blanket over the damp grass and warmed by the fire. Clean, wrapped up in Bodie's scent, and surrounded by a pristine Montana morning, she watched the sun grace the top of the mountains in the distance. When the bubbling brew turned dark, she poured her coffee and set the rest aside to keep warm for Bodie.

Well timed, the wolf raced off the ledge over the water. In midair, the wolf transitioned to the man and splashed into the water with an exhilarated whoop. She knew he patrolled as the wolf for their safety, but she was beginning to think he did it more because he craved it. As much a prisoner to responsibility as she was, maybe more, he made the most of freeing moments like his high-speed sprint across the field, the enthusiastic leap over the waterfall's edge.

This was no longer a job. The stakes were so much higher now. Those ferals were incomprehensibly, terrifyingly, beyond anything she could have imagined. Her team was a relatively young team, yet one of the best. For a lot of reasons. But one was that they genuinely cared about the people they protected.

This time... it was too personal. They had essentially agreed that anything personal between them needed to wait until after, if ever.

Too late.

Rising from a long underwater soak, Bodie shook the water from his hair. Lips turned up in a devious grin, he strolled out of the river, downright lickable again, his skin moist and... damn, those muscles were ridiculously toned.

When did she get so shallow?

As he approached, he had that bottom lip pulled into his bite with an adorably sexy grin.

Perhaps it was a newfound sense of existentialism that made her do it, or perhaps it was the instinct to lose oneself in acts of love in the face of an impending, unwinnable battle... or, more likely, it was the naked lust that was becoming too hard to resist. Gaze locking on his sky-blue eyes, Astrid unbuttoned the shirt. A wanton seductress, or so she had suddenly become, she leaned back on her elbows and beckoned him closer.

Not one to mince words, Bodie's grin morphed into a hungry growl and he stalked toward her. Without hesitation, he crawled across the blanket. Taking her lips, his body hovered just over hers, she arched to meet him.

Sweeping his tongue over hers, he groaned. His kiss already familiar, his taste as invigorating and soothing as the alpine air surrounding them, he lowered her down to the ground. His stubbled beard rough against her skin, he trailed kisses down her neck, along her collarbone.

Her hands explored his skin, his taut muscles that moved him so powerfully, landing on his rock-hard cock, tracing her thumb along the shaft.

Nipping at the curve of her breast, he shifted out of her reach and slid the borrowed shirt off her shoulders so she lay naked on the blanket, then took her breast deep in his mouth. Heat radiating from the intense point of contact, her breath halted in her throat. Tormenting with his touch, he proved his appreciation they'd joked about that second morning. Watching his hungry expression as he kissed the narrow between her breasts, traced his thumb over peaked nipples, wrapped his hands around her, her arousal spiked beyond lust, her heart tripping over itself.

As her brain swirled around waves of surprising sensation, heat building, he shifted down her abdomen, pressing savoring kisses as he followed the curve of her ribs, her belly, her hips, before settling between her legs. Tormenting her with playful kisses to her inner thigh, the sensitive skin above her ankle, he drove her mad with anticipation. She found herself begging for exactly what she wanted, daring in a breathy request she'd never heard from herself. His teasing smile swiftly darkened, and he pressed his mouth to her core.

Pressure, the radiant heat from his velvety tongue... he lingered, unhurried. Vibrating with sensation that built like an orchestral crescendo, she relinquished to ecstasy. Circling, sweeping, he responded to her soft sighs, her accelerated cries.

When she teetered on the edge of control, he slid his fingers into her and stroked. Wild, soprano moans escaped her lips in response to every lick. Cresting, soaring, she crossed the line between wavering and claiming.

Still coasting over the clouds above, Astrid felt Bodie caress her body with his hands, his tongue, his lips, as he moved up her torso.

Searching hers, his electric blue eyes sparked. The fire crackled nearby. Heavy between them, regret threatened to rear its ugly head. They wordlessly sat up.

She pulled his flannel shirt back on while he snagged his jeans from the tent. She warmed and poured his coffee while he heated their breakfast.

Letting out a long exhale, she said, "We can't—"

"I know."

"Not just distraction, but your pack—"

"Yeah, I know. You saw how furious Raulf was when I held your hand in front of him. He might spontaneously combust if he caught me kissing you. Raulf hates demon hunters enough as it is, and now that one is seducing his son." He raised his eyebrows suggestively. "Well, he hates just about everyone that isn't a tame werewolf. But demon hunters rank lower than humans, ferals, and even vampires."

Her gut filled with lead. She was glad he was on her same page, but hated that they would have to put this blossoming *something* on the back burner. Doing the wrong thing had felt so damn good, she wanted so much more. "And we need his buy-in."

"Yep. Things are tense enough in the pack right now." He poured the boiling water into their astronaut scrambled eggs. "I... Man, I suck at this." He shook his head again. She could tell he was no better at relationships than she was.

Astrid held onto the perfection of the moment, pushing away the sad. Savoring the complete contentment... and sexual gratification, she let herself focus on the moment. On the mountains glowing majestically purple all around. On Bodie wearing nothing but un-buttoned jeans.

He shifted toward her and pulled her legs around him as they sat together on the blanket. Lips resting against her temple, he kissed her softly. "If we live through this, can I take you out to dinner sometime? Far from werewolves and demon hunters and certain death?"

"Anytime, anywhere."

"My dad's a hard-ass and my mom, although human, isn't much more understanding. Your parents won't be thrilled with you dating a werewolf, will they?"

"On the bright side, they don't hate anyone. In contrast, they don't love anyone either."

His brow scrunched together. "Not even their daughter?"

"Not any of their four children. Not each other. I'm honestly not sure they are capable of such emotion."

He kissed her again. "I'm sorry you had to grow up with that. Once this shit is done..." He paused, biting his cheek.

For one last moment, she trailed her fingers over his corded arms, letting herself feel every bare scrap of his skin. As her fingers trailed along the waistline of his jeans, he sharply inhaled. Groaning, he took her mouth with his. His hands slipped under her top, taking her breasts in his hands.

Exploring, indulging in one last touch, the heat of their connection fused them irreversibly. Leaning his forehead to hers, Bodie groaned, "Damn, I'm having trouble caring what everyone thinks. They can get off their high-horsed asses and do what's best for the pack by joining forces with a dreaded team of demon hunters."

Astrid pulled away just enough to hand him his pouch of scrambled eggs and a fork. She took a bite of her own, even though she wasn't hungry anymore. "Let's just see how the next few days go."

He laughed mirthlessly. "Yeah, we're great at waiting. How long have we known each other? I'm a damn walking erection around you. I might be the first guy on the planet to die of blue balls."

She rolled her eyes, but didn't hide the grin. "We can hold off until after the fight... don't you think?"

Things were going way too fast. They needed to slow down, anyway. Right?

She pushed away the heartache at the idea of waiting. For what? Dinner and a hotel room in Kalispell before she flew back home? A night together every few months when she happened to be traveling east?

8

THE HOUSE WAS A welcome sight after another damn day and a half of travel. Clear skies and no scent of rain in the air, Bodie didn't bother to put away the quad.

Grammy had left the porch light on. Each grabbed their backpacks. His hand ached to link with hers, but on the off chance anyone had seen them arrive, he didn't dare risk it.

Dammit, he'd worked his ass off to learn to keep his temper in check. He hadn't been kidding when he told Astrid how important his early education in meditation and martial arts had been. Maybe a werewolf thing, but equally likely a Raulf thing, Bodie, Noah, and even little Jessie had inherited his short fuse. Not exactly a safe thing, considering what he could turn into if he lost it.

Fucking eh, Noah. Why did you have to run off and ruin my *future?* Exhaling heavily, he forced the obtuse thought from his mind.

Astrid trudged up the front steps ahead of him and disappeared from sight. He dumped his backpack in the entry and filled fresh glasses of water for them both. The shower was already going when he got upstairs.

Fuck it. They were in the privacy of his own home. No one would know. He set their glasses on a nearby bookshelf and snuck into the bathroom.

Steam clouded the shower door, but he could see enough. Hands kneading her hair with the sudsy shampoo, her body arched back.

Dumping his clothes on the ground, he stepped into the shower.

Eyes closed, Astrid stood in the spray, the warm water flowing over her lithe body. He knew she was aware of his presence by her soft smile, but she didn't falter in her routine. Stepping closer, he wrapped his arms around her.

He inhaled the lingering scent of his skin on hers.

Astrid opened her eyes and shook her head in a feigned reproach. "You're really not a patient person, are you?"

"Until you? I was the most patient person on the whole damn planet. Now? Every time I use my brain, I can convince myself of all the reasons I should keep my hands off you. Then, well, when it comes right down to it... I don't want to."

She reached behind him and took the soap from the tray. Focused on her efforts, she worked the soap into a lather and slid her slick hands over his skin, not missing an inch. Already hard before her clever fingers reached him, she tormented him with an extra slippery wash. "Should we keep arguing with ourselves for the next few weeks? Perhaps we could set an hourly alarm so we don't forget."

Groaning, he snagged the soap from her grip and ensured she hadn't missed a spot on herself. "Good idea. We'll wake up every hour and remind each other that we shouldn't be fooling around."

"Just to be safe, we'd better stay close. For clear communication."

Shutting off the faucet behind her, he scooped her up, soaking in his arms, skin against skin. Her legs roped around him, her mouth locked onto his.

Intertwined, he couldn't pull his lips away as he carried her to down the hall to his bedroom. The waning moon glowed through the glass door and illuminated the white sheets. Powerless to break away, he kept kissing her as he lowered her onto the bed.

Rock hard and fucking desperate, he trailed his lips along her skin, her breasts, her everything.

With one last, lingering kiss, her lips warm and pliant as they connected, he barely managed to pull away. Turning her in his arms, eliciting a chuckle from her at his blatant attempt to end things before they got any steamier, he spooned tight against her backside.

Damn, he needed to slow down. He tended to be a three months of dating before sex sort of guy. With Astrid, he knew that the moment he crossed that last line, there would be no going back.

Sleep came quickly but was agonizingly restless. Erotic fucking dreams haunted him all night. At least it wasn't nightmares, but his pulse pounded, and the sheets ended up at the foot of the bed, anyway.

He'd missed his patrol last night and couldn't skip it this morning. Brow relaxed, lips slightly parted and turned up at the sides, Astrid was still out cold.

Bodie slid his arm out from under her and walked straight for the deck door. He leaped over the balcony and changed midair to the wolf.

His senses came alive, the last traces of moon flooded him with energy. Full speed, he raced across the valley. Night owls, he knew the rest of the wolves would still be sleeping. Out of habit, of desire for solitude, he tended to stretch his wolf legs at dusk or dawn, rather than during the night like most werewolves.

Satisfied that the area was clear of ferals, of threat in general... not to mention his own edginess that had been calmed by the wolf run, he returned home.

At the back door of the house, he slipped inside and grabbed a pair of sweats from the shelf. Yeah, he was spoiled. He knew he wouldn't always have Grammy to do so much of the cooking, folding laundry, whatever chores she could manage. Her creaky joints reflected the aging state of the rest of her.

Dashing up the stairs, he slowed as he found Astrid just leaving his bedroom. She wore nothing but one of his flannel shirts, her hair rumpled from the night before. He bit his lip as he grinned and admired those long legs attempting to sneak to the kitchen, undoubtedly for her morning coffee fix. And he thought he was a caffeine addict.

Their lips connected like magnets as they reached each other, lingering before parting again. Without a word, she continued downstairs, and he to his room. After a quick rifle through his dresser, he tossed his clothes for the day on the bed and hunted for his deodorant.

Astrid returned just as he was pulling on his jeans. Did she have some sort of psychic connection to his nudity? Every time he was in a state of undress or even half-dress, she appeared. Not that he was complaining. Her satisfied grin told him she didn't mind either.

She handed him a steaming cup of coffee and set hers on the bedside table, exchanging it for her phone. "I need to call in my team."

The honeymoon of the trek back and last night had been a much-needed break. But it was time.

He lowered to the bed at her side. "How soon can they get here?"

"A few days. They're all on the West Coast and will meet up and fly out together in Bennett's plane."

Sipping a quick sip of coffee, Astrid set the mug back down and pulled out her phone. "Wow, how do I have full bars?"

Bodie grinned. "Life's pretty simple around here, being so far out. But we have some basic amenities and a big-ass budget for things like renewable energy and cell towers."

Nodding appreciatively, Astrid dialed. A grouchy voice answered, "Do you have any idea what time it is in Sitka?"

"Hey Lana. Sorry, I forgot I'm an hour further east than usual. Rally the troops. It's time to mobilize."

Long pause, then a much more wakeful voice chimed back. "Okay, I'm awake now. So this werewolf expert is really onto something?"

"To say the least. I'll explain when you get here. But... it's bad. Come prepared for the worst."

"Apocalyptic?"

"Not exactly, but we may have bitten off more than we can chew."

"How many?"

"A hundred or so. With above average intelligence."

Lana gulped audibly on the other side, clearly doing the same imbalanced math that Bodie and Astrid had already come up with. "We're fucked."

"That's a fact. Be quick. We're going to need a solid plan."

Bodie smiled at the change in Astrid as she spoke with her friend. Both used truncated sentences, somewhere between speaking in code and cutting out unneeded fluff when talking to a so-close-we're-family friend. At ease, she scowled, groaned, and laughed out loud, all within a matter of seconds.

"Ha. Sure thing. The gang's all waiting. Well, Ryan has another few days at sea before he can get away. I tried to convince Quinn we don't need any pregnant help, but she claims she's working until delivery. Directions?"

His eyes had wandered during their conversation and were lost on Astrid's spectacularly sculpted thighs. Blocking his view, she handed him the phone. Blinking, he tried to focus. Smiling sheepishly, he traded his coffee for the phone.

"Hey, this is Bodie," he said.

"Hey yourself. I'm Lana," a flirty voice responded.

Moving along, he gave directions to the nearest airfield, transportation recommendations, and the roads, mostly unmarked, to Connery Ranch. He agreed to email a detailed map so they wouldn't get lost. They had enough bedrooms. The team would be able to crash here. Not that he'd ask any of his pack to house a mortal enemy. As he spoke, Astrid wrapped her bare legs around his torso and kissed along his neck. Giving up on his ability to concentrate, he handed Astrid back the phone.

Yeah, they were doomed. And not just because they were going to get flattened by a massive feral pack. Raulf would see their connection no matter how hard they tried to hide it, and all hell would break loose. How was he supposed to concentrate when he knew how smooth that skin was? That she tasted as sweet as the honey of her eyes?

Lana must not have realized he was sitting so close that he could hear everything she said. "Your new friend sounds hot. Taken?"

Astrid swallowed a giggle as he unhooked the buttons of her top. "Just move your ass." She clicked the *End* button and tossed the phone, sliding her hand around the back of his neck and pulling him close. He grinned at her possessive claim.

Her shirt followed in half a second. Gloriously naked aside from the flimsy excuse for the lacy panties she favored, she wrapped her long limbs around him.

Nothing unnatural about it, their connection was easier than breathing. Patience his ass. This was a hell of a lot more than lust. Lust, he could resist. He was getting more and more attached by the second.

FRIED EGGS, BACON, AND hash browns annihilated, the kitchen was a delightful mess. Bodie's little sister, all of age six, and his cousin, age seven, had appeared at the backdoor this morning, pleading for Grammy to fix them breakfast. Without pause, she invited them in.

All giggles, they thought Grammy was psychic for having their plates already set. Flashing Astrid a conspiratorial wink, Molly typed in a quick text, *Packages received,* to their parents and returned her phone to its charger on the entry table.

Astrid hadn't spent much time with children. None at all, actually. Who knew bacon could be made into a goofy mustache or eyebrows when held in front of one's face? Or that the egg yolk couldn't run, even a little, or it was suddenly poison that risked the safety of the rest of the food on the plate? Incredibly patient, Molly had swapped plates so Jessie didn't have to eat the yolk-tainted hash browns.

Molly ran a tight ship, too. Even the little ones cleared their plates and dumped their leftovers into the pail for the chickens. Bodie jumped right in with scrubbing the dishes, threatening any improperly scraped plates with a spray from the faucet to the bearer of said plate. In the family room rocker with her coffee, Molly simply listened and smiled.

Astrid had never laughed so much drying and putting away dishes before. When the kitchen gleamed like new again, Jessie and Marcus ran toward the front door, only called back to grab the chicken pail. Grumbling, they changed course and headed out the back door, still fighting over who had to carry the stinky thing.

Carrying her own coffee to the family room to join Molly, Astrid settled on the couch where she could see out to the small garden and nearby chicken coop where the kids were dumping the scraps. Bodie sat on the opposite end of the couch, and joined them in watching the kids out the window.

"Go ahead, Bodie. You can sit next to her. I certainly don't mind a little hand holding." Molly smiled knowingly as she continued to rock and sip her coffee.

His eyebrows shot up in feigned dismay at her comment. "See why I can never get away with anything?" Grinning, he scooted closer and linked his fingers with Astrid's.

Molly chuckled. "The longing looks across the breakfast table were telling enough. This sort of thing doesn't happen every day, especially for hybrids like us. Hell, sometimes I think our lives are so long to give us a chance at finding the right mate." She read them both like a seasoned fortune-teller. "Stop worrying, the ferals don't give a darn if you two are getting it on, and the pack will get over it, eventually."

A blush flamed over Astrid's cheeks. She tried to say something, *anything*, but was too humiliated. Glancing over at Bodie, she raised her eyebrows, demanding he say *something*.

No help at all, his eyes were searching the ceiling as if it contained the answers to all of life's greatest mysteries.

"I know Bodie well enough, and, Astrid, I suspect you're just the same. You'll do the job right, no matter your personal distractions." Molly lowered her coffee to her knee, her lips drawing tight. "Raulf will take some convincing, but he's a romantic at heart."

Bodie cringed. "He'll flip his lid and disown me. Banishment might not be so bad, but I'd miss you. And most of the pack."

"Boden Connery, don't you talk like that. I know you don't want to be alpha, but that's not something you need to worry about just yet. I'm still in charge around here, and no matter how bossy your father is, he'll do what I say."

"Thanks to Noah, I don't have much choice." Bodie gently pulled his hand away and set his coffee on the end table. Tightening his fingers in his short hair, he buried his head in his hands.

"Noah screwed up. Doesn't mean you have to answer for his mistakes. I've told you once and I'll keep on telling you, you don't owe the pack anything. Sure, you better come 'round even after I'm gone, but there are plenty of others that can lead this pack and do it well. You're not the only one with brains and heart around here."

Astrid sat back and took it all in. There was so much about Bodie she didn't know. "Who chooses the next alpha?"

Molly paused before answering. "It won't surprise you that we are a rather conventional bunch. Werewolves are in general. Chain of command, tradition, that's what we know. Usually, alpha falls to the oldest grandchild. Noah wasn't ready, which is a big part of why we lost him. So now it's supposed to fall to Bodie. Normally, there's more time for the grandchild to grow into their own before taking on the role, but Thomas and I were in no rush to have children, then Raulf and Felicity waited like we did. As I keep telling Raulf and the others, we're not the royal family. They're our rules, and we're allowed to break them. Bodie didn't ask for this. Hands down, he'd make the best alpha, but I won't force him into it."

An ear-piercing scream ricocheted across the yard. Moving before she knew the cause, Astrid was out the door. Bodie was immediately at her side, running ahead as the wolf. Two ferals held the children. Two others watched, ready to strike from their positions in the distance.

The two that carried the children leapt over the garden fence and took off at a run, either intending to eat their meal in peace or to take hostages. Sprinting, Astrid caught up to the one that held Jessie. Bodie continued on for the other that held Marcus.

Leaping onto its back, she wrenched its head back.

Howling, it dropped Jessie.

Brave little thing picked up a stick and started swinging.

"Run," Astrid yelled as the feral writhed in its struggle to throw her off its back. This would be easier if she'd brought a weapon.

Jessie ran full speed for the house, Marcus trailing close behind as Bodie finished off the feral that had taken him.

Kicking and snarling, the feral reached around and sliced Astrid's leg with its claw. Ignoring the pain, the blood she knew drained from the wound, she tried to get a grip on its jaw.

It snapped its jaws, flailing and nearly knocking her off. Grabbing hold of its arm instead, she jerked its shoulder out of joint.

It howled and doubled its efforts to shake her off with a belligerent rage.

Linking her arms around its neck and chin, she spun and tugged.

With just the right torque, she snapped the neck. With pressure, she continued to twist and pull until she felt the crunch in her arms, and the cervical spine extruded from its skin in a compound fracture.

She leaped off and searched the field for Bodie and the remaining ferals. Springing through the air, he locked his jaws around one of the spying pair.

Jessie ran from the house, yelled for Astrid, and tossed her a kitchen knife. Astrid caught it from the air without pause and sprinted after the fourth. Although this one was smaller, he was fast. Legs burning, arms pumping to propel her faster, Astrid caught up as he crested the top of the hill.

Before she could leap on his back like the other, the feral turned toward her and swiped its claws at her.

Astrid ducked and rolled. Popping up, she sliced the knife across its back as it spun around.

It lashed at her. A claw sliced across her abdomen. Superficial only, she wasn't slowed by the wound.

Dodging another blow, Astrid twisted and jabbed a bloody gash deep into the feral's gut.

That slowed it down.

She grasped its wrist. Yanking it close, she sliced through its neck.

Twitching as the life drained from it, the monster collapsed at her feet.

Bodie came running over and stopped at her side. He looked over the dead ferals around the yard, then looked up at her with heavy blue eyes. She felt it, too. They'd been seconds away from losing the kids.

Driving the knife into the ground, she pulled it back out, the blood replaced by dirt. As she turned to walk back to the house, three other wolves were running their direction. They slowed when they realized the battle was over. Breaking away, the newcomers combed the hills, ensuring the area was secure. Bodie took off and joined them.

Astrid continued back to the house. Molly held the back door open for her and took the knife. "I'll clean this up. Why don't you go get yourself cleaned up?"

Nodding softly, Astrid headed toward the stairs. Before she reached the bottom step, four tiny arms wrapped around her. She immediately knelt down to hug them back, and found herself enveloped by two tearful kids. Jessie and Marcus spoke so rapidly over the other, she could hardly make out what they were saying. Each told the tale of how the ferals had surprised them while they were playing in the garden.

The back door opened and Raulf rushed in, Bodie right behind him. Bodie was already pulling on the jeans and t-shirt that had been left on the ground where he'd changed into the wolf. Raulf stopped at the shelf just inside the door and snagged a pair of Bodie's pants. She almost laughed at the oddity. Did all werewolves keep spare clothes by the door for moments like this? Although effective and logical, the transition details were dang inconvenient. Nothing was ever as simple as fantasy made it sound.

Jessie leaped into her father's arms. Tears streamed down her face as she clutched him fiercely.

Bodie scooped up Marcus and nearly reached for Astrid. Balling up his fist, he stepped away. He wiped a tear from Marcus' cheek. "You okay, buddy?"

Marcus nodded pitifully and clung tight to Bodie. Well if that image didn't stir a pitter patter in her uterus, nothing would.

Raulf nodded to Astrid. "Thank you for my daughter's life. I owe you a debt I can never repay."

"You'll never have to. She's an amazing kid. Marcus too. Your family has already carved out their own niche in my heart." Astrid held back the tears that threatened to boil over. The love and affection in this family was infectious, so different from what she'd grown up with. "And, as I said before, this is what I was born for. I won't stop until the ferals are no longer a threat. Your pack is in danger, and that's why I'm here."

"And then you're off to the next threat?"

"That's how it goes." What was he getting at? "Your secret will be safe with my team. We have no wish to endanger you, or any other peaceable werewolves."

Nodding, his lips remained pursed tight. Jessie nuzzled further under his chin so he could hardly maintain eye contact. "Thank you for that. I..." Raulf swallowed a tough lump before continuing. "I admit that I misjudged you based on the behavior of others. I'm sorry for that."

Astrid was taken aback. Her face scrunched with wonder and relief.

Marcus's father came running in from the front door before Astrid had to answer. Bodie turned and handed him to his father. His mother came a moment later, pulling a sweatshirt over her head as she'd clearly just changed back to human form. She pulled Astrid and Bodie in for tearful hugs and thank yous, then the little family disappeared as swiftly as they had arrived. Marcus flashed them a watery-eyed wave over his father's shoulder as they walked out the door.

Clenching his fists, Bodie held his shoulders stiff. "Dad, there are nearly a hundred of them. Organized. A damn army."

All the air in the room seemed to drain away as Raulf struggled to catch his breath. He gripped Jessie tighter and kissed the top of her head. He took a step forward, then paused before heading toward the door. He turned to Bodie. "I messed up with Noah. I thought I was doing right by you, Bodie, but, well, I'm often wrong." He smiled against Jessie's head. "Maybe I'll get it right with this one."

Silence reigned over the house, Raulf's presence in the room lasting long after he'd left. Astrid struggled with the frustrating sensation that she was missing something. What had happened to Noah that everyone talked around it? What had he messed up with Bodie? That Bodie didn't want to be alpha? That he turned to demon hunters for help, insulted him for the decision, but now realized Bodie was right all along?

Molly finally cleared her throat, providing a much-needed distraction. "We have guests arriving soon, I expect?" she asked Astrid.

"In a few days. You'll have six demon hunters ready to fight. I am not sure that will be enough, but we'll figure it out. I need to research and plan. What do you have on ferals?"

Grinning from ear-to-ear, Molly led her to what she lovingly referred to as, the *Den*. "Just like Bodie. Nose always in a book." She chuckled softly as they followed behind. "Poor boy. Didn't hit six feet until he was nineteen and was thin as a rail. Raulf was fit to be tied, convinced his son would forever be a skinny bookworm."

"Hey, there's nothing wrong with that," Bodie muttered as he followed them down the hall to the mysterious room across from the kitchen. He may have been a late bloomer, but he'd passed six feet and had filled out more than satisfactorily.

Astrid's eyes lit up and her heart skipped a few beats as they stepped inside the library. Transported to another realm, she nearly burst into song like a princess in a fairy tale, although her off-key tone wouldn't have quite captured the moment. The airy room was filled with bookshelves as high as the ceiling, a massive fireplace on one wall, a cozy window seat on another, and three plush leather couches surrounding a reclaimed wood coffee table. Lamps, throw blankets, and cozy pillows invited her to savor.

"I think I'm in love." She wasn't sure if she spoke out loud or just in her head.

Bodie came up behind her and wrapped his arms around her middle. "I'd never been jealous of a room before now."

Leaning into him, she snuggled close. "I'd marry you just for this room."

"Even if I turned feral?"

"I'd let you curl up at my feet and I'd pet your mangy fur."

"I'm not mangy."

"Ferals are mangy."

"Fair point."

Molly flipped on a few lamps and hobbled back to the door. "I'll bring some coffee and let you two get started."

9

Bodie hadn't studied so hard since college. Nor had he seen such an efficient, satisfied reader. The stack of books she'd poured through, barely taking breaks for lunch and dinner, was impressive. Was it a demon hunter thing, or an Astrid thing, to be able to read so fast?

Eyes blurred from hours reading up on ferals, he added the leather-bound text onto the stack of already-reads on the coffee table. Curled up in the opposite corner of the couch, Astrid looked as fascinated with this sixteenth book as she had with the first she'd read this morning. Rising from the table, he held out a hand to drag her to bed. Well after midnight, and he was toast.

Glancing up at him, her honey eyes warm and gooey with satisfaction, she smiled. "What time is it?"

"Late. I'm wiped. Let's go to bed." He wondered if she'd ever go to sleep on her own, so happily surrounded by so many old books.

In the books he'd finished, he hadn't found anything useful. Doubted there was a useful passage in the entire library regarding the mess they were in. This pack was unlike anything else. Instead, he'd been caught up in worrying over the cluster his life had become, and it had started even before the gorgeous demon hunter had walked into his life.

"I thought we were backing off after indulging last night." She raised an eyebrow at him, the corner of her mouth quirked up in amusement.

"Yeah. Then you were so damn hot, reading and concentrating all day. I think I need you to lie next to me all night and remind me how we're not supposed to be fooling around." He flashed a wink at her, but he was too tired to maintain the bright mood. He rubbed his hands over his face as he fought to pull it together. "My dad's going to kill me."

"Maybe we should stop. It's not like this can go anywhere, anyway."

"I'm a grown up, I shouldn't be afraid of my father. Yet, here we are. I'd like to tell him to fuck off, but we need him on board. I think the others will come around with a little convincing. I'll talk with them, let them know the plan. But when this is over..." He didn't want to say it.

As if reading his mind, she tapped her fingers on the book as she closed the cover. "If we survive this? Even then, your life is here. Mine isn't." Rising to her feet, she stopped in front of him and reached to give him a boost up. "Even if we survive the fight, we still don't have much hope for anything beyond an occasional late night when I'm on my way through town. We've skyrocketed past calling this a distraction, but I think ignoring how we feel is far more detrimental to the mission at this point. How about this? Until the fight is done, we savor what we have together. That's it. No promises, no expectations. Just, enjoy."

"You're really good at talking yourself into things."

"Same," she said, and curled into him.

"Let's get some sleep." Not that either of them would be able to shut off like that, but at least they could pretend every kiss wasn't increasing the inevitable heartache down the line.

Fingers laced together, they headed upstairs, and he closed the bedroom door behind them, turning and expecting to stumble right into bed.

Astrid clearly had other ideas. She pulled her shirt over her head and tossed it aside. "If you're so tired, I probably ought to assess werewolf stamina now, so I know what I have to work with." She raised a haughty eyebrow. Holy shit, she was a constant surprise. That standoffish prissy exterior had opened up to an arrogant temptress.

He rubbed his eyes and shook his head to wake himself. He wasn't about to miss out on more naked Astrid.

She teased as she unzipped her jeans, revealing a scrap of black silk that barely covered the good stuff, held together by crisscross laces. Did she own any uninteresting underclothes?

"Why Mr. Connery, are you not up for the challenge? Perhaps I should evaluate werewolf mental acuity as well as endurance."

Chuckling, he found his second wind as she continued her deliberate striptease. Stalking closer, he pulled his shirt off and flung it across the room. "Actually, that's Dr. Connery."

"Really?" Those watermelon-pink lips curled up in the awestruck smile he'd been hoping for.

He reached around her and unhooked the flimsy black bra that matched her why-bother-except-they're-fucking-hot panties. Sliding the bra over her shoulders, down her arms, he kissed her neck as he spoke. "School was my escape from here. After Noah joined the military, I wasn't allowed to go far. So, I stayed at the University of Montana as long as I could."

"I get it. Your home is beautiful, but it's nice to experience the world." She brushed her lips along his jaw, trailing down his sternum. "Doctor of what?"

"Anthropology." As she grazed her tongue down his abs and knelt in front of him, he inhaled sharply and kept talking as a necessary distraction... before he embarrassed himself by coming in his jeans before she even touched him. "Specifically, my dissertation explored how contemporary, remote cultures perpetuate ancient beliefs in the paranormal."

As she lowered his zipper, sliding his jeans over his hips, she tormented him with a feather light touch. "Keep talking. I'm liking Professor Connery." She flicked her tongue over the tip of his cock and winked at him.

He lost his grasp of the entire English language as he watched her. Hottest fucking vision of his existence. Wearing nothing but those clever panties, Astrid gripping his cock, her blond hair playfully tousled... she sat back on her feet and looked up at him, mischief brewing behind her honey eyes.

"Can you expound?" she asked, gliding her tongue hungrily over those lush pink lips, her intentions clear.

He nearly came at the sight. No dummy, he continued quickly, attempting to remember the key points. "Inherited traditions and legends can tell of dangers."

She ran her tongue along the length of his shaft. His breath caught in his throat.

As soon as he stopped talking, she stopped again.

"Were you born this cruel?" he asked, his voice hoarse as his entire focus shifted south.

"Perhaps." She waited a breath away until he started talking, then took him in deeply, driving him on further.

Hardly able to breathe, let alone think or even speak, he gathered a long breath and said on a long, groaning exhale, "For example, remote villagers survived the Indian Ocean tsunami of 2004 because stories had been passed down, warning that a lowering tide meant a tsunami was approaching, so they ran uphill rather than marveling over the uncovered sea life."

Hot against him, her mouth covered his cock, gently tugging and tightening. If this was her idea of testing endurance and mental acuity, he was one hundred percent on board.

As he stopped, distracted, she slowed.

Quickly, he found his voice again and said, "While those tales protect, others can become corrupted when cultures clash and cause harm. For example, stories of werewolves became twisted, vilifying them all, and accusations of lycanthropy led to the annihilation of hundreds of werewolf families concurrently with the Salem witch trials, a terrible time that revived ancient parables asserting that lycanthropy is a disease contracted through a bite wound, rather than the birthright it is."

As she gripped him, sucking with those watermelon-pink lips gliding over his cock, he could hardly speak, let alone stand. Whenever he stopped talking, she stopped. Evil woman.

As he recited the key points of his dissertation, she continued her fucking incredible efforts to drive him wild. "Which led to increased isolation and secrecy, driving the paranormal to become even more engulfed in misconstrued myths."

No longer able to hold back at the... enthusiastic movements of her tongue, her mouth, as she practically swallowed him, he groaned and backed out of her grip.

Kneeling in front of him, she licked her lips in smug satisfaction. So, so not the librarian many must mistake her for, thanks to her prim exterior when she felt shy or distrustful. Rising to her feet, gloriously naked except for that scrap of silk and ribbon she called panties, she wordlessly walked to the bed and elevated a haughty eyebrow in challenge.

Rubbing his hand over the back of his neck, he grinned and muttered, "You know, payback for that's going to be a bitch."

THE SUN ROSE OVER the jagged horizon well before Bodie was ready. Had they slept at all? Early rays of warmth graced their entangled limbs as they lay sprawled on the bearskin rug in front of the deck door.

Dead weight, Astrid was plastered to him. Cold from the crisp night air, he had dragged a quilt over them at some point, but it had just tangled around them. He managed to free himself and pulled the blanket back over her.

Diving off the deck, he landed on four legs and took off at a full sprint. He'd missed the predawn darkness, but the moon was waning anyway and down to a sliver. Nothing invigorated him quite like a full moon. Well, maybe Astrid in epic orgasm, but otherwise, the moon filled him with a vibrance he couldn't describe. He considered timing their attack on the ferals with the full moon so the wolves would be at maximum charge, but so would the ferals.

Accepting that he was a complete mess, mentally, emotionally, Bodie ran harder and faster than he had in years. Pushing his legs, his muscles burned, his paws nearing raw from the brutal pace. Increasing his circles, he checked the ranch for signs of feral activity.

He felt bile rising in his throat at the thought of what would have happened yesterday if they hadn't been close enough to hear the kids screaming. Had it been intentional? The kids? The ranch? Or had those four stumbled upon a fortuitous breakfast? The way they were set to run with the kids, he feared it was very deliberate.

The light was on in the bedroom when he returned. He paused before going inside. He could just make out Astrid's silhouette as she pulled on a sweater to fight the morning chill. He watched her graceful movements as she got ready for the day, until the light flicked off and she disappeared.

What was he going to do about her? As she'd put it, her life was… everywhere. And his was here. He was stuck in a stupid cycle of letting himself hope for a future with her, then right back to remembering all the reasons they wouldn't work.

Sisyphus just had to worry about a stupid rock in his unending torture. If it had been a woman, he would have blasted that boulder off the mountain top and thundered after his persecutor. Yeah, that was it. Bodie just had to throw a big-ass rock at someone, and he'd feel much better.

He was done doing the right thing. He wanted to claim her, marry her, bond with her as a mated pair, consequences be damned. Come on, it's not like they weren't committed already, emotionally and physically. Fooling around all night, comfortably working together all day, learning every detail about each other with every word, every touch.

Following the path to end up another tragic fairytale about love and loss. If refusing to think about the future made her happy, he could keep his thoughts to himself.

Swallowing a bitter lump, he dragged his paws as he approached the house. Bodie shifted back to the man and opened the back door, its familiar whistle comforting to his ears. Snagging his jeans from the shelf inside the door, he pulled them on and found a clean t-shirt in the laundry room. He'd become accustomed to going commando years ago. The first few times he'd shifted, he'd found that his boxer briefs clung to his wolfy hips, and, well, it was a little embarrassing.

Across the house, he heard his father's voice awkwardly attempting conversation. "Is, uh, is Bodie around?"

Astrid's equally self-conscious voice responded, "Um, no, he's out for a run." Long pause. "Would you care for some coffee?"

Taking pity on the pair, Bodie walked down the hallway to the entry.

Raulf immediately loosened up, releasing his tightly crossed arms. "Hey, you're back. Jessie was, uh, wondering if the two of you would consider joining us for dinner. She wanted me to tell you that she's making French toast."

He was a decent dad. Understandably protective. Most kids complained that their parents needed to get with the times. Being isolated in rural Montana, with a father pushing two hundred and a mother over eighty, although neither looked it, Bodie had run into that issue more than his fair share.

"French toast for dinner?"

With a shrug, Raulf said, "It's the only thing she knows how to make. Other than mud pie. She insisted."

"Sounds great."

Raulf backed toward the door. "Six o'clock."

"We'll be there."

As the door clicked closed, Bodie turned and saw Astrid letting out a long sigh, as if she'd been holding her breath all the while Raulf had been there.

"That okay with you?"

She nodded. "Of course. I only have the next ten hours to freak out."

From the kitchen, Grammy hollered, "Breakfast is getting cold." Yeah, she'd heard the whole thing. Bodie could scent her amusement from here, tickling his nose like he'd sniffed a bouquet of dandelions.

After filling up on one of his favorite comfort-food feasts involving a mashup of eggs, cheese, and breakfast sausage, Bodie spent most of the day going from house to house, talking to his pack about the plan. About the ferals. About Astrid and the other demon hunters that would arrive soon. Wanting them to speak openly about any concerns, he'd gone alone. They'd been surprisingly open, but there had been a lot of questions. After the attack on the kids, they were scared.

Aunt Lilith had already been on board, after seeing how Astrid had protected Marcus. Rain had seen her share of the world and was more openminded than the rest. Uncle Angus, being from Raulf's generation, had stewed on it for a bit, drilling Bodie with tough questions about demon hunters and the ferals themselves. Nash rolled with everything, sometimes too much. He'd nodded and said, "Sure," without seeming to care about the fact that they weren't going to win, and they were trusting strangers with their safety.

Astrid had been eager to return to the library anyway, but only read two books and skipped lunch entirely, claiming she was saving room for French toast. The clock in the corner chimed five. Astrid practically leaped off the couch and raced upstairs.

She reappeared at half past five in a delicate white sleeveless top, light colored jeans, and brown leather ankle boots. She'd even added a splash of makeup on her eyes that added a hint of sultry to her appearance. Her hips swayed wickedly in the jeans. In those boots, she walked like she could crush a man with just a look, but the top and her natural demeanor added an air of geniality.

Did he say willowy bombshell before? Siren was more like it. Like the gorgeous nerd-next-door had a secret badass spirit and a mouth that could... *whoa, down boy*. Not the time.

Bodie glanced down at his own jeans and wrinkled t-shirt. He set down the book he was working on and pulled his shirt off as he stalked to the laundry room. He dumped the wrinkled tee in with the dirties and pulled a blue button-up from the freshly ironed pile. It wasn't even plaid.

While he was there, he took an extra moment to move the laundry along. He pulled the clothes from the dryer and piled them on top, moving the wet clothes in.

By the time he made it to the front door, it was another twenty minutes until dinner started. Astrid was pacing back and forth in the entry, her shoes clicking with each step. He moved in front of her path and she ran right into him. He traced his hands along the skin of her bare arms.

She was practically hyperventilating, her breath forcibly slow and steady, but her eyes were wild as a rabbit on the run.

Cradling her face in his hands, he softly pressed his lips to hers and said, "It's a peace offering, not an ambush. Trust me."

Nodding, she finished her long exhale. "Just don't sit next to me. Your relationship with your father appears tenuous enough. Despite the attack yesterday, he still doesn't trust me. We need his complete buy-in if we're to take on the ferals together. If he knew we were... if he finds out, we risk the success of the mission."

He knew she meant well, but her words ripped at him like claws digging into his chest. "No. Before everything... before I realized how much you mean to me? I would have said the same thing. Hell, I did say it. It was easy to tell myself we were just fooling around, no harm no foul and nobody's damn business. I was stupid to think we could or even should hide anything. He's my dad. He has a big bark, but he's not a biter."

Glazed over, Astrid's honey eyes searched his. "His hatred for demon hunters is not unfounded. I can't come between you."

"Too bad. You're already part of me, like he is, and you both may as well get used to each other. If we make it out of this alive—and I don't mean dinner tonight." He laughed at his own joke. "You're going to disappear from my life. Give me tonight to see what it feels like to bring someone home. I've never gotten to, and it may be another hundred years before I get the opportunity again." Brushing a stray lock of blond behind her ear, Bodie ran his fingers over the curve of her jaw. "Give me the next few weeks to pretend I get to keep you."

She still looked ready to run, but instead, she turned her nose up in that haughty way. "I thought we weren't thinking about *after*."

"I'm not, I swear. I'm just trying to experience *now* to the fullest." He grabbed their jackets and extended his hand for her.

If they could get through the next few hours, he had no doubt it would all be okay. Well, maybe not with the ferals, but at least with his parents. If they tried to keep this secret, and Raulf found out anyway... yeah, his dad might just go feral.

Golden rays fingered across the landscape, teasing that night was coming. He clung to the last of the day's warmth. They walked hand-in-hand down the road. They reached the house two minutes before six.

His childhood home stood before him, the place he'd lived until he'd run off to college. Sure, he'd endured a lot of high-decibel lectures under that roof, but there had been mostly laughter. Weekly board game night. Interesting concoctions his mom had let him throw together. Some were even edible. Chasing up and down the stairs with Noah. Despite the five-year age-gap, they'd been good buddies.

And then they received word that Noah was missing in action, along with most of his squad, shortly after they'd returned from a deployment. Majors didn't just disappear during routine training ops, and routine training ops didn't take the lives so many soldiers. A darkness had fallen over the house that day. Rather than showing signs of lifting, the melancholy was about to contort with exquisite dejection, and not because he was dating the wrong woman.

Bodie hadn't realized he'd stopped in the middle of the porch until Astrid tugged at his hand. "I'll follow your lead. Let's head in."

His nose scrunched up. "Follow your own lead. They might as well get to know *you*. To see why I like you so well." He pulled their joined hands to his mouth and kissed the back of her knuckles.

Her cheeks tightened as she swallowed. Straightening her shoulders, she rose her hand to knock. She was fighting the instinct to run from the big bad wolf. Nothing scared her, at least, when something did, it was mostly social interactions, and she wouldn't let it rule her.

Opening the front door before her fist met wood, Bodie called out, "Something smells good in here." Jessie's cooking must be coming along. It actually did smell good. Warm peach compote and French toast casserole, judging by the scent. Their mom must have convinced her it would be more convenient for entertaining than frying each slice separately.

The little chef came running out, her oversized apron gooey with said peaches. Rather than leaping into his arms, as she usually would, she launched straight into Astrid's. Without missing a beat, ignoring the potential ruination of her pristine top, Astrid caught her and spun her in a circle. "Astrid, you came! Dad and Mom argued all morning—"

"Remember what we talked about, little one?" his mother asked as she came strolling out of the kitchen in a matching apron, her dark wavy hair tied loosely in a ponytail, eyes amused despite her stern expression. Where Bodie was Raulf's spitting image, Jessie was their mom's miniature twin.

Jessie slid to the ground and shrugged, her missing front teeth pricelessly adding to the picture. "I wasn't tattling, promise."

Crouching down next to her, Bodie whispered not-so-discreetly in her ear, "Kinda sounded like you were."

She glared back. "Hey, you're supposed to be on my side."

He nudged her shoulder. "Always."

Before he could greet his mom, she sighed heavily, wiped her hands on her apron, and extended her hand to Astrid. "I'm so glad you agreed to come for dinner. Or 'brinner' as Jessie's calling it. I'm Felicity."

Shoulders back, expression polite, Astrid accepted the handshake and responded, "Thank you for inviting me. I'm Astrid." At least she was following her own lead, but she was so stiff.

While his mom and Astrid made overly polite, nervous conversation, Bodie took Jessie's hand and dragged her to the kitchen. He quickly checked that they were alone and asked, "What were they arguing about?" Despite Astrid's subtle scent as a demon hunter, he was so in tune with her, he could pick up her anxiety from across the house.

"Thought I wasn't supposed to tattle?" She glowered, hands on her hips.

He scooped her up, set her on the counter and raised one eyebrow, mouth set firm.

"Fine. They were fighting about you. About how they can't lose you, too. Mom cried. I said they were being really childish, and that Astrid was really nice so her friends are probably really nice, too."

Bodie mussed up Jessie's hair, earning himself one of her infamous death-glares. "Thanks, little one. Now, why don't you stir those peaches and I'll pour some drinks? Astrid gets really nervous around strangers, and she really wants Mom and Dad to like her."

Jessie scooched closer to the stove, still sitting on the counter. Carefully, she mixed the fragrant mixture with her wooden spoon.

Bodie pulled four beers from the fridge, plus a sparkling water for Jessie, and started pouring. He heard Astrid and his mom approaching.

"Where did you grow up?" Felicity asked.

Shoulders back, Astrid still hadn't relaxed as they rounded the corner and entered the kitchen. "Georgetown."

Both were clearly maxing out on polite conversation. Astrid's face lit up when she saw him, almost overcoming the pasted-on smile she'd been wearing. She gratefully accepted the beer he shoved in her face and drank it down by half before coming up for air.

His mother laughed out loud and held her hand over her abdomen to tame her reaction. "Oh, thank goodness."

Astrid paled so not even her typical blush reached her cheeks.

Felicity said, "I was so afraid you hated us. We have heard such awful rumors about demon hunters. Are you as nervous I am?" She accepted a beer from Bodie and took a long pull from the frothy glass. "I guess I was expecting a fierce warrior dressed in head to toe leather with a gruff exterior, judging us and our quiet lives." His mother was rambling more nervously than he'd ever seen. "Then here comes this shy, polite woman that put her life on the line for my daughter and my nephew."

Astrid palpably relaxed. "I shouldn't say that I'm glad you're nervous, but I really am. I'm socially awkward at best, and..."

Nodding, Felicity finished her thought for her. "And Raulf was not exactly welcoming."

Bodie cleared his throat. He'd planned to break the news to his parents together, but, actually, divide and conquer might be the way to go. "Mom..." Wow, this wasn't easy. He'd never brought home a woman before. He slipped his hand into Astrid's.

Felicity knew when to hold her tongue, and she looked like she was near biting through it at the moment. At least she wasn't yelling. Actually, she seemed to be biting a smile.

"I know the timing sucks, with things so hectic and who knows what the next few weeks will bring, but we, uh, kind of like each other. A lot." Wow, he sounded like Jessie, just needed to add a few reallys and actuallys.

Astrid stiffened at his side, her panic ripe on the air.

Releasing her tongue, Felicity tried to speak, but Bodie needed to finish before any possible lecture or tough questions that he already tormented himself with. "We don't know where this will go, but, for now, we wanted to be honest and let you know that we're seeing each other. For however long we can make it work."

Her expression softened, but her eyebrows drew together. Relief? Concern? Bodie didn't recognize this of his mom's many expressions. "When Raulf saw you two the other morning, when you were headed out on the quad... I shouldn't say it, but I want you to understand where we're coming from. When he saw you together, clearly interested, he was terrified. We've already lost one son." She looked away when her eyes got misty. "Bodie, you already leave at any excuse to hunt ferals. You're a born fighter. For that, I want you to be able to spread your wings. But that spirit is also what makes you an incredible leader, our best hope for the future of our pack. When Noah left, then Morrison, and then Rain was gone for so long... too much of the next generation is leaving. We need to stay together."

"Mom, can this—"

"Hang on, Bodie. I'm sorry, Astrid, but we immediately feared you were putting thoughts in his head of leaving his family. Already, we knew demon hunters to be capable of terrible deception and violence. I have no doubt that Bodie dated while away at school, but he's so trusting."

So far, this was going well. His mother was only half crying. But he hadn't told Raulf yet. He leaned against the kitchen counter and pulled Astrid next to him. "You may be the first demon hunter I've met, but not the first my parents have met."

"Exactly. I am truly sorry for judging you without getting to know you. If we want Bodie to lead, we have to trust him. And he trusts you. Molly already thinks the world of you. You didn't hesitate to save our daughter. And, you didn't shy away from a little peach compote." She grabbed a dishrag and handed it to Astrid to clean the smear of peach from her top.

Relaxing at his side, Astrid melted into him, gripping the cleaning rag. "Since meeting Bodie, I have discovered that werewolves are not the monsters we feared them to be. That only a small percentage are a danger. I hope that my team can show you that demon hunters can be decent people. And I have no intention of stealing away Bodie. We've already concluded a future together is bleak, but we wanted to make the most of the time we have."

Bodie found himself breathing easier than he had all evening. "Keeping it from you and Dad felt wrong. Please tell me we made the right decision to tell you."

His mother slipped her arm around his other side. "I love you, Bodie. No matter what, I want you to be deliriously happy, in whatever form that takes." She leaned across him and said to Astrid, "I'm really glad you're... normal."

"I don't know about normal."

His mother looked up at him and shook her head. She reached across and hooked her hand around Astrid's elbow. "Come on. Let's go sit and chat. Tell me all about the moment you knew you were in love with my son."

Astrid blushed beet red as she was dragged to the living room. He heard her back-pedaling. "I'm not, I mean, we're not—"

As his mother dragged Astrid to the couch, she tsked. "Of course. It's too soon. A mother fears her son picking a woman she can't get along with. Imagine my horror when his father tells me he saw some sparks between Bodie and the mysterious blond demon hunter. Tell me all about yourself. I've got a feeling we're going to get along beautifully."

Behind him, Jessie hopped down from the counter and brushed past him. With a disgusted groan, she dashed upstairs. Kissing, or romance of any kind, was downright gross to the little one. She would definitely not want to hear a love story.

A massive sigh of relief passed Bodie's lips as his mother and his lover relaxed on the couch and chatted easily. Felicity's warmth rapidly melted through Astrid's prissy exterior. He'd never brought home a girlfriend before. Hell, Raulf was over a hundred before he met Felicity. Every time he came home on a break from college, his mother had lectured him about not falling for the first girl he met, but to take his time to find the right one, even if it took a century like his dad.

Now, if only it were so easy to win over Raulf. Felicity had spent her first thirty years without knowing the paranormal existed, until she met Raulf. Recently divorced and done with men, she had traveled with some girlfriends on a road trip across the states. She'd run into Raulf at Glacier National Park. Her friends thought she was nuts, but she claims it took one look, and she'd known he was it for her.

Bodie heard footsteps lumbering down the stairs. He snagged his and the beer he'd poured for Raulf and met his father before he reached the great room. Bodie pulled his dad aside and dragged him out to the front porch. Raulf didn't argue, but followed his lead and sat in the neighboring chair.

They stared out at the evening glow.

"Ready to start the lecture?" Bodie felt himself asking, despite his many lectures to himself that he wasn't going to start a fight.

Raulf snorted. "You already know everything I'd come up with, anyway." Yep, confirmed. Raulf knew.

"My place is here, not with some snooty demon hunter, running amongst those that would destroy us, and cousins to those who have killed a lot of us. That about it?"

"Pretty much." Raulf sipped his beer slowly, then wiped the froth from his thick beard. "Or that's what I had been planning. Until yesterday. Can't exactly curse someone that fought so hard for Jessie. Bare-handed, she put herself at risk for my youngest child."

"She's a fighter. Stubborn as they come, too. I'm not sure she's capable of giving up. Even for an unwinnable fight." Bodie felt an unfamiliar clench in his chest as he considered what they were up against, the risk of losing so much more than he'd realized.

"Sounds like someone else I know," Raulf snorted, raising his glass in satirical salute.

"You want me to protect the pack. I will. Always. Whatever it takes."

Both sat silently, watching the sun lower behind the mountains.

Raulf lifted his glass, then set it back down. Exhaling slowly, he picked up the glass again and downed its contents by half. "Smelled you all over each other yesterday. Not exactly taking things slow, are you?"

"Like you? What, were you a hundred and twenty when you met Mom?"

"Something like that."

"Can't exactly say this is permanent, as much as I'd like it to be. I'm not that naïve. I can see 'doomed' written all over the relationship."

Raulf snorted and shook his head. "Now that, that I can relate to. If she means that much to you, you'll make it work."

"Odds aren't exactly in our favor. Literally and figuratively. At best, we've got thirteen against a hundred. Not exactly normal ferals either. These are trained and patient. A normal feral, yeah, we could each take two or three no problem. Four would be a challenge, but doable. Five, next to impossible. Against these? No fucking way. Astrid and I together had trouble with four." Keeping still, Bodie forced his jaw from ticking, his knee from vibrating, his growl from exploding.

Sneering, Raulf's breath moved swiftly in and out. The spice of his fury, his fear, emanated off of him like burnt stew. "There's never been a pack like this. Someone did this. Someone made this happen."

Bodie didn't hear the frogs croaking at the pond across the yard, didn't feel the shadow creeping across the landscape, didn't feel his breath moving in and out of his lungs. "Do you think..." He hated even saying it out loud. "Do you think it's him?"

"Do you?"

"I'm not sure. I wasn't close enough to tell, but I think I caught a whiff of him on the drive over. He makes the most sense. So close to the ranch, the timing."

"That's what I've been afraid of."

"How would he have figured it out?"

Raulf raised an eyebrow in question.

"Being with it enough, even as a feral?"

Raulf took a long pull of his beer. "Every so often, a werewolf keeps enough of their mind after going feral. He changed once, to the feral, not long before he left."

"What? How?"

"Furious with me. He wanted to use this power to save the world. You know Noah, he was always the hero. Don't know what I did, probably all your mother's influence." Raulf quirked a half-smile, knowing it was his temper plus Felicity's spirit combined. "All three of my children dive headfirst into a fight. But you, you steady it. Noah never had that restraint. I wanted him to see the world and realize that home was where he belonged. But joining the Army? No way I'd let him risk our secrets like that. We'd been sitting by the bonfire out back. You and your mom were in town at the time. It just came over him, the fury. He let it happen."

"That's why you let him leave."

"No choice. Took everything I had to calm him, to get him to change back. Hurt like hell, holding onto him and talking to him while he lashed back at me. I wasn't giving up on him."

"The scar on your neck?"

Raulf nodded. "I'm just lucky he took it out on me rather than running off. A few more minutes like that, and he wouldn't have been able to pull out of it. It's rare that anyone can go back from the feral state, but fuck, he did it."

Bodie refused to say it out loud. That maybe he should have let him be. Raulf had been so badly wounded and wouldn't tell anyone but Felicity what happened. He said he'd run off a damn cliff by accident.

"You've always been restless. Hell, you're always off exploring. I thought college might be enough of a journey to satisfy that craving. You get that from your Grammy. I've never wanted to be anywhere but right here. Right now, more than ever, we need you here. Grammy's not going to be around forever"

"Dad, I just... I will." Because they were counting on him.

"I hate that the responsibility falls to you."

Bodie's heart lurched in his chest.

"You've always been the steady one. Even when you boys were kids, I knew you'd be a better alpha. You keep that temper in check and take care of things. Like this whole feral situation. You didn't ask the rest of us what you should do, knowing we'd argue. You just acted. And, I'm beginning to realize you made a good decision, one that I would never have considered." Raulf leaned forward and ducked his head, as if trying to not pass out. Inhaling deeply, he sat up. "I'm so sorry for pressuring you like I pressured Noah. Should have learned my lesson."

Raulf seemed so torn, like he would start to say something about letting him off the hook, then right back to all the reasons Bodie needed to stay and lead.

Crumbling, the vision of an impossible future burned away as he recalled why they were having this conversation in the first place. "We need to take out those ferals."

Raulf rose to his feet and grabbed his half-consumed beer. "Let's see if your girl's as good as Grammy seems to think."

By the time they got back inside, Astrid and his mother were giggling like a duo of misfits. Before Raulf cleared his throat to get their attention, he heard Astrid chuckling something about a sphinx, and his mother snorting with laughter.

Well timed. The oven declared dinner was ready with a rhythmic beep. Jessie came thundering down the stairs to check on her masterpiece.

They ate in relative peace. It was great to see his parents relax. Things had been beyond tense since Noah was reported missing. Even Astrid let her barriers drop. Hell, it was great having fresh stories at the dinner table. For all his parent's hatred of demon hunters, for all Astrid's nervousness around strangers, they got along great. Maybe it was starting off on the wrong foot that made the rest of the journey flow so easily. All the resentment was out in the open and brushed away with humor and acceptance.

After shoveling in final bites of dinner, his mom waved them off from helping clean up and scooted them out, claiming it was already late. As they stepped onto the front porch, Raulf walking them to the door, he cleared his throat and said to Astrid, "Your team will be here soon? We have about seven good warriors in our pack, including me and Bodie. A few younger and older that aren't fit for war, but they can stay behind to defend the others, if it comes to that."

Jessie's jaw set in determination, hands on her hips, she declared, "I can fight."

Raulf smiled softly. "I have no doubt about that, little one."

Bodie moved closer in the dim porch light and scooped his sister and tossed her in the air, letting her hair sweep the ceiling before catching her again. "You're the bravest of us, so we need you here to protect the pack."

She giggled and rolled her eyes. Bodie lowered her back to the ground, and she took her dad's hand. "Come on, Dad. We've got battle plans to make."

Raulf rolled his eyes. "Not a great bedtime story." Before he let her drag him back inside, he said, "Again, Astrid, thank you for my daughter's life. You're a good fighter. I'm glad we have you on our side."

Walking out into the night, Bodie laced his fingers with Astrid's. The frogs croaked in the distance, a cacophonous orchestra of woeful bedtime tales. Astrid leaned into him. They walked hand-in-hand back home, neither daring to break the peace of the evening by continuing the conversation that Raulf had started.

10

THE WALK BACK HOME felt so incredibly normal, like an evening stroll with her boyfriend, beaming after a successful meet-the-parents.

Fingers laced with his, the easy connection so stirring, Astrid almost laughed at how her body reacted to him. Somehow the intimacy of handholding had become equivalent to foreplay.

"That wasn't so bad," he said. "We only endured a few lectures, but I think they were supportive by the end."

"You were right to not keep it from them. They clearly love you and want you to be happy. Raulf is just torn between the good of the pack and keeping his son happy. He's right. You're a natural leader and the pack already looks to you."

"Hey, no seriousness."

"Sorry. I keep forgetting." She stared up at the stars. How is it, the second she told herself to not think of the future or anything serious, that's all she could focus on?

"Your team arrives tomorrow?"

"If they can make sense of the map you drew."

"Hey, it was a great map."

"Sure it was. I mean, I'm not saying you're a terrible artist, but you fortunately have other talents."

"Much to my mother's dismay. During art class, she had us studying the classics and doing charcoal portraits of the family. Noah's were really good. Mom's could be in the Louvre. Sadly, I take after Raulf and can't do much more than stick figures."

As they reached the house, she hung back, not quite ready to go in. He leaped up the stairs, turning back when he realized she wasn't following. Hands buried into his pockets, he waited.

"My parents hired professional artists to make a genius out of me. Like so many of their attempts, I fear they were disappointed in the end. I can say that charcoal is not my medium, and I am a disaster at watercolor and oils, but I can do a topographical map pretty well." She waited on the bottom step.

"How about dance class? Ballet? Tap?" And there went that lip, neatly tucked between his teeth as he dared her to refute.

"Ballet, yes. Tap was too noisy. Jazz was too risqué. A few years ago, Lana enrolled us in a hip-hop class." Feeling energized at the easiness between them, she strolled up the stairs and stopped in front of him.

"Yeah?" he grinned. "A child of the forties, my mother insisted we knew how to dance. Although... I hear pole dancing is becoming popular. Maybe you could try it out sometime. I'm a great teacher."

"Within seconds, you take us from ballet to ballroom to pole dancing, yet I remain unoffended. Somehow."

"I'm a charming guy."

"I believe we established *charming* is not the right term."

"Hey, Prince Charming comes in many forms." He leaned down and took her mouth with his.

"I'm not a princess." Too many had mistaken her for one, too many times.

One hand sprawled over her back, his other skimmed along her arm and took her hand. Swaying, he pulled her in for a light waltz. "You're so much more interesting."

Swirling on a cloud, she hardly noticed as he danced them in the front door. Her jacket slipped off her arms, her shoes dropped one at a time along the path. Halfway up the stairs, her shirt went missing.

Lips never leaving hers, he somehow had her completely undressed aside from her panties by the time they reached his bedroom. Sliding her hands down her sides, she tried to shed them as well.

"No wait, hang on. I haven't seen these yet." He stepped back and looked her up and down. "Where do you find all of these? Honestly, I can't even figure out how these are even staying on. There can't be more than three square inches of satin altogether. Genius, that's what they are."

Loosening the pale pink tie at the sides, said panties drifted to the floor. "I confess, I'm addicted to pretty underwear."

"I'm not complaining."

"Wait a moment, how are you still dressed and I'm the naked one?" She'd rather enjoyed that he was rarely fully clothed, but now that their roles were reversed, well, she didn't mind at all.

"We could start those pole dancing lessons," he suggested, running his hands along her bare hips.

"I don't see a pole."

Devious grin teasing at his lips, he went for his zipper. "Oh, sorry. I can help with that."

A fit of giggles erupted from deep in her belly. Merry butterflies danced in amusement as she took in his goofy grin.

Fading, sweetly, his expression grew hungry. Despite the darkness, his eyes glowed as blue as the rare moon.

The distance between reduced to nothing. Buttons flinging off into the far corners of his bedroom, she tore his shirt off and tossed it aside.

His mouth was everywhere, her jaw, her collarbone, her shoulder.

Overcome with urgency as need took over, she tugged at his zipper, sliding his jeans over his hips. He took her breast deep in his mouth, a hand covering the other.

He scooped her up and laid her on the bed, following close behind. Lips everywhere, the tip of his tongue grazed down her abdomen, her thigh, her core, and he took her higher than before, an impatience she hadn't seen in him. She reveled in it.

Trembling from the rapid orgasm, she felt every breath pass in and out of her lungs. He kissed every inch of her as he moved up her body.

His voice heavy with gravel, he teased, "We really, really shouldn't."

"Let's not do the right thing, just this once." Gripping his hips, she pulled his him closer and pressed against his hardness.

"Going to be more than once." He kissed her again, his gaze resting on her lips.

He slid into her in a smooth, consuming plunge, then immediately stilled. She gasped at the startling pressure, igniting an inferno that pulsed through her.

He chuckled softly against her, as if in delirious shock. Both held still, stunned.

Astrid found herself laughing with him, the shock driving the laugh as much as his surprised smile.

He murmured softly, his voice hoarse, "I, uh, you..." He rocked inside her, then paused again, holding his breath.

She wiggled and pulled his hips closer, the subtle movement sending liquid heat curling through her. Breathless, she couldn't find the words. Neither needed to say it out loud. The electricity of their attraction, the zing she felt every time their eyes met... their connection was like nothing else. Stirring and stunning, and holy shit she was aroused beyond reason.

He moved again, smiling wickedly. Shocks of heat, of pure energy, radiated through her at the electrifying movement. Smiles quickly fading, they were swept away into the dizzying, dreamy haze of it.

Pace quickening, deeper, thicker, they moved together. Ascending rapidly, cresting over the highest mountains, they climaxed together.

Breathless, limbs intertwined, they held each other.

What was that? From the moment their eyes had met, the shock at the first time his skin touched hers, the heat of his lips on hers... there was no going back, and there never was.

THE NEXT MORNING CAME early. He'd been right, it hadn't been just once. Astrid hadn't slept a wink last night. Werewolves absolutely had comparable stamina.

Already, she craved him again. Astrid wrapped the quilt around her shoulders and moved to the glass door, watching the sunrise. Purple and pinks swept behind the mountains in the distance, teasing at the coming day.

Bodie slipped back in the house half an hour later, just in time for breakfast. "No activity around the ranch. I can't scent anything on the air, but something isn't right. Like they're taunting us."

Astrid took a testing sip of her coffee, feeling a sense of dread deep in her gut.

Molly sat across the kitchen table and held her mug with both hands. "I feel it, too. Like they're staying just outside of where we can smell them."

"Let's expand our circle then. Let's see what they're up to." Astrid's legs shifted in her seat, her back aching as she couldn't seem to get comfortable. While demon hunters held no superpowers as far as knowingly sensing danger, sometimes she felt this inescapable dread, like an ominous change in the wind.

Bodie nodded, sipping his coffee before speaking. "We know we can't assume they're normal ferals that wouldn't care that four of their own went missing. From the army we saw, they'll want to maintain their numbers and watch their perimeter. They'll investigate."

"Will they scent you as werewolves?"

Molly nodded. "If they're as smart as they look in the video you took, it won't take much to discern wolf intertwined with human means werewolves. If they can remember their own lives before they went feral."

"I've read through half your library already, and I can't find anything on ferals behaving this way."

"They... I fear there is something in them beyond feral." Molly glared into nothingness, calculating.

"Like raptor?" Bodie grinned, eyes twinkling in amusement over the rim of his mug.

"See *Jurassic World* too many times?" Astrid chuckled. "Actually, that's a great point. Demon hunters were bred very intentionally by our demon ancestor to protect humans from the evil of her realm that crosses over. Could these werewolves have been bred to be more aware, in the event they turned feral... then, I don't know, maybe they are provoking the feral side in the rest of their pack?"

Scowling, Molly shook her head. "Not by breeding, no. I wonder more if they are finding and training werewolves who have already gone feral, or finding werewolves in general and provoking them."

Bodie tilted a look and calculated in tune with his grandmother. "How would they keep finding ferals to train? And this level of training, for this many would be impossible. Maybe medications to calm them? I couldn't tell you where to find even fifty werewolves that could be changed and trained so readily, and there aren't any other packs around here."

Astrid stared at her coffee that had grown cold. "There are demons of all sorts in this world. Vampires are a dime a dozen. Sirens and other sea monsters, yeti, banshees, many that aren't too hard to find. Werewolves, for all their fame in Hollywood, actually are few and far between. I've maybe come across a dozen in as many years. How can there be so many in one place at one time?"

They all drifted their attention to vague focal points around the room. Astrid's mind went everywhere except anywhere useful. Comic book serums, radioactivity, witchcraft. Nothing reasonable.

After a massive breakfast of eggs, sausage, and fried tomatoes, thank you Molly, she returned to the library to look for anything that might explain modifying or even recruiting a feral werewolf. Molly's library was half the size of hers at home, but she had an extensive werewolf history that most demon hunters could only dream about.

Bodie took off again, expanding his search to see if he could find evidence that the ferals were moving closer. Probably a good thing he was gone all day. She had no idea what to say to him. But she was more than tempted to drag him back upstairs. Or lock him in the library with her all day.

As she poured through every relevant text in the house, she kept the door open to hear comings and goings, knowing the team would arrive soon. She heard Molly puttering away in the kitchen, then back to her bedroom for a nap, then to the kitchen again. Since their arrival, Astrid had observed Bodie moving laundry along, cleaning the kitchen, tidying various messes around the house before Molly could get to them. With each thoughtful act, Astrid's heart tripped a little further.

Brain mush from another day of study, as she had done her utmost to not get distracted by interesting but irrelevant tales, Astrid tossed down her latest book and rubbed her eyes. She ventured out just in time to see Molly in the entry, seated on the cushioned bench and pulling on her tennis shoes.

"Where are you off to?" Astrid asked. Not many choices, as she wasn't likely to be heading out shopping with how remote they were.

"Dinner with Eliza. My late brother's wife. Our standing Sunday date."

"Sounds fun. Don't stay out too late now."

"Actually, after all the whiskey that enabler pours in me, I've learned to just crash at her place. If I'm not home by noon on Monday, Bodie usually swings by in his truck to give me a ride home."

Not at all what Astrid was expecting her to say. She supposed at nearly three hundred fifty, Molly could indulge in drinking to excess, smoking, whatever. Astrid waved goodbye to Molly for the evening, watching as she shifted into a glorious, graying wolf, and carried her cane in her teeth as she jogged down the driveway. Astrid had offered to drive her on the quad or in Bodie's truck to Eliza's place. Nope, Molly declared if she couldn't take her evening walk, she may as well change into the wolf one last time and run off into the woods.

Curling up in the library window seat, Astrid watched for her team. The road should still be clear. They hadn't had any torrential rains since she and Bodie had crossed, so they should make good time. Especially without her along to barf up her lunch.

She couldn't read another page today. It was astonishing how naïve demon hunters were about their fellow hybrid. Reading werewolf history was painful; they seemed to lose every time. To humans, demon hunters, other werewolves. The werewolf-vampire war of 1426 was well known in the paranormal world. This version of the tale was far more tragic.

Even now, their population was substantially lower than it had been before the globalization of civilization. No wonder they isolated in packs, distrustfully secluded in the mountains.

Still, she hadn't found anything about ferals organizing to form an army. Something was different about these ferals. Nothing in the books provided any solid leads, like why they were able to live together without killing each other, how so many had been changed, and how they were so well controlled.

Regardless, they were intelligent, and they were united. A solid plan of attack was needed, and without any underestimation of their abilities.

She had watched and re-watched the videos they'd taken, and she still couldn't come up with anything definitive. If they could collapse the mine while most were inside sleeping, they might be able to wipe out half of them. The numbers wouldn't be so lopsided then.

She was going to lose her mind, going over every possibility. If they failed, not only would they lose their own lives, but if the ferals were as intelligent and devious as she suspected, they would come after the pack. And then the nearby towns and tourist hubs. None could make get past them.

As HE ROUNDED THE edge of the ranch, the sun was already lowering in the sky and making its nightly farewell before hiding behind the mountains. Dust from an approaching truck fanned out from the far forest. A group of four bounced in the cab as they drove over the last of the deep ruts before reaching the smoother, gravel top of the main drive. Running faster than the truck, Bodie raced for the house and came in the back door.

Astrid beat him to greet their guests, rumpled from reading all day in a sweet pair of ripped-up jeans with a white cotton tee. Feet bare, her toenails were painted hot pink. Who knew that the smallest of details could get to him like that?

He dashed into the laundry room and pulled on a jeans and a black t-shirt as the troops flooded in the front door. A bubbly shrimp of a woman, all curves and dark hair in a miniskirt and hiking boots, bounced spritely into the house.

Bodie paused at the foot of the stairs, leaning on the rail to watch the show.

Behind the vixen came a shaggy-haired guy with a tight-trimmed beard. Next came a red-headed, porcelain-skinned woman who ex-uded confidence, the corner of her mouth turned up with a hint of amusement.

Last, a tall guy with a stealthy way about him. He tapped Astrid on the shoulder with a playful fist and said, "Still mad at me for sending you first? I think you're enjoying the fresh air." The rumble of his voice was rich and unassuming.

The bubbly one patted Astrid on the cheek. "Fresh air looks good on you. I think you even have a little sunburn. Maybe a few more freckles."

Astrid blushed as she closed the door behind them. "Where'd you guys find that truck? A bit spiffy for a rental."

The bubbly one beamed. "I've always wanted one. After you warned us about the road to get here, well, I ordered the pretty thing and had it waiting at the airport for us." Turning to check out the rest of the house, the woman caught sight of Bodie and stalked over, her hips swinging in invitation. "Hey," she said. Flirty, but reminded him of some of his college friends. Comfortable with everyone, and defiantly her own person.

"Hey." Extending his hand, he said, "Bodie." She shook his hand half a second longer than was appropriate, and her eyes lingered an extra moment on his.

"Lana, hands off." The shaggy-haired guy shook his head and pulled her back by the shoulders.

"I'm just saying hi."

At last, Astrid walked over to him and rescued him from her curious friends. "Bodie, this is Lana." She pointed to the flirty one. "She's chronically horny and just got back from Northern Alaska, so she's probably a bit twitchy."

Lana snorted. "I'm not that bad."

Bodie rubbed a hand over the back of his neck and shrugged. "Sorry, no single guys around here."

Astrid blushed again and continued. Pointing to the shaggy-haired guy, she said, "This is Bennett. Hunter with sword and shield and determined as they come."

Bennett said, "Often to a fault. Hey, man." He shook his hand with a firm grip. Despite the shaggy hair and casual introduction, he had a snooty quality about him. His Southwest Canadian accent was startling, as he seemed more posh English.

"Vann is the one Molly spoke with. He's fought more than his share of ferals."

Firm handshake and ironic half-smile, Vann said, "Although I bet you've got me beat there." Did he know what Bodie was? No way he knew, as he would have given Astrid a heads up, but he seemed to sense Bodie wasn't just a rancher. If the lack of horses and cows hadn't tipped him off.

"And Quinn." She pointed to the redhead with a hint of belly peeking out from her snug shirt. "Quinn's husband, Ryan, is our sixth and should be here in a few days."

Quinn shook his hand and chuckled. "Wow, now I'm the married pregnant one, with no comments on *my* skills."

Astrid quickly amended her statement. "And she's a badass with whatever weapon she wields and has a fondness for decapitation."

"Thank you." Quinn smiled and nodded proudly.

"Anytime."

Despite the introductions being finished, Astrid kept her distance. Was she embarrassed by him? What gives? He was surrounded by her people. A little help would be nice. He had no idea what to say to a demon hunting team. They were clearly tightknit. As cool as they seemed, he was the outsider.

Actually, she'd been quiet all day. Last night had been incredible. He'd known things would be different after, but he didn't think she was one to run away scared.

"Beer?"

"Please." Bennett nodded and immediately followed Bodie into the kitchen. Bodie popped the top off the simply labeled bottle with a charcoal sketch of a wolf and *IPA* written on it. Bennett raised an eyebrow. "Yours?"

"Nah. My dad and my uncle have a little brewing hobby. We live a long way out, and a fifty-mile beer run in four feet of snow just sucks."

Bennett took a long pull and nodded appreciatively. "Good stuff."

Bodie kept passing out beer until he got to Quinn. She pouted melodramatically. "Stupid pregnancy rules. Come on, the girl's got a lot of demon, you can't tell me just a sip will harm her."

Patting Quinn's hint of pregnant belly, Lana rolled her eyes. "My tiny cousin deserves the best. That means lots of water and lots of veggies."

"I know," she grumbled. Quinn snorted and thinly masked her disappointment when Bodie offered her a cup of tea.

The timer blasted an urgent chime. Astrid jumped and immediately grabbed a hot pad holder and pulled a lasagna from the oven. He raised his eyebrows in question.

"Molly," she said, as if it answered everything. Well, he supposed it did. Grammy didn't miss a trick.

After an awkward dinner, on his part anyway, filled with superficial conversation about Montana scenery, the weather, the rough drive here, they all pitched in and quickly got the dishes done, then grabbed another round and slowly migrated to the family room. They were a great crew, and he liked them already. It was Astrid's aloofness that threw him. She was so stiff, he'd have assumed she wasn't as comfortable with her friends as she'd implied. It was clear her friends knew something was up. Worse, he was worried he didn't mean as much to her as she did to him, not wanting her friends to know about her little summer fling with a dreaded werewolf.

Although they were new, both had implied this was beyond anything they'd felt before and had hovered just shy of the L-word. He'd been shaken to his core last night, in deeper than he could have imagined. Had she changed her mind? Had it not been the same for her? Maybe it was his ego, but he thought last night was pretty fucking spectacular.

Vann crossed his arms at his perch on the edge of the couch and said, "Your grandmother didn't go into much detail, and I suspect my dad has some explaining to do. What is this place?"

Bodie sat up in his chair and gulped a mouthful of hops. His dad and Uncle Angus really had nailed it with the latest recipe. He hoped they didn't modify it again. "What do you know?"

"Just that you are a rare werewolf expert. And, apparently, live in a commune in the sticks."

Rubbing his hand mindlessly over the back of his neck, Bodie didn't know how to tell them. Astrid had been so shocked at the truth. If she hadn't seen the change for herself, he doubted she would have believed him.

Astrid attempted to enlighten them. "He's a... I mean, there is so little that we know about... well... Bodie, you explain." She shrugged and blushed, fading into her corner of the couch.

What was her deal? She sat clear across the room and looked anywhere but at him. Her cheeks had been red all evening, and she'd hardly said a word. Those she did speak were uncharacteristically inarticulate. For all the talk of how awesome her team was, she seemed weirdly awkward around them.

He took a measured breath, feeling the last of the setting sun filtering through the lace curtains behind him. "Fuck," he muttered under his breath and stood from his seat. He could talk until he was blue in the face, but a demonstration would answer half their questions without saying a word. He pulled off his t-shirt and tossed it onto the arm of the couch.

Not a whisper could be heard from the silent team, undoubtedly confused as he backed up a few feet. Knowing further beating around the bush would just confuse things, he shifted into the wolf.

Each swallowed their surprised gasp at the unexpected change. Man, his kind had done a little too good of a job protecting werewolves from the world. He inhaled deeply, trying to get a sense of their reactions. Damn demon hunters, he had to be within about twelve inches to get much off them. At least frank revulsion wasn't evident.

Vann nodded leisurely, already accepting as if he had suspected before he'd even arrived.

Bennett scooted forward in his chair and rubbed his hand over his face, staring with complete bemusement.

A pensive look on her face, Quinn's puzzled smile quickly morphed into impressed. "Well, that's not what I was expecting."

Astrid flashed him a gratified grin from her spot in the corner. He still had no idea what she was thinking.

Lana asked, "Can you understand us like that, and can you speak?"

He nodded yes, then shook his head no.

Noting that his jeans were on the floor at his feet, Lana's eyebrow raised in question, her nose scrunched in enjoyment. "Do those clothes magically appear back on you, or do we get a show?"

May as well be one hundred percent honest. One thing about the shifts, he didn't give a shit about walking around naked in front of others. Werewolves tended to lack modesty for just this reason.

Actually, it always amused him seeing the ripped, stretched clothes on the ferals, like they were too preoccupied with their anger to realize they looked ridiculous in their tattered clothes and smelled even worse. For all that this army of ferals seemed organized and more intelligent than average, they still smelled rank and didn't think to ditch their tattered human garments.

Bodie shifted back into the man and raised his shoulders in a nonchalant shrug.

The corner of Lana's mouth quirked up in appreciation, her eyes not shying away as she perused the goods. The others didn't seem to care about the nudity and were a bit more appropriately astonished regarding their preconceptions about werewolves. Astrid still wore her shy smile in the corner.

He pulled on his jeans. "Any questions?" he asked as he pulled his t-shirt over his head.

"Just one. Can you do it again?" Lana asked. Quinn chucked a couch pillow that smacked her in the face.

The corner of Bodie's lips quirked up in a half grin as he plopped back onto the couch. "Another time."

Rising to her feet, Astrid moved and sat close to him, but just out of reach. Was she embarrassed that she'd been getting it on with a werewolf? She spoke softly to the team. "We are entirely uninformed about werewolves. What we know are feral werewolves, those have become trapped between human and wolf."

"Trapped?" Vann asked, catching the key word.

Bodie amended for her, "As in, it's nearly impossible to break free from the state. Halfway in between man and wolf." He explained the acute fury that drove a werewolf to such a state, and the near impossibility to pull out of it, as the adrenaline from the conflict it created was beyond addicting and overwhelming. The power, the destructive nature of it was an outlet few could shake once they'd tasted it.

"When you say halfway in between, you went straight from human to wolf and back again. I didn't see... the creepy-looking werewolf that we've all fought." Bennett drained the last of his beer and set the empty bottle on the side table.

"It's actually not a transitional or a natural state but more of a beast state, like our demon ancestor was said to have been... sort of. Anyway, it's not hard to avoid with decent training. Most ferals end up in the state because they were reckless and lacked control, or they wanted it. From what I hear, it's a heady sensation, bringing both the power of the wolf and the man. The shift between man and wolf is fast, but exhilarating, and we get a small taste of it. But there's also no control in it, no mercy, and no humanity to tell you how to pull yourself out of it. Hence, *trapped*."

Vann nodded. "You ever try it?"

"And risk permanently becoming a smelly, belligerent monster? Hell no. I've only heard of anyone coming back from it a few times."

Lana giggled and rose from her seat on the couch. "That's exactly how Astrid describes werewolves."

With a wide, noisy yawn, Quinn rose from the couch. "I don't know about you guys, but that was a long-ass trip to get here, and I want sleep."

Bodie hopped up. "We have two bedrooms down here and more upstairs." The team disappeared outside for a few minutes and returned with backpacks and massive trunks. He hoped they were packing as much steel as Astrid had implied. They were going to need it.

Bennett tapped his fist on Bodie's shoulder. "You know, that far field would make a great landing strip." Not a bad idea. Bennett sauntered into the nearest downstairs bedroom.

Quinn grabbed another of the downstairs bedrooms and mumbled a sleepy, "Thank you."

Awkward didn't begin to explain the current situation. Astrid had escaped to the kitchen, doing who-knows-what, leaving him to flounder. Only three bedrooms left, and one was his.

He directed Lana to what had been Astrid's room and Vann to the other. Hearing nothing from downstairs, he figured Astrid would either climb in with him or bunk with Lana, depending on how far she was taking this unrehearsed secrecy. Here they'd been, worrying about his pack's response, but in the end, Raulf had almost easily accepted them.

She could have at least given him a heads up.

11

Draining her glass of water, Astrid looked longingly up the stairs. The second the team had arrived, she panicked. Thanks Mr. and Mrs. Edmonds, for making her a complete idiot when it came to relationships.

When it was just the two of them, everything seemed fine. It had been awkward as hell with Bodie's parents at first. But they'd been strangers. They didn't know what was going on in her head.

Around her team that knew her so well, she didn't know how to say, *Not only am I fucking the werewolf, but I have completely fallen for him.* How did one start that conversation? With a subtle hand-holding and see who notices? By making a formal announcement? Either way, she was going to be the center of twenty personal questions.

Instead, she'd drifted back into her untouchable shell and probably drove Bodie away. Her last date had been... Wow, it had been too long. Eight years? She really liked romance, sex, love, all of it. But she had never been any good at it.

In college, she'd pretended to be so worldly. It had been draining to feign comfort with the entire process.

Her friends *knew* her. They'd question and pester and fuss and applaud that she had found someone. Very pressuring.

Once she was sure everyone was securely in their rooms for the night, she went upstairs and slipped into Bodie's room. He was lying on the bed, the sheet draped low over his hips. She wanted so badly to join him. But she'd probably driven him away with her frigid freak-out.

At her arrival, he sat up and watched her move across the room, his blue eyes warm with sympathy, but the spark of uncertainty stabbed right into her sternum. Did he have to be so understanding before she even spoke?

With upright posture, she sat on the edge of the bed. "I'm sorry," she began.

He drew back an inch but didn't run. "What happened? Are we...?" He didn't finish his sentence. Didn't need to.

"I'm scared," she admitted.

"We've got a hell of a battle ahead. We're all afraid."

"Not that. I mean, yes, that is an ominous cloud hanging over all of our heads. What I mean is... I suck at relationships. I can't even admit that I'm seeing someone out loud in front of my best friends. I panicked."

He scooted closer but didn't prod, waiting for her to explain what shouldn't make any sense.

"Before they arrived, I was in the middle of nowhere with an amazing man no one has ever met. No rules, no expectations. I could just be me."

"And you can't be you anymore?"

"That didn't come out right. I can be me... I'm more *me* with my team than with anyone else on the planet. They *know* me. Do you know the last time I dated anyone?" She found herself rambling unintelligibly, trying to explain to Bodie what she could hardly explain herself. "I can tell you exactly how many times I saw my parents hold hands, hug, kiss," she snorted with a cynical shudder. "Never. They prepared me for everything else. Music, dance, science, math, and demon hunting. But they didn't think interpersonal interactions were relevant to raising a child." She swallowed and turned toward Bodie, knowing she'd bungled it. "When my friends, my *world* walked in today, I didn't know how to even broach the subject. It was like all those years of repression my parents drilled into me resurfaced. My team is awesome. I love them dearly. It just threw me, not knowing how to explain how I feel about you. Knowing even touching you would be *noticed*."

Bodie flipped off the sheet and wrapped his body around her, meticulously peeling off her clothes, trailing kisses along her shoulder. "You scared the hell out of me. Thought you'd changed your mind once your friends arrived. Or that you were too embarrassed to admit that you're falling for a werewolf."

"Never."

"How about we just have really noisy sex, and they'll get the idea?"

Astrid couldn't help the laugh that bubbled up in her throat. "At least I won't have to see their initial reactions. Seriously, though. I think I'm the only demon hunter in history that has anxiety and gets carsick and overthinks absolutely everything."

Cradling her cheek with the palm of his hand, he wouldn't let her look away. "Or, you *feel* everything so fully. Every movement of the car, every detail of the room, every look from others, especially those important to you. It's not a bad thing. Makes you a hell of a warrior. But it must get intense."

She felt the racing of her heart slow to a steady, grounded beat. "I like that better than calling me an anxious mess."

"You are not an anxious mess. Now, let's see how deeply you feel me." He bit his lip in a sexy grin.

"Nice segue. So charming."

"That's me, Prince Charming."

"I would never have imagined a werewolf for my Prince Charming, not even in my wildest dreams."

"Then let's get wilder."

She giggled and lowered onto the bed, wanting to feel every inch of him.

BODIE LEAPED OFF THE balcony, shifting midair. and took off into the predawn darkness before his hind legs even hit the ground. In full sprint, the crisp breeze ruffling his fur, he let the energy from the slivered moon pump through his veins. Dew glistened on the tall grass, morphing into damp pine needles as he entered the forest. Fine gravel barely shifted under his swift strides as he ran along the creek that crossed the property, destined to intersect with the river where he'd fallen for Astrid.

About to turn away from the babbling stream, he caught scent of a putrid odor that reeked of feral. Dammit. He'd hoped the others coming so close to the house had been a coincidence. Hope was just that, full of floating fluff.

Following the scent, he felt the air grow thick around him, their irrational animosity saturating the atmosphere. He slowed his pace as he neared the epicenter of the stench. A high-pitched yelp stopped him in his tracks, the subsequent menacing growl making him think twice about diving in headfirst.

Sneaking closer, camouflaging himself in a fragrant patch of bluebells and heather, he watched. Two nasties were chowing down on the remains of a cougar. At least it wasn't a person. Bodie's stomach wrenched and recoiled, flashing back on the countless meals he'd stumbled upon. *Meals*, that's not right, sometimes they just gnawed on mangled playthings.

Another paced back and forth on the edge of the creek, the remnants of a denim jacket forming a punk-style vest with cuffs at her wrists, her ripped khakis stretched and shredded beyond repair. Behind her, sitting on a boulder and burying his face in his hands, a feral was muttering something under his breath. It wasn't a growl, but... no, that couldn't be right.

"I can't. I remember—" the feral mumbled.

The female rotated on the muddy bank and snarled at him. "Nothing. Gone."

"The... kids. Wife... We need to..." The feral glared at his clawed fingertips, shaking his head with uncertainty.

The female slurred something under her breath, then continued her pacing.

One of the ferals that snacked on the carcass tore a chunk of flesh, chomped his jaws over the hunk of muscle, and swallowed the throat-full. Growling, he stepped back and barked at the others. He nodded upstream, then looked at the brightening sky as if to convey the urgency of his order.

The hungry ones vaulted over the nearby log and took off into the far forest. The female paused at the confused one and growled under her breath. "Now." Giving up, she disappeared into the forest after the others.

Bodie rose from his cover and snuck through a shallow in the creek toward the feral that seemed to have some self-awareness, questioning the unnatural state. Dumb idea. No doubt about it.

Bodie shifted into the man, but kept a safe distance, offering, with hands held out in a gesture of peace. "I can help."

The feral muttered, "Too late." He looked up at the purple sky, then to Bodie. His eyes remained clouded with bewildered rage, but something behind his look projected a remarkably human desperation.

From the forest, the female bounded over the log with exceptional speed.

Arms slashing, she aimed straight for this throat.

Bodie ducked and rolled, dodging her wild attacks.

Half a second too late, he sensed the confused feral appear behind him with renewed ferocity. Bodie moved to avoid the attack, but one of the feral's claws lashed deeply across his side.

Pain burned before the wound numbed, blood trickling out from the long gash. *Fuck that hurt.*

Pissed, he grabbed the male's other arm and smashed his jaw with an uppercut.

Fist tight over the feral's wrist, he dodged a hit from the other side as the female leaped at him.

As the feral in his grip lashed back at him, Bodie yanked him closer and wrapped his arm around the feral's neck. Jerking its head with an efficient twist, Bodie winced as the spine ruptured in his hands.

Showing remarkable intelligence as she'd calculated her timing this go around, the female launched at him as the male dropped to the ground. Knowing he would dodge the blow, she spun around and bashed him in the head with a blunt fist that knocked him to the ground.

Pissed as hell, he flipped up and slammed his elbow into her nose. As he'd done with the male, he yanked her close and snapped her neck.

Blinking away the blinding fury of his own, Bodie stood over the neat pile of smelly ferals at his feet. He scanned the forest for signs of the other two. They didn't return, their scent fading into the distance.

His side throbbed, the warmth of his own blood flowing over the skin below. Knowing it would sting like a son-of-a-bitch, he paced into the creek and rinsed the wound with the glacial meltwater. Fucking freezing. Should have changed back to the wolf to get his teeth in the fight, but it hurt like hell to shift with a wound this deep, and every movement widened the gash.

Slightly cleaner now, with slightly less risk of unhygienic feral-claw germs getting into his bloodstream, he braced his hand over the wound and limped home.

BODIE WAS GONE WHEN she awoke. Astrid was getting used to his morning routine. The balcony door was open, and the curtain twirled with the cool morning air in a delicate pirouette.

Knowing hot water would be limited with so many people in the house, Astrid didn't linger in the shower. Nor did she waste time drying her hair, accepting that it would end up pin-straight and part exactly where it wanted to. A few weeks ago, she'd even added a few layers, but it didn't seem to change much. She threw on a pair of her favorite jeans and a short sleeved black v-neck, feeling a bit darker today.

In the refrigerator, another casserole waited with a handwritten note from Molly in her antique script, *Hope your friends settled in okay. Can't wait to meet them this afternoon. Heat on 350 for 45 min, let sit for 10 min.*

Smiling, Astrid shrugged at the sweet note. Growing up, her breakfast was served promptly at 0800, a light meal of oatmeal with berries and walnuts, served by the housekeeper, and no one to dine with, whether her parents were home or not, and her siblings had long since left the house.

As instructed, Astrid preheated the oven. The sun was already starting to warm the earth outside, and morning blooms were opening to attract the birds and the bees that would be arriving for their daily pursuits soon.

Quinn ambled out of her bedroom as Astrid put the casserole into the oven. Quinn poured herself a cup of coffee with rebellious intention. "Stow it. I get one cup." She curled into one of the mismatched dining chairs. There was now a piano bench at one end of the table and two stools crammed in so there was seating for seven. Astrid suspected the library had once been the formal dining room. The current arrangement was much more to her liking.

The rest of her team filtered into the kitchen as the scent of eggs and sausage from the breakfast casserole wafted through the house. Where was Bodie? The timer alarmed. She almost missed it for watching out the window.

Astrid mindlessly set the casserole dish on top of the stove. Her brain raced in every different direction, not liking a single answer of where he might be.

Bennett sat at the table with a massive cup of coffee while Lana brewed a fresh pot. His eyes swept across the room before asking, "Where's Bodie?"

"He normally goes for a run in the morning, but he doesn't usually stay out this long." A hollow pit of worry was intensifying in her stomach.

Enough.

She tore up the stairs and threw on her boots. Sprinting back downstairs, she found the team already tossing on their shoes. If they spread out, they could find him quicker. "I'll get his dad to help. He should be able to track Bodie's scent."

The back door swung open, the loud crack as it hit the wall jarred through her. Spinning on her heel, she saw Bodie holding his side as he stood in the open doorway. At first, his eyes were unfocused until she came into view, then he flashed a devious half-smile in her direction that washed the fear away.

She rushed to his side and threw her arms around him. "What happened?"

"Whoa, watch it," he warned but pulled her close against him with his free arm. Trembling, every muscle in his body tense, he leaned into her.

Astrid pulled back just far enough to move his hand so she could see what he was covering. Blood oozed between his fingers, a huge laceration spanned across his left side over his ribs and abdomen.

"You scared the hell out of me," she muttered as she scanned the rest of his body for injuries.

Despite his pale complexion, he smiled at her frantic inspection.

"Where's the first aid kit?" she managed to ask, feeling faint at the sight of blood for the first time in her life.

Bennett appeared at her side with a clear plastic tub filled with supplies. "Got one. Kitchen?"

"Mind grabbing me some pants?" Bodie motioned to the shelf by the door.

Astrid couldn't seem to let go of him. "Now you're modest?"

His voice was hoarse, but he laughed. "Don't want to intimidate your friends."

Quinn grabbed him the nearest pants from the shelf and handed them to Astrid. While Bodie pulled on the jeans, Astrid steadied him.

"Come on, let's get to the kitchen and clean and dress that wound." Astrid steadied him as he followed along. He grumbled as she made him sit on a stool. She pulled up a chair so she could evaluate the injury.

Wincing, he drew his hand away from his side at her urging. Immediately, blood poured from the deep laceration. Lana passed her a clean, white hand towel soaked with hot water. Bodie let out a brief cluster of expletives and paled as she cleaned the wound, but he didn't flinch.

"Well, Dr. Connery, you've really done it this time. What happened?" Astrid was astonished at the lack of life to her voice, but she needed him to keep talking until she was convinced he was okay.

"Little lightheaded here, give me a minute..." He trailed off, his face paling to a clammy ghost white. Vann moved to steady him from behind, but Bodie waved him away. "I'm good. I'm good. No problem."

Vann nodded with a slow smile, but he stayed close.

"Sure you don't want to lie down?" Bennett asked.

"No, no, just keep talking and be normal." Bodie grinned.

While the others gathered around the table, Quinn slid the casserole in the oven to keep warm and topped off coffees. She said, "Although I admire the tough guy act, feel free to pass out. We'll only mock you a little."

"In front of a team of demon hunters and stoke those egos? Hell no."

Astrid rolled her eyes and tried to still the trembling of her hand as she finished cleaning the wound. Others offered to take over, but she wouldn't let them.

Besides, she did the best suturing of the team. She did let Bennett assist and set up her sterile field. "We don't have any lidocaine." She scrubbed her hands under the kitchen faucet while Lana held pressure with a fresh towel.

Bodie flashed her a wink. "That tiny needle sounds much less painful than a feral claw." Wow, she should not be so attracted to a pasty, wounded man in a kitchen, but he was half-naked and joking about his bravado and pretending he wasn't on the verge of passing out.

He silently winced each time the needle dug into his skin. "Okay, I was wrong. That hurts like a son-of-a-bitch. I think we have some liquor in the cabinet."

"I already cleaned it."

"I mean could use a drink."

"Sorry charlie, but I need your brain."

"No fun. I thought you guys healed so fast you wouldn't need stitches."

Concentrating on her task, Astrid didn't look away, but it was hard to see for the flashbacks of Bennett bleeding out while she fruitlessly held pressure over his abdomen for hours as they sailed to medical care a few months back. "Not usually, but sometimes it gets bad."

Bennett crouched at her side and studied the wound. Astrid tried not to laugh at the spectacle Bodie had become. He didn't seem to mind, but simply chuckled. She envied his comfort with attention.

Still inspecting the injury, Bennett asked, "How quickly do you guys heal?"

Bodie shrugged, then winced as the movement pulled at the wound. Astrid glared up at him for interrupting her work and pulling loose the suture she had yet to fasten. He grinned down at her, an azure gleam in his mischievous wink. At least he wasn't as pale as he'd been.

"Not as fast as you guys, but faster than humans. This should be good in two, maybe three days. Can someone grab me some coffee?"

Quinn was at his side in seconds with a fresh cup. He sighed, gratefully saying, "Thanks."

Astrid finished her last stitch and dressed the wound.

"What about ferals?" Vann asked. "I've seen them with their arm hanging off and they keep coming."

Bodie stilled his shoulders instead of shrugging this time. "They don't sit still for long, so I'm not sure on healing time. You're right though. They're so primed with adrenaline, they probably wouldn't even notice they were injured with a gash like this. I would expect them to heal faster, as everything about them is amped up, but they also wouldn't sit still long enough to let the wound close."

After ensuring the bandage was secure, Bodie rose from his stool and disappeared into the laundry room.

Astrid sat back in her chair and sipped her coffee that had grown cold while she worked. All eyes stared at her. Quinn's eyebrows were raised in exaggerated question. The corner of Vann's mouth was turned up. Long silence, but they all looked pointedly amused.

Great. This was exactly the attention she had been avoiding.

Lana leaned back in her chair and raised her eyebrows up and down. "So, you and the sexy werewolf, huh?"

Here came the blush. She took a cautious sip of coffee. Deciding it was undrinkably cold, she dumped the rest in the sink.

All eyes watched her every movement.

She poured a fresh cup for something to occupy her. "Um, well..."

Returning miraculously fast in a crisp white t-shirt and non-bloody jeans, adorably barefooted, Bodie slipped his arms around her waist and pulled her against him. She could feel his grin against her temple. "Yep," he said, rescuing her. Or threw her to the wolves. Either way, she melted into him and let the blush drain down her neck. "As we discovered, werewolves and demon hunters can be... remarkably compatible."

Biting her lip, Astrid stared down into her answerless coffee.

Bennett laughed out loud, a massive smile on his face. "Ha. That's what you get for ragging on me for the vampire. What was that you said? 'Anything's better than a smelly werewolf?'"

Bodie's arms wrapped tighter around her middle as he shook with quiet laughter. He whispered in her ear, sending shivers down her spine. "Not in your wildest dreams."

12

Static electricity stirred the air. Every hair on Bodie's body stood on end. The odd sensation filled him with dread, but the others in the room seemed to relax, setting down their books at the change in the atmosphere.

Appearing from the thick of the charged air, a muscular guy in a Coast Guard t-shirt and cargos appeared down on one knee in front of the fireplace, an unearthly black sword strapped to his back.

Bodie struggled to calm the thundering in his chest at the invasion. Feigning a smile, he gathered this must be the sixth. Or he hoped anyway.

The new guy rose to his feet and casually extended his hand. "You must be Bodie. I'm Ryan." When they said he'd arrive in a day or two, Bodie had expected... well, he hadn't expected him to materialize in the library.

Bodie stood and shook Ryan's hand. "Hey. Uh, make yourself at home." He dropped back onto the couch and gulped his beer in a long, collect-your-thoughts swig. Glancing around, he realized that truly, no one else was surprised by the fucking bizarre arrival. As the static faded away, he sniffed. He was slowly beginning to be able to pick up demon hunter scents, but it took effort. "You smell different," he blurted out.

The new guy laid his sword on the mantle, then dropped onto the opposite couch next to Quinn. Ryan ran his hand through his military-short hair, his dark irises flashing as his grin widened. "Oddly enough, you stink a lot less than I'd have guessed."

"Okay, slow down. Can someone bring me up to speed here?" Bodie was still new to demon hunter culture, and the rest seemed so comfortable with each other. But he was lost.

Now that Astrid had settled in, she'd been snuggled against him all evening, happy as a clam with her team and a good book. Miraculously well timed, she reappeared from her beer run and handed him a fresh drink, placing a few spares on the coffee table. She curled back into the corner of the couch, draping her legs over his lap. "Ryan is a demon hunter, but his father is Bain, king of the demon hunters, whereas we come from his lover, Deandra."

"Okay," he said again. "That would explain the difference in smell. But how can he materialize in my home?"

Ryan shrugged. "Not easily. Thanks to my father, I have a little control over the veil and can pull myself through it, with the right motivation." He pulled Quinn closer and kissed the top of her head. "It leaves a ripple that will eventually fade, but I shouldn't do it often, and make sure the ripples calm down before I travel again, or I can create weak areas in the veil that take even longer to repair. My captain was not thrilled that I was leaving so early in the deployment, but from what I hear, this qualifies as an emergency?"

Bodie nodded. "Got that right." Tossing his book onto the coffee table, he wrapped his free arm around Astrid's legs, brushing his hand along her calf.

Ryan snagged a beer from the collection Astrid had set out. He ignored the bottle opener and easily popped the top with the ring on his finger. Ryan looked from Bodie to Astrid and back again. He laughed out loud. "Astrid's nailing a werewolf. I'm deployed for a few weeks, and the world turns upside down."

Quinn flipped her wavy red hair. "How did you know he was a werewolf?"

He shrugged. "You didn't? Look at him. It's obvious."

Everyone stared at him like he was nuts.

"Seriously?" Ryan sighed, clearly surprised by their cluelessness. "Even in human form, their eyes glow and, I don't know, they move different. Wolf-like."

Bodie hadn't thought about it, but he was right. "Most of the rest of the paranormal world only knows about ferals. Where have you seen others like me?"

Expression darkening, Ryan scowled at his half empty beer bottle. "I, uh... long story, but I used to be part of a violent demon hunting team—"

Quinn cut him off. "Not part of. Victim of."

"Either way... shit, I'm so sorry man, but I..." Ryan buried his head in his hands, exhaling slowly through pursed lips. "I grew up a pretty normal kid, not knowing what I was until I'd graduated from high school. My first team knew I was different. Initially, I was eager to learn. Eventually I realized, they enjoyed killing demons a little too much. They kept a tight leash on me, a demon-spawn, a perfect plaything for their vicious games."

Bodie's throat filled with bile, dreading where this was going.

Ryan's eyes darkened to an unearthly black, his gaze met Bodie's. "I'm really, really sorry, but I've killed a lot of your kind."

Air leaching from his lungs, Bodie's vision faded red. Breathless, he uttered, "What?"

Astrid took his beer and set it on the coffee table, then rested her hand on his jaw as she turned him to face her. "*They* are why Raulf has every reason to be afraid of demon hunters. Most aren't like that. Ryan least of all."

Ryan continued, leaning forward in his seat, his lips pulled tight as he strained to keep it together. "I don't want to dig the knife in any deeper, but I want to be completely up front with you. Before I ran—probably what haunts me more than anything of the other nightmares they put me through—they once pitted me against a pack of werewolves. Made me watch while they tortured them until they turned feral, and then they unleashed them on me a few at a time. Testing them or me, or both. Or, more likely, just enjoying the show." He paused, his jaw pulsing. "Didn't matter what I did, I couldn't turn them back."

Lana asked, "Did any of them have control?"

"Most wouldn't have acknowledged their own mother, but there were two that seemed to have some awareness outside of the irrational rage. One even talked."

At his side, Astrid was all ears, her posture erect as she took in everything that was said. "Were you able to successfully communicate with it?"

Ryan snorted, snagging his beer again and settling into the couch. "Sure did. It said, 'You're dead,' so I said, 'In your fucking dreams.'"

"Witty." Astrid rolled her eyes.

Ryan took a long pull of his beer. "Sorry. Not exactly a time in my life I like talking about."

Bodie nodded. "You're not wrong. Even one coherent enough to speak would be so far gone, no matter who they were before the change, and wouldn't hesitate to kill mercilessly. The fact that Ryan had even tried to change any? Fucking fearless."

Nodding, Ryan said, "Nearly died trying. After getting my ass kicked again and again, my sympathy waned. Feral claws don't just slice, they shred."

Bodie laughed ironically, his wound throbbing again.

Astrid sighed heavily at his side. "What we really need to know before we risk trying, is whether any can be pulled out of the feral state?"

Bodie answered, needing the connection as he laced his fingers with Astrid's. Hating the truth of it, he shook his head. "As Ryan discovered, it's too dangerous to even try. That's how I earned my merit badge this morning."

Rubbing a hand through his shaggy hair, Bennett plopped his feet onto the coffee table next to Ryan's and shoved Ryan's feet off. "I take it we can pretty well count on *not* having an ally among the ferals."

Ryan plopped his feet back up and kicked Bennett's feet off. Bennett repositioned his feet back on the table, this time on the other side of Quinn's, capping off the move with a smug grin on his face. Ryan flipped him off, sporting a wicked grin. Bodie watched the curious interaction. Clearly, there was a history there. "How many are we talking?"

Bodie quickly brought Ryan up to speed, laying it out again for the others. And for himself. Didn't matter how many times he went over it. Even if they succeeded, they weren't all walking away from this.

Vann spoke up from where he sat stretched out on the window seat. "Let's say a hundred of them from your count, maybe a few more by the time we get there—if they're still actively recruiting. Six from our team plus seven werewolves. That leaves seven to eight ferals per warrior. If we can knock those numbers down a bit, we got this."

"Knock those numbers down a lot. Plus, we can't let any past us," Lana said.

"Bennett's mom and my dad's team should be back in town in a few days. Lana, your dad's team is home, right?" Quinn picked up her tea that had long since gone cold and glowered at it, then set it back down again. "We could almost triple our numbers by having them join the fight, but even that won't be enough. If the feral pack is truly more intelligent and organized, it may not matter what the ratio is. I think… I think more important than more warriors, is backup in case we fail. Let's see if our parents' teams can cover the valleys between the ferals and the populated areas in case any get past us."

Bodie felt a nagging jealousy, sitting and watching the team brainstorm in action. He'd always gone on his vigilante missions alone. Noah had always said he'd bring Bodie along when he was old enough, but Noah left just as Bodie was learning to shift. "Good plan. In case they've got an ace up their sleeve, I'd rather we have a strong defensive line."

Lana scowled, pulling her feet under the blanket on the corner of the couch near Bennett. "I don't know. If we could recruit as many teams as we can, and Bodie, you call in as many werewolves as you know, we could form a hell of an army."

Astrid shook her head, loosening the braid under the force of it until her hair drifted into her face. "I wish. It's too big of a risk, after what happened during the vampire uprising of 1207." Clearly accustomed to few knowing the details she had stored in that steel trap, Astrid expounded, "Terribly outnumbered when the vampires united, dozens of demon hunting teams joined forces to counter with an army. While they succeeded in defeating the vampires, thousands of humans died in the regions of the world that were left unprotected, and the demon hunting population was cut in half."

Vann nodded. "Even if we could count on the humans protecting their own while we gathered, if word got out of multiple teams of demon hunters in one place, more than likely, our enemies would take advantage and converge. Imagine adding a few hundred vampires to the fight?"

"Not in my backyard." Bodie shook his head and tried to bring levity to the conversation, but the desperation in his voice probably outweighed his poor attempt at a joke.

Astrid pulled out the map they'd made again. Sketching in the possible exits, the activity patterns they'd recorded, she laid it out. "It's up to us. Now, most of the ferals sleep in the old mine. If we can get someone in there before sunset, we could eliminate half or more at once. They seemed pretty nocturnal, and, if there's a full moon, we can almost count on it. Anyone have access to explosives?"

Everyone looked up at Ryan. "Don't look at me. I can move in and out of the veil, with difficulty. I'm not taking anything explosive that way. Nor do I want to create a ripple right in the middle of baddie central. That's just asking for bigger demons to follow."

"Rain, my cousin, is a total pyromaniac. Bet she can come up with something."

From his corner, Vann asked, "Timeline?"

Bodie shrugged. "Although the ferals will be stronger on the full moon, so will we. I expect more so, as we can double the strength we gain from it with focus."

Brow scrunched in curiosity, Lana brushed her hair out of her face and asked, "Is that why you all howl at it?"

Chuckling, he rubbed his hand over the back of his neck. "No, uh, that's just for fun."

Quinn laughed with him, then asked, "I've always wondered, what is the connection between werewolves and the full moon?"

"That's an excellent bedtime story. For another night. For now, I'm toast." Bodie drained the last of his beer and rose to his feet.

Lana added a sleepy goodnight, and said, "Don't go out alone again. We're shy on warriors as it is."

"Not a problem. This hurts like hell. Raulf organized the others to monitor the perimeter after I talked to him this morning. They'll work in pairs and alternate shifts. Eyes only."

Vann said, "We'll do the same."

Astrid rose and linked her hand in Bodie's. The others were starting to pack up and would likely be heading to bed as well. Bodie had hoped to feel more reassured after meeting with Astrid's whole team. And, well, he did. But now that he had a feel for their own small army, he realized just how horribly outnumbered they were. Tomorrow, he'd talk with Grammy about her thoughts on calling in Morrison and some of the others from the pack that were away, but even then, they'd only add three, maybe four to their numbers.

As they reached the stairs, Vann called softly after them. "Hey, Astrid. Got a minute?"

Astrid released Bodie's hand. "I'll be up soon."

Vann nodded his head for Astrid to follow. He led the way out the front door. The crisp midnight air prickled over her skin. In the distance, she could see the lights of Raulf and Felicity's front porch, further along through a cluster of trees was Marcus' house. Peace and quiet tonight, or so it seemed. Although, she imagined the world could be burning, and this corner of it would remain serene and untouched.

Vann leaned against one of the posts that framed the front porch. Glancing around, he ensured they were alone.

Astrid crossed her arms and looked out over the ranch. "What is it?"

His voice was quiet, rumbling, "You trust him?"

"Of course." She wasn't sure what he was getting at. "I wouldn't be sleeping with him otherwise," she said.

"Come on, Astrid. It's more than sex."

"Yes."

"He loves you."

Among the oddities not daring to appear in her wildest dreams, Vann commenting on her love life was unexpected. "I think so."

"It's pretty obvious. Which is part of why I don't think he's got any malicious intent."

"What are you getting at?"

"He's hiding something." Vann didn't have extrasensory perception. No magic powers above any inherent demon hunter abilities, but he was remarkably intuitive, so Astrid couldn't help but trust his instincts.

"You may be right."

"We can't go into battle with any secrets."

"And you want me to get it out of him?"

"Nothing so devious. He's hurting. Protecting himself or someone else."

"I'll see if I can find out what's bothering him."

Astrid moved to go inside, but Vann hesitated. He looked into the night, a distant look on his face. "He's a good guy."

"I know," she said as she went back inside. The downstairs bathroom light flicked off, and Astrid stayed in the shadows as Quinn and Ryan came out together, already absorbed in each other.

She felt a growing ache deep in her belly as she looked up the stairs.

She slipped into the bedroom and found Bodie staring out the window at the empty sky. The moon was a mere sliver, partially obscured by a cluster of clouds that weren't letting on if they planned to accumulate or dissipate. What was it about that man? Didn't hurt that he was rarely fully clothed. The soft glow from outside cast a striking shadow over his muscular back, the bandage secure across his side and a few inches above his well-worn jeans that draped low over his hips.

Knowing he'd already sensed her, she moved to stand behind him and slipped her arms around his waist, resting her head on the back of his shoulder. His hands immediately covered hers, completing the connection. "You okay?" he asked, his voice gravelly with exhaustion.

"Yeah. Tired. Let's go to bed." She slipped into the cool sheets, and he followed right behind. Wrapping her long limbs around him, she rested her head on his chest and let sleep wash over her.

Cloud-covered sunlight diffused into the room through the open deck door, announcing morning was breaking. Despite the damp chill, she was toasty warm with Bodie wrapped around her. His arm tucked under her head, she felt like a melting scoop of chocolate peanut butter ice cream spooned deliciously in his arms. She relished the lingering scent of alpine forest that she suspected was more a part of him than a result of his environment.

Although she would happily stay in bed with him all day, she wiggled her way out of his arms. With a sleepy groan, he stole her pillow and wrapped his arms around it instead. She grabbed a cozy flannel shirt from his closet and slipped it on. Remembering the full house, she pulled on a pair of jeans and tossed her hair into an easy ponytail as she headed downstairs.

The coffeepot announced a successful brew the moment her feet touched the cool tile of the kitchen floor. The cabinet creaked as she snagged what she'd already learned was Bodie's favorite mug, as well as one for her. She hadn't yet decided between the national park themed sturdy mug versus the more delicate one with hand-painted flowers.

Behind her, a meaningful throat-clearing caught her off guard. Whipping her head around, she found Lana in yoga pants and a cotton tank top grinning at her. "The ever-vigilant Astrid Edmonds caught by surprise? What could be working your brain so hard you forget to watch your own six?"

Astrid snorted in amusement and poured her coffee, but left Bodie's empty for now. "Isn't it obvious? I'm standing in the middle of the homiest kitchen on the planet, wearing a werewolf's flannel shirt, while trying to suppress the sensation of my soul being ripped in half at the impossible duality of staying here indefinitely and keeping my day job."

"That's it? Didn't you forget that's only if you survive the mission?"

"That too. Just another day at the office."

Lana reached into the cabinet and pulled out a serviceable stoneware mug. She filled her own cup and sat at the kitchen table.

Shuffling steps, echoed by a sleepy groan, preceded Bennett as he rounded the corner. "Can't this damn region decide to be hot or cold? I'm cooking by noon, then freezing my ass off by dawn. What elevation are we at, anyway?"

"Good morning," Astrid said with a snarky grin, pouring Bennett a cup of coffee as he dropped onto the sturdiest of the wooden chairs at the table.

His smile reached his eyes as he wrapped his hands around the steaming mug. "You're a goddess. Thanks." He took a long, testing sip that seemed to wake him a bit, catching Astrid and Lana both watching him with amused grins. "What? Am I interrupting? Dammit, I'll go back to bed."

Astrid was glad he was getting back to his pre-Quinn, affable Bennett self. Yeah, he'd always been intense, but he and Quinn had both repressed parts of their personalities in a foolish attempt to make the mistake of a relationship last. Since their breakup that occurred only days before Quinn was blasted across the arctic to Ryan, Bennett had been bitter and irritable. Day by day, Bennett seemed to be coming back into his own.

She leaned against the counter. "You're welcome to join in."

Kicking him gently under the table, Lana chuckled. "We're just pontificating on Astrid finally meeting her match, but predictably dwelling on the impossibility of it."

He snorted in a terribly un-Bennett-like manner. "Isn't that the bitch of it?"

Astrid and Lana both fell silent. He wouldn't say it. When he and Quinn broke up, his heart hadn't been broken as much as bruised, as he'd given it away years before.

Ryan's sleepy voice rumbled from the hall as he approached, "Not another damn Kumbaya moment." He shuffled to the coffee pot and poured two massive mugs.

Lana cleared her throat at him.

"Hey, she threatened to name the baby Seven if I don't bring her a 'gargantuan cup of black coffee.'"

"Then water it down."

"Good idea." He filled half the cup with water and paused. "Well? What's the deal?"

Shifting her chair so she could face the entire, now bordering on crowded, kitchen, Lana shrugged. "Impossible relationships."

Ryan swallowed his sip so fast he cringed, the scorching liquid burning his throat. "Yeah, that is a bitch. Fate had to launch Quinn across the fucking Arctic Ocean and wipe her memory for us to make it work." He glanced over at Astrid. "And you have to survive a hundred ferals, then decide if you want to make a life with a smelly werewolf in the sticks. You'll figure it out."

Bennett shook his head in amusement. "And there's Sunshine the optimist coming out."

Ryan flipped him off and took a long, piping hot sip.

Stumbling in, adding to the embarrassingly theatrical scene, came Quinn. "Don't talk smack about my mother-in-law. That woman's tougher than the rest of us combined." She grabbed her cup from the counter next to Ryan, scowled at it, then silently traded mugs with him. "What's with the heavy talk this morning?" She leaned against the counter next to her husband.

Vann followed in, the room silent as he poured his coffee, knowing it was his turn. He took a sip from his mug and let out a satisfied sigh, clearly enjoying their impatient waiting.

He topped off all but Quinn's coffees and then methodically prepped the machine and turned it on for a fresh pot. Watching all of their reactions, the corner of his mouth quirked up as he answered Quinn's question. "Astrid's fallen in love with the werewolf and is scared shitless."

Astrid parked on the stool in the corner of the kitchen out of pure spite, knowing Vann had his eye on the perch, then flashed him a daring eyebrow raise. She announced, "You know what, you can all head back home again. We'll just call in the national guard to launch an air strike on the ferals, so I won't have to listen to all of your witty comments on my sex life."

Lana grinned. "I believe he said *love*, not *sex*. But we can change the subject. Tell me, how is sex with the superbly built werewolf?"

Icing on the cake, Bodie strolled in. "Fucking spectacular." He bit his lower lip in that ridiculously adorable way of his, adding a wink for Astrid. He dropped onto a chair at the kitchen table.

Ryan took pity on her. "Okay. As much as I'm sad to have missed out on Bodie's nakedness and can't pass judgment on his 'ripped' body—thanks for the graphic description on that, Lana—I think they can figure this one out on their own."

Snuggling against him, Quinn whispered loud enough for the rest of the room to hear, "We were lucky they were all across the Gulf of Alaska when we went through the lots-of-sex, worrying-about-the-future stage."

"We're still having lots of sex," he said, sliding his hands under the edge of her shirt to splay his hand over her belly.

As if her entire team and her lover weren't enough, Molly came limping into the room, dressed in cheetah-print fleece pajamas. "Tell me about it. Their room is above mine." She winked at Astrid and headed for the coffee pot that was sputtering as the pot finished brewing.

13

THE FOLLOWING MORNING, ASTRID awoke to the subtle, electric sensation of Bodie's fingers grazing along her waist. Her eyes fluttered open, adjusting to the dim light, the cool of the air contrasting the heat of his body spooned around hers. "You want to get out there, don't you?"

A chuckle passed his lips, tickling across her ear. "Yeah."

"Are you healed enough?"

"Mostly. I need to see if they came back."

"I want to go with you, but are you sure you wouldn't rather go with another wolf? I won't be nearly as fast on my two feet to your four."

"I want to be with you."

Butterflies fluttered in her belly at hearing him say it. "No coffee as bribery this time?"

As she turned in his arms, she realized he was already dressed and grinning at her, his hair wet from the shower. Their coffees were waiting on the bedside table behind him. He sat up and passed her coffee over.

"How long have you been up?"

"An hour. I was trying to let you sleep."

"Thanks, I guess."

Fifteen minutes later, they were out the front door. He slipped into his backpack, loaded with water and snacks as they'd skipped breakfast, and he shifted into the wolf. The team, the werewolves, would all be plugging away again today, attempting to come up with a failsafe plan. Tentatively, they were planning their attack for the upcoming full moon. Assuming Rain could come through on explosives in time.

Bodie motioned to the trees beyond. They set out into the forest, exploring just beyond sight of the ranch. Circling the area, Astrid watched as Bodie would follow a scent, confirm it wasn't a feral, then move on. As they continued their fast clip across the area, she scanned as far as she could see, checked the ground, and the trees for signs of disturbance.

As they neared the familiar trail they'd taken the quad down, Bodie's ears pricked up, and he sniffed the air. A low growl passed his lips. Stalking off the trail, he followed the scent.

"Wait, I want to know how many first."

Halting, he whipped his head back and nodded toward the woods, insistent.

"Okay," she said with a sigh. He tracked better as the wolf, but communication was terrible. Part of her wondered if he stayed in wolf form to avoid telling her what was bothering him.

Last night's wind had brought in a thicker, blacker sky that wasn't letting up. The sun had risen, as she could tell by the gray glow over the forest, but it was suppressed behind heavy clouds.

Bodie raced faster as the scent grew stronger. Astrid had to sprint to keep up, but she felt his mounting fear. The feeling of something different resonated deep in her gut. Nothing she could pinpoint, but she didn't like it.

BODIE HADN'T KNOWN WHAT to expect, Astrid on foot while he was the wolf. Amazingly, they'd made a good team. She was a machine on the job. And fast, despite her fear that she would slow him down.

The scent was painfully familiar. He had no doubt as to the source this time.

In the distance, he heard a whimper. His ears trained in the direction of the sound, but his nose yearned to follow the familiar scent instead.

Turning her head left toward the cry, Astrid was clearly as confused as he was. "Come on."

Teeth bared, sniffing hard, he was already losing the scent, the risk of never reaching him threatening to shred his soul. Changing, he became the man. "Go. I'll join you soon as I can. I don't want to lose this trail. It's... please."

With frank irritation, she bit her tongue and didn't argue. She wouldn't have missed the desperation in his tone.

Sprinting full speed toward the cry, she disappeared into the thick aspen grove.

He shifted back into the wolf and followed the odorous trail, the waning scent of humanity laced into each track a knife in his heart. He chased the lead until the trail ran cold at the creek. Nothing. Bodie scanned the far bank in both directions, but there was no scent to pick up.

He'd disappeared.

Lightning flashed in the distance, drawing closer with each rumble of thunder. He could head up or down stream all day, but the chances of picking the scent back up were slim to none. Heart thundering in his ribs, he took off after Astrid, acutely aware that his sentiment had landed them in the middle of another fucking trap.

Fat raindrops fell from the sky, darkening the boulders that surrounded the creek. Wind gusted through the trees and pulled the weakest branches to the ground.

Fading faster than the feral's trail, Astrid's scent was almost undetectable. If he hadn't known her so well, the taste of her skin, her subtle fragrance, he wouldn't have been able to track her at all.

As the rain dumped harder and faster, the trail to Astrid became almost imperceptible... until it ran cold.

Ears turning up, he listened through the pelting rain. Nothing.

Like a curtain at the end of an epic tragedy, his vision began to darken as panic set in.

Then he heard it. Her footsteps striking the rocky riverbank resonated in his ears. Picking up the pace, he took off toward her. The scent of feral and blood emanated off of her.

What had he been thinking? So fucking obsessed, his suspicions finally confirmed, he hadn't had the common sense to put his emotions behind him, risking her life.

Bodie changed to the man, and his backpack dropped to the gravel at his feet.

As Astrid reached him, she stopped in her tracks and put her hands on her hips, pacing with as much fury as was boiling under his sternum. "We walked right into that trap. They separated us with so little effort."

His voice came out in a harsh whisper, "How many?"

"Just one. Whimpering like a hurt child to draw me in."

"And?" He snarled, hating himself more than ever.

"And I took care of it. She attacked the moment she saw me. As you see, I am unharmed." She gestured to her soaked but intact tank top and running shorts.

His jaw was clenched, fists at his sides, fighting an unwinnable battle against himself and his own stupidity. "Why just one? What kind of trap leaves us both unscathed?"

"Maybe their intent wasn't to hurt us. Perhaps to study us or... try to determine our tactics? Our weaknesses?"

Hands on his hips, he glared into the dense shadows of the forest across the river.

"What did you find?" Her usual calm voice was gone, her words clipped. She paced the riverbank like she'd just lost the race.

"Nothing," he said with a sneer. "Trail ran cold."

"But it was just one you scented? And I only saw one. The last few sightings have all been groups of three or four. Something's different about today."

"Yep," he responded in a harsh tone. The self-loathing curtain still clouded his vision, thickening as he imagined what could have happened to her, what a fool he'd been, how close he'd come to losing everything. Yet he needed to keep going, to follow that scent... his vision burned red.

Unable to even look at her, he scanned up and down the river in livid desperation.

Ferals weren't smart enough to mask their trail when they chose. Or to set traps.

"Bodie, what is it? What aren't you telling me?"

Knuckles white as his fists refused to unclench, his throat swelled and words wouldn't come out.

"And do you plan on sharing this information?"

Dammit she needed to know. He should have said something, but he didn't dare even think it too hard, or he'd be wrong. "It's Noah." He forced breath in and out of his lungs, feeling his control slipping away.

"Your brother? Here? He's... he's one of the ferals?" She stepped closer, reaching for him.

Knowing he was too far gone, he backed up and shook his head.

"When you said he had disappeared..."

He backed well out of her reach, fearing his boiling rage, his regret. Emotion coursed through him, and he breathed slowly in and out, struggling to contain the fury that gripped him. Not wanting to hear his own affected voice, he shortened his words, hissing, "MIA." Bodie struggled to suppress the anger blistering in his gut, the heat of it threatened to combust as it burned into his throat. "When I saw the feral army... the military fatigues... I..."

"You knew it was him?"

"Not for sure. But I... I hoped." Tears seared down his cheeks. "Fucking stupid of me."

Noah had always looked out for him. Had taken him on crazy adventures. Had taught him about the change much more patiently than Raulf had. Then he'd ditched him for the military, rebelling from their entire way of life as the angsty youth he was. "I'd know his scent anywhere, in any state. He's leading the feral pack."

"Not a coincidence they settled so close then."

"He's testing me."

"Why?"

"Don't know."

"If he could chance turning you?"

"Always said he'd come back for me."

"What will he do if he finds out your priority is the pack? The humans they threaten?"

"I don't know." Torrential, the storm drenched the rocky banks of the old debris flow around them. His focus aimed upstream in his continued search for any sign of Noah. Helpless to save his brother. Foolish enough to risk his lover. Himself. His pack.

Astrid murmured so softly he almost didn't hear her for the thundering in his ears that had nothing to do with the storm. "Are you going to be able to kill your brother, if it comes to that? If he's too far gone?"

If he'd had an ounce of control left, it abruptly washed away. Tension filled his limbs, his fists aching as he fought the loss of control and its vertiginous feedback loop. Liquid steel filled his chest, pulling him into territory he refused to succumb to. "He's not Noah anymore." Forcing his breath in through his nose, out through his mouth, he fought the monster inside him.

Astrid reached for him again, her expression drawn with pity.

He backed up and shook his head, his lips pulled back over his teeth as he growled at her in a voice not his own. "Don't touch me."

"Okay." She clenched her jaw and nodded. "Let's head back." The lightness of her voice tugged at him. She knew he was on the edge of completely losing his shit and couldn't know it would be impossible to calm the wild rage that flooded beyond his control.

"Go," he said through gritted teeth. The molten steel entered his veins, pumping into his body as he struggled to push back the nightmare of slaughtering his big brother. Of letting sentiment win and losing his pack, of losing her.

Every brush of wind prickled over his skin, each drop of rain set him on fire as his control slipped further and further away.

Goddammit, Noah.

Astrid stepped a few paces toward home as he'd insisted, then turned back. "Bodie, I'm not leaving you. No matter what."

A tear of burning acid trailed down his cheek. He shook his head.

She ignored his plea and closed the distance between them. Eyes meeting his, she held his gaze.

His voice was hoarse as he felt the connection to her washing over him. "I don't want to hurt you." One wrong word, one wrong thought, and he'd be lost.

She traced her hand down his arm, his skin slick from the storm, and smiled fiercely. "I think I made it clear when we first met, you don't scare me." She flashed him a sweet wink, bringing back the moment they'd met. The haughty warrior, stubborn as hell. She'd turned his world upside down with one blushing ogle.

Focusing on her honey eyes, he inhaled deeply, taking in the clean scent of the rain on her skin, her familiar, wildflower scent.

The red began to fade from his vision, the curtain beginning to recede. Cool beads of rain trailed over his skin.

Goosebumps danced over her bare shoulders, her white tank top clinging to her. Chest rising and falling with each breath, her breasts drew his complete attention. Shallow, but he was grateful for the distraction.

Pushing back the beast inside him, focusing on the desire for her above anything else, he caught her by the waist and pulled her against him. He buried his hand in her hair and palmed the back of her neck, then took her mouth with his.

Fury still coursed through his veins, refusing to let him go.

Her hands gripped his waist, exploring his body, her fingernails dug into his shoulders, her hold on him flooding him with heady sensation.

Redirecting the adrenaline that wouldn't be suppressed, he swept his tongue over hers, funneling the energy into her.

No light brush of lips, she devoured. Heart pounding in her chest against his, giving him everything, as she must have known that no less would pull him back from the brink. Her kiss floored him.

Savagely, she took his bottom lip in her teeth. She swept her tongue along the thundering pulse of his neck, then nipped his collarbone.

Volatile, hungry, he clutched his hands around her hips and tugged her tight against him. Stroking his fingers over her skin, the craving for her overwhelmed him, washing everything else away. Impatient, he ripped away her top. Her bra was gone and lying on the rocks at their feet in an instant.

The storm raged over their heads, vibrating the world around them. Astrid let go of him long enough to slide her shorts down, pulling the wet fabric over her toned thighs. Rock hard, his breath rushed from his lungs at the sight of her.

Clouds opening above them, rain streamed down her skin, forming rivers around the contours he'd tasted so many times.

He scooped her up and drank the water from her skin. Her legs wrapped around his waist, and he pressed her up against the nearest boulder. Pulsing with raging need, he plunged into her.

Crying out in an electrified soprano, Astrid's hands were everywhere, clutching his hair, his shoulders, gripping him tight against her. Lightning flashed as the thunder bellowed around them. With an urgency, a reckless determination, he took her against the rock.

Ravenous, she took on the fire that burned through him, transforming the energy into passion. Wet, skin against skin, the rain pummeled over them. Roaring as heavy as the storm above, as the rapids of the raging creek, they echoed each other's climax.

Quieting with them, as if they alone had caused the explosive force of nature, the storm eased to a delicate mist. Her fingertips trailed down his back, her cheek pressed against his, as they caught their breath together.

As breathing came more easily, his pulse slowing, Bodie pulled away to see if she was okay. Her eyes were still clouded with post-orgasm haze.

Feeling similarly off balance, yet miraculously settled, he said, "Thanks for not leaving me."

Eyes searching his, she shook her head with a resolute smile. "Never."

Astrid loosened her grip as Bodie relaxed against her. His breath came fast and heavy, from exertion rather than fury now. "Bodie?" She asked, her voice strong for them both. She'd been so afraid of losing him.

"Yeah, I'm good. You okay?" His voice was no longer laced with the growl, but his eyes still glowed blue as the moon.

"I'm good." She grinned at him, her cheeks flushed and pupils dilated. "Really good."

He lowered her to the ground, hands lingering on her waist before pulling away and picking up his backpack. She grabbed her bra and shorts from the rocky ground and pulled them on. She held up her torn-up tank-top and raised an eyebrow at him.

He smiled sheepishly. "Sorry."

Rolling her eyes, she stuffed it into his backpack.

He tossed her his t-shirt before pulling on his jeans and sneakers. His scowl returned, and he blindly scanned the opposite riverbank.

"You didn't lose control." She watched as he looked everywhere but at her, as he finished tying the double knot in his laces. "You didn't change."

"I've never come that close to losing it. That was... scary."

"Yes. But it was understandable." She started back toward the house.

"I can't get that close again. What if you're not around to ground me next time? Worse, what if I lose it anyway, and I hurt someone? If I hurt you?"

Glancing back at him, she watched as he put his hands on his hips and scanned the area one last time. Finally, he rubbed his hand over the back of his neck and watched her watching him.

"Sorry charlie, but I'd kick your ass." She cocked out her hip and raised a haughty eyebrow. "Are you coming?"

He tossed his backpack over his shoulder and bit his lower lip with an arrogant smile as he caught up to her. Walking side by side, he laced his fingers with hers. Clearly needing levity, he said, "I believe I just did, and it was epic." He flashed her a devious wink. He was still shaky, but she could feel him coming back. Beating back the beast.

"Ha ha. You fought it, and you won. You were able to shift your focus, to... well, to burn off that edge."

"I believe that was your pussy."

Stopping in her tracks, she raised her hands in shock. "Really? I'm still deciding how I feel about the word *tits*, and you use the p-word?"

"I didn't say cunt." His ornery grin was infectious.

"Fair point." She found herself chuckling in response, her heart tripping an irregular rhythm as she watched his blue eyes settle to the same precise shade as the scrap of Montana blue sky that peeked through the clouds.

Clearly, he wasn't ready to talk about it. Levity was a lifesaver when the darkness was too heavy to face. "Vagina just doesn't have the edge to it that I was going for."

A delighted laugh tickled across her cheeks. Ahead, the trees thinned as they approached the valley. "I suppose it is a bit sexist of our society, that dick and cock, and sometimes even the term prick, are perfectly acceptable slang, sometimes even appealing. Yet, most terms that refer to a woman's anatomy are so easily used as insults or sound infantile. I think I prefer the p-word to hoo-ha or lady-bits. At least it sounds stronger. Perhaps I'll use it more, and reclaim the narrative."

"If it helps, I'm fond of the entire region, no matter what you want to call it. The look of it, the feel, the taste..." He grinned again, this time with a sexy wickedness that fueled heat coursing to her fingertips and toes.

"Okay, I get it."

"I may be losing control again. I think I need another round of rough sex to save me from myself."

"Nice try. I can see the house, and we've been gone long enough. The others are probably worried."

"Cockblocks." He raised their joined hands and kissed the back of her knuckles as they approached the house.

Ryan and Quinn were curled up on the porch swing, and Lana and Bennett were settled into the cushioned chairs, resting their feet on the rail. The group was peacefully sipping lemonade.

Bodie asked, "And you thought they might be worried about us?"

Quinn overheard and laughed. "We were thinking of worrying, we just hadn't settled on it yet."

Eyes panning up and down Bodie as they walked up the steps, Lana grinned. "Wow, Astrid is a lucky woman. Do you ever have a shirt on?" She glanced at Astrid, her smile widening and eyebrows raising up and down. "Oh, there it is. Those woods are treacherous to the safety of one's clothes, I'm sure."

They joined the others on the porch and leaned against the rail. Vann must have heard them approaching and came out the front door, taking position leaned against the wall.

"Her lost shirt was my fault." Bodie bit his lower lip as he winked at Astrid, then his tone darkened. "But there's more to the mission that I can now confirm and need to disclose." He swallowed loudly, his eyes glazing over. Astrid squeezed his hand and nodded, letting him know he didn't need to say it yet if he wasn't ready. That she could bear the weight of the truth for him.

Which wasn't Bodie's style.

Which was part of what she loved about him.

"My brother was supposed to be alpha of our pack. Number of years back, he refused the role and ran away to join the Army. He'd always been restless. Convinced we should be doing more than hiding to protect ourselves." Pausing, he scanned the attentive audience. Astrid held his hand firmly. "We thought he'd been killed in a training op. Well... turns out he, uh, must have gone feral then or sometime after. He's... Noah is leading the feral pack."

Ryan sipped his lemonade, clearly trying to keep things calm, but the ticking jaw muscle gave him away. "That's what took you guys so long getting back today?"

Bodie nodded. "I thought I'd caught a whiff of him now and again the last few months, but convinced myself it was wishful thinking. The scent I caught today? No doubt it's him. Left a fucking obvious trail, sent me on a wild goose chase, then I stupidly continued to track his scent when we heard what we thought was someone in danger. Astrid went to check it out, and it was a feral luring her away."

Astrid shook her head and said, "Like Noah, I fear many of the feral pack have an unprecedented intelligence and control. We cannot underestimate them."

Footsteps crunched in the gravel drive behind her. Turning, Astrid saw two people she hadn't met before approaching the house. Their expressions were drawn, as if they'd heard the entire conversation. The woman was strikingly pretty, with wavy amber hair and penetrating green eyes. Alongside her, clearly related to both she and Bodie, was a man shorter but solid muscle with a chiseled jaw and a sturdy build.

The woman spoke first. "How long have you known it's Noah?"

Bodie didn't let go of Astrid's hand, but turned toward the newcomers. "I suspected but wasn't sure. After today, I know. It's him. Nash, Rain, this is Astrid and her team."

Astrid released his hand long enough to shake hands with his cousins. She introduced everyone.

Rain nodded. "Glad you guys are here. I heard you were hoping for some explosives?"

Hopping onto the railing, Astrid rested her toes on the bottom bar. "Bodie says you're our best hope on that end of things."

"That's right. It gets... boring around here."

Bodie cleared his throat. "Not to mention, she studied chemistry for her undergrad, then got her master's in applied physics at Cal Tech."

Smiling, Rain shrugged. "It's more of a hobby. From the sound of things, our timeline is pretty tight and resources are lacking. I've been sorting out what I have and what we need, some basics already put together, but it's not enough. I made a grocery list that's only moderately suspicious. I was just going to head into town for supplies… if there's time?"

His voice resonating from the corner, Vann said, "We'll make time. Do you have anything to collapse the mine they're holed up in?"

Bennett said, "Plus some for misdirection?"

Astrid scrunched up her brow, hating her own idea. "And, although I would hate to cause a forest fire, but something to burn the place down when we're done?" Astrid leaned into Bodie, soaking up his energy. He slipped his arm around her. "We'll need to destroy the bodies."

Rain nodded. "Give me five days, and I can cook up some chaos, destruction, and oxy clean."

Nash spoke up for the first time, "My brother's a fire jumper out of Billings. I'll give him a heads up."

Quinn said, "That should be good timing for the other two teams to get into place. I spoke with my dad and my uncle yesterday. Their teams are already on the move."

Nash nodded. "A week then? I'll feel better with the full moon overhead, anyway."

Bodie agreed. "We'll nail down the timeline, get together and formalize the plan over the next few days."

Rain and Nash took off down the road.

Bodie dropped his arm and rose from the railing, pausing at the front door. "I've got to go tell my parents about Noah. I already told my dad about the possibility, but I wasn't sure." He chewed his cheek and hesitated. He went inside for a shirt and returned a moment later.

"Want me to come?" Astrid offered. Not the kind of news parents would want to hear. Or that Bodie wanted to tell. He'd been playing it cool, telling the others. She knew the grief still raged under the surface, but he wouldn't let it boil over again.

"Nah, thanks though." The side of his mouth turned up with a regretful smile in a subtle signal that he'd be okay.

14

WELL, THAT HAD GONE about as horribly as he'd imagined. Bodie stepped out into the darkness, the frogs croaking in a morose chorus. He hadn't meant to stay so long, but it had taken a good hour to even work up the nerve to say anything.

At the news, Felicity withdrew to her bedroom, watching out the window in shadowy solitude. Raulf raged and cussed and threw things. No surprise there. Bodie stayed long enough to relive every moment of Noah's departure all those years ago. Later, the news of his death. Then, the speculation of what he must have been up to since.

Something wasn't adding up. His parents had been too upset to delve into how Noah could have pulled it off, not ready to face that he was the brains of the operation.

Gravel shifted under his feet as Bodie left the front porch, heading back home. The front door creaked open behind him, and a teary little voice asked, "You're not ever going to go away, are you Bodie?"

He turned back and saw Jessie holding her favorite stuffed wolf tight in her arms, her eyes as red as their parents'. He'd hated her hearing it, but she had her ways of listening in anyway. Another cautionary tale every werewolf should know. Dashing back up the porch steps, he knelt in front of her. He shook his head. "Never, little one. I might come and go, but this is my home."

"What if you turn feral? Like Noah?"

"Something happened to Noah, and I wish I knew what. I won't let it happen to me. You, mom and dad, the pack... you're too important to me."

"Don't forget about Astrid. I like her."

He chuckled softly and wiped away the latest tear from Jessie's freckled cheek. "I like her too. I'm hoping she'll stick around when this is done, but she might not be able to. But, yeah, she's important to me."

"What if Noah comes after me?"

No child should have to worry about darkness like that. "It's not Noah anymore. It's the feral controlling him." Poor thing had never even met her oldest brother, so she didn't know what a decent guy he'd been, just, restless and unsettled like so many at that age who lacked the power of choice. "Noah would have loved you like crazy. Would have tossed you in the air and caught you like Dad does, making you giggle until you lose your voice."

A soggy smile showed her front teeth just starting to grow in. "Okay. 'Night Bodie." Appreciating her endearing way more than ever, Bodie pulled her in for a squeeze hug before ushering her back inside.

As he walked down the driveway toward home, he found Astrid waiting on the porch swing for him. She was curled up in a red log cabin quilt, the swing's chain creaking with a familiar cadence, a pleasant melody in concert with the frogs. When he curled up on the seat next to her, she stretched her long legs over him and rested her head on his shoulder.

"How did it go?" she asked.

"About like you'd imagine. I'm surprised Raulf didn't go feral himself, hearing his fears confirmed. He was livid."

"You know, for that man's temper, he has a remarkable sense of control."

"Apparently." Grazing his thumb over the curve of her jaw, he felt the heartache intensify, knowing she'd have to leave when this was all over. And he'd be stuck here, mentally reliving every moment of the last few weeks, both good and bad.

She wrapped her hand around the base of his neck, teasing her fingers over his short hair before pressing her lips to his. Soft or hard, greedy or selfless, each time they kissed, he was astonished at the headiness of their connection, the electric tremors that rushed through his veins. "Let's go to bed."

Scooping her into his arms, he carried her upstairs, and they slipped into the cool sheets together. The night sky was black as midnight, thanks to the dense cover of clouds. He was starting to feel twitchy already, knowing he'd have to miss out on his habitual morning sprint as the wolf.

He had no doubt Noah would be waiting.

The familiar nightmare overtook him. Claws lashing at him, feral growls drumming in his brain. This time, it was Noah slashing at his throat, not fighting at his side or the object of his endless search, as he'd been in the prior nightmares. When he looked down at his own hands, they were covered in patchy fur with long, yellowed claws. Panting desperately, he felt his lungs fill with a dreadful power, and a bitter howl rose from his chest, shattering the moon.

Sweet crooning reassurances, soft fingers grazing over his skin... Astrid was there, pulling him from the nightmare again. "It's okay. You're here with me."

As his eyes came into focus, he swallowed the terror that had been choking him. The moonless night still penetrated the room, but he could make out enough to see her sad smile. He sighed. "I'm sick of waiting."

"Me too. But we don't stand a chance without the explosives, nor should we move without protection for the nearby people at risk if we lose."

Bodie sat up and flipped on the lamp, taking a gulp of water. "I think we're missing something. The how and the why. I don't want to go in, without knowing what's really going on."

"Knowledge is power, I'm a firm believer in that. But we may never find the answer, yet the fight will still happen."

"You're not wrong. But... I'm just going over all the possibilities. Noah always said he'd come back for me. Now I'm wondering if he went feral, and he's trying to follow through on that promise, however messed up it is now. How does he have so much control? Was this planned, or did he lose himself to the feral and have enough control to build an army, but not enough to overcome the mindlessness of the beast?"

"We've searched every book in the library. This feral pack is entirely unprecedented."

"From the sounds of things, there are a rare few that show some control, albeit the angry, violent sort."

"We'll go back and look through the library again from another perspective. Not if or when this has happened, but how the feral state could be controlled. Historic experiments."

"Trust me, I know that library backwards and forwards. There's nothing in there that's going to help." He flicked the light back off and laid his head on the pillow. Breathing in her scent as she snuggled into him, he said, "I have no idea where you live."

"Seattle."

"Tell me about it. You just bought a house, right?"

"I did. House hunting, via the internet, was a stress reliever when we'd lost Quinn a few months back. Of course, we know now she was safe and happy with Ryan, but it was awful, not knowing. I found this gorgeous house with loft-style with cedar and steel construction overlooking Elliot Bay. A huge library, floor-to-ceiling windows, a deck I can sit out on and read all day."

"I can picture it. You all curled up on a cushy chair, watching the world turn. Maybe I'll come visit someday. We'll cozy up and watch the sun set, then off to fight a few monsters."

"Then back home for a good night's rest, and you can bring me coffee in bed the next morning."

He wrapped his arms snug around her and sighed. His heart rate finally began to calm to a subnormal, sleepy rate.

AFTER ANOTHER FEW DAYS of absolutely no progress, the current alpha was putting her foot down. Literally and figuratively. With her gnarled wooden cane in one hand, she marched out to the big field behind the house. Obediently, in her wake trailed six locked and loaded demon hunters.

Strapped to her legs in her latest modification to improve her flexibility in combat, Astrid's twin blades were easily accessible, moving fluidly with her legs. Similarly, Quinn had her favorite twin swords crossed over her back à la *Deadpool*, as she described it. Ryan and Vann both preferred massive great swords. Vann's was centuries old but as sharp as he was, and Ryan's blade was as black as the demon realm. Lana strutted with an extra swing in her hips with a battle axe that was taller than she was, and Bennett sported his traditional sword and shield. Demon hunters were designed to blend in, so the eclectic group looked like a well-armed, fit, albeit ordinary group of humans.

Ahead stood five ordinary looking people with brilliantly reflective eyes, ready to shift to wolf form at a moment's notice. Rain and Nash hadn't returned from their "grocery shopping" trip, but they were due back anytime. Raulf looked as troubled as Astrid had imagined. Angus, the brew master, nodded in silent friendship. She'd briefly met Marcus's mother, Lilith, already. One of the few non-related pack members, Stevie, with her wild red hair and mischievous smile, quietly joked with Angus as they waited.

Bodie flashed Astrid a panty-melting grin as she approached with her team.

After too many days of physical inactivity, topped off with mental strain, Astrid was glad to be out in the fresh air. No recent feral activity. Groups of two and three scouted the area of their own, the grounds never unmonitored, but nothing was coming close.

"Alright," Molly began. "We have a battle coming up. One we cannot win. Not without each other, and at that, we don't stand much of a chance."

"Great pep talk, Grammy," Bodie whispered loudly.

"Hush, child. Rain will do what she can to cut the feral population to a more manageable size. But we cannot count on anything going our way." For a wrinkled thing, her voice was filled with vigor. "What are their weaknesses? We've all taken out our share of ferals here." The silent crowd looked to each other like a shy group of high school kids, afraid of embarrassing themselves in front of the stern teacher. At the lack of response, she pointed with her cane. "Vann. How do you kill ferals?"

"With a sword," he said with a smartass monotone.

She moved her head in an invitation for more information.

Quinn said, "I'm fond of decapitation."

"All good answers. Not what I'm looking for, but we'll get to that. Basic feral safety?"

"Don't let them get behind you," Astrid answered.

Lana added, "Watch out for the claws."

From Molly's other side, Angus said, "Make every gash deep. A superficial wound won't even slow them."

More voices added helpful tips like, "Negotiating won't get you anywhere... don't let them get their teeth on you... they're wicked fast."

Molly cleared her throat and brought their attention back. She smiled at her active class. "What's different about this pack?"

"There are too many of them."

"They're smart."

"They're organized."

Molly continued the rapid-fire pace, but the next sentence sapped the energy from the air. "Where did they come from?"

Everyone looked around, unsure of how to respond.

Bodie broke the awkward silence. "Noah brought them." He stepped forward and looked around. "Noah's not Noah anymore, so don't give him a moment's pity. He won't be reasoned with. More... I don't know how he pulled this off. Do any of you know of a hundred werewolves that he could have recruited? Or even fifty?"

More silence.

"I can't say for sure, but this is far from a normal pack of ferals. Doesn't matter. Astrid and I have taken out eleven of them together. They're tougher, stronger, and smarter than most, but they can be killed. We have backup between them and populated areas, but let's not let it come to that."

Angus cleared his throat, resting his hands on his hips. "Why didn't we act sooner, when their numbers were smaller? Let's go now, before they grow larger, before they get smarter."

Bodie chewed his cheek. "It's not about numbers. Yeah, I'm as fond of statistics as the next guy, but we've always had the disadvantage. Assuming is with it enough, he knows what our pack is capable of. Even when we first discovered them, we didn't know the half of what they were capable of, but they were clearly different. When we called in the demon hunters, the ferals still held advantage in numbers and mystery. We still don't know enough, but at least now we know what we're up against. When Rain and Nash come through on their science project, we'll have another advantage."

Nodding, Molly smiled regretfully. "Not one of these ferals can make it out alive. We cannot risk this happening again in another time or place, without a pack as tough as ours nearby to stop them. We'll have demon hunting teams covering the exits, and Morrison will ensure we can burn it down when we're done. Now, you're probably wondering why we're out here in the blazing hot sun, rather than relaxing in the family room over a pint for this conversation. We think we know what they are capable of, but do we know what we're capable of? We need to trust each other. I've been saying it for three damn centuries, but at least you're listening now. Who's ready to take on Bodie?"

Astrid slunk back, hoping she wouldn't be pitted against Bodie. Really not her thing in the first place, sparring, but she didn't want to actually hit him.

Bennett raised his hand.

"Yes, Bennett?"

"If we're learning to work together, why are we fighting each other?"

She tsk'd sarcastically. "How can you trust your new friend to have your back when you don't know what kind of warrior they are? And thanks for volunteering."

Shrugging, Bennett stepped forward. After tightening his shield, he drew his blade. "Can't we use fake swords? I really don't want to hurt anyone. We heal faster, and we're armed."

Bodie shifted his weight arrogantly. "You'll have to catch me first."

"Says the guy with stitches in his side."

"I learned my lesson, feeling sympathy. Not to worry, it won't happen again." He winked at Bennett, then shifted into the wolf, his clothes crumpled at his feet. Circling, they studied each other's moves.

Bodie was as fast as he promised. Leaping, jagging, each dodged the other's strikes.

When Bennett swung toward Bodie with the sword, Bodie's mouth clenched over his wrist and shook until Bennett dropped the sword. Snarling, Bennett wasn't fooling around anymore. Swinging his shield, he cracked Bodie in the jaw.

Bodie was tossed twenty feet across the field. Rising, he blinked a few times, then shook off the injury and ran back into the fight, diving between Bennett's legs, sinking his teeth into his thigh as he passed.

Bennett howled and dropped to the ground, snagging Bodie's leg. Quick as a blink, Bodie shifted into the man and clocked Bennett in the nose.

A trickle of blood flowed from Bennett's nostril. Glaring, he wiped away the blood. A satirical smirk graced Bennett's face, seeming to enjoy the fury. He rose to his feet and unstrapped the shield. Without more than a glance, he tossed it aside.

The warriors circled like a couple of boxers, each getting a few good licks in. Astrid had seen Bennett fight bare knuckled for fun when they sparred in his warehouse. Years of intensive training paid off, and the air itself vibrated from the power of each swing.

Bennett knocked Bodie on the lip.

His head recoiled, but he didn't waver.

Sparks glinted in his eyes, and he flashed Bennett a wink.

Shifting back into the wolf, Bodie zagged and juked, then leaped at Bennett and brought him to the ground. Spinning, Bennett shook him off and tossed the massive wolf a few dozen yards. Tearing back at each other full speed, Bodie rammed him and they were both sent spinning across the field. Where Bennett outmatched Bodie in strength and recovery time, Bodie won out in speed and agility.

Sprinting back, Bennett's fist flew out to connect with the wolf's snarling mouth, but Bodie shifted back to the man and dodged the blow, spinning back around and knocking Bennett to the ground with a well-placed kick.

Bennett rolled to his sword and sprung up from the ground with the blade ready.

Molly started clapping, ending the match. "See my point? Pretty evenly matched, don't you think?"

Predictably horny, Lana said, "We should all get naked for the fight. That was way more fun."

Ryan ran a hand through his hair and winced. "Nah, I'm good."

Biting his lower lip with his adorable grin, Bodie raised an eyebrow. "Worked for the ancient Celts against the Romans."

Shrugging, Quinn griped, "See? None of the convenient paranormal stories are true. Nobody turns to dust, the good guys aren't always good, the evil not always bad, and no one's clothes magically disappear and reappear when shifting."

"I'm not exactly going to stop mid-fight to put my pants on. 'Uh, hang on ferals, just need to maintain my dignity.'" Bodie didn't bother getting dressed, but stalked over to Astrid and stood with her.

The werewolves and demon hunters got along remarkably well. Each had their own brand of humor. Molly divided the rest and switched out pairs now and again like an efficient athletic coach. Maybe she wasn't too terribly near the end of her life. She was rather spritely when she put her mind to it.

As the sun set, all were sweating, wiped out, and nursing sore muscles after a long day of sparring. Although Astrid wasn't thrilled to fight her friends, she was wired after stretching her skills to the limit. No breaks for hydration, snacks, or even bathroom breaks, as Molly insisted that wouldn't be possible in battle, anyway. Where was she to help them prep for so many battles before?

Raulf caught up to Astrid as the others headed across the darkening field. He gestured to the wide valley, its scattered forests making way to rugged slopes on either side. "Pretty around here, isn't it?"

Did he really just ask if she liked the setting? "Gorgeous."

"Your friends, Bennett and Lana were scoping out the field, saying how this would make a decent landing strip."

"That would cut down on your drive time in and out of here. Anyone have a pilot's license?"

"Not at the moment, but I'm sure most would be more than happy to learn. What about you?"

"Me?"

"You fly?"

"I've been thinking about it." What was he getting at?

"Might be fun. You and Bodie could take lessons. Maybe..." he trailed off as they drew nearer to the house. Felicity was parked out front and sitting on the tailgate of her truck. Bodie sat next to her, both of their feet dangling as they watched the setting sun burn orange over the rugged peaks beyond.

Raulf trotted the rest of the way to the truck. Two generic file boxes sat in the truck bed.

Felicity looked up when she arrived. "As I was telling Bodie, I dug out these boxes while you were training. I'm not sure if there's anything helpful in them, but I... you all can sort through them." On the side, in permanent marker, was a name, *Noah Connery*.

Nodding, Astrid agreed. "Of course. Thank you. We'll return it all to you."

Lips drawn so tight they blanched white, Felicity nodded. Raulf took her hand and they climbed into the truck together as Astrid and Bodie each carried a box into the house.

15

Each page held some piece of Noah. From a random doodle of a leafless tree to a rather salacious sketch of a nude woman, and another of a curious wolf, Noah's personality shined through every drawing.

No one had even opened the boxes, as Bodie had unsealed them this morning. He'd barely slept, dreading what he might find in them.

Astrid sat curled up on the floor of the bedroom with him, methodically sifting through the pile. She silently passed him a photograph of Noah, age nineteen, and Bodie, age fourteen. Noah sported a smartass grin as he rested his elbow on top of Bodie's head, where Bodie grinned like a fool, loving the attention from his cool big bro.

Bodie flipped further through the sketchbook. The first half was filled with clever and, clearly bored, sketches. After a while, the subjects turned darker. Corpses rotting alongside a burn pit. Children kneeling at gunpoint. His stomach churning with helpless pity, Bodie could hardly draw in air, imagining what Noah had gone through overseas.

Always the leader, the tough guy, the one to never-say-die, Noah had joined an elite force that he 'wasn't allowed to talk about.' Though there were no dates, Bodie could feel when Noah's calls home had dwindled, then ceased entirely as Noah became lost to them.

Astrid shifted through more photos and showed him one of Noah and another soldier he'd never seen before. She squinted as she looked closely, and read the name from his uniform. "Do you know this guy? Simmons?"

"No. Shit. Those are werewolf eyes." Bodie held the photo closer. "See if you can find anything more on this guy. Maybe we can find him to see if he knows anything. Or, worse, maybe he and Noah are still working together."

"Did he keep a diary, by any chance?"

"Noah Connery share his feelings, even with an anonymous blank book? Not a chance in hell."

"That would have been too convenient." She kept digging in her box as Bodie flipped through the sketchbook.

He came upon a page with a sketch of a feral in uniform.

Shit. He forced the air from his lungs, his ribs burning as he lost the drive to breathe. No doubt about it, Noah had done, whatever he did, on purpose.

Dammit, Noah. He couldn't be that stupid.

Still, they needed something, anything, and knowing Noah hadn't gone feral by accident... fuck. After pouring through the dozens of journals Grammy had in the library, they'd been less than a mile from the right one.

Astrid pulled out a flask, its contents sloshing inside. Untwisting the lid, she sniffed it. Nose scrunching, she grimaced as she recapped it. "This is not whiskey."

Bodie reached for the flask and took a whiff. "Smells like... sweaty feet... with a metallic undertone. And some other nasty stuff I don't want to think about." Like a feral on chemical steroids.

"That's disgusting. Why would he store that in a flask?"

Lana knocked on the open door. "Hey guys. Take a break for lunch?"

"Here, smell this." Astrid held up the flask.

Lana jumped back and held her nose. "Gross. It smells like a feral or something. A little warning next time."

Bodie's brain raced in too many directions to keep track of, his thoughts boiling into a slurry of nonsense. "I... I don't know." It was too farfetched to say out loud. He looked back at the sketch of the feral in uniform, then flipped through the next few pages. More ferals, like it had become an obsession, each a bit more chaotically drawn, less artistic than the next.

The next page answered the question he didn't want to ask. A deranged sketch of a group of ferals in uniform. Astrid took one look at it and pulled a photo from the pile. "It's his unit. There was only one other werewolf in the photo, but they're all feral in the drawing."

Ryan came into the bedroom behind Lana. He bent down and studied the photo, comparing it to the sketch. "Did he find a way to turn them?"

Lead seemed to coat Bodie's skin as he felt energy sapping from his body. "I guess. Using whatever shit is in this concoction."

"Could he or his werewolf buddy have gone feral and used something from their feral state to make this?" Astrid asked, glaring at the foul liquid.

Despite the horrific odor, Bodie sniffed it in detail this time. "Blood, saliva," he began, inhaling again. He cringed at the foul odor. There was something else in there he couldn't place. Not just bodily fluids. "Snake venom? There are some chemicals in here I can't place. Maybe if I'd done more drugs in college." Bodie rolled his eyes.

Pursing her lips in concentration, Astrid responded, "Snake venom would kill some of their pain receptors. Slow down their rapid pulse rates so they might have more control. Could they have used this to control the feral?"

"Maybe. Hurts like a son-of-a-bitch, even thinking of changing." Which he had recently discovered. Though he'd stayed just on this side of feral, he'd felt the strain on his bones, his skin as he became charged with volatile adrenaline from both the wolf and the man.

Lana pulled out a neatly folded uniform with a unique Ranger insignia. "If they were getting creative, who knows what they would have added."

Ryan continued to set the pile of photos back in the box. "I actually took a course about smuggling illicits for the Coast Guard. They could have used any combination of nasty shit. Ketamine, MDMA, PCP. Add some less shady shit like human growth hormone and epinephrine. Any of those could manipulate their brain chemistry, their physical capacity. If they were creative enough, they could create something useful that might help them to control and even bring on the feral side. Maybe some downers to contrast the uppers."

Astrid sniffed again and visibly gagged, then adopted her proper expression to mask her disgust. "Could he have found a way to create ferals from ordinary humans?"

Next to Astrid, Ryan looked inside the box. "I'm thinking that's exactly what he did. Maybe he and this other guy. Something in there must be able to alter their DNA."

Frowning, Astrid calculated. "Gene editing is extremely complicated, even for top scientists. If he were involved in any military experiments, had high enough clearance, he may have been able to access experimental materials. If they'd managed to create a virus that would imbue werewolf DNA into ordinary humans, it might be possible. Or, maybe they figured out how they change humans into vampires, and tried to replicate it?"

"Add the drugs to turn them crazy before they even changed, they'd go straight to feral." Bodie scowled, his gaze glued to the sketch.

Lana leaned against the wall, watching. "With the army he's got, he must have made buckets of the stuff."

Ryan asked, "I want to know why. Bodie, was he... was Noah the kind of guy to do something like this?"

"No. No way. I mean, he was restless and Dad said he changed once, not long before he left. He seemed okay though, actually, even happy when he'd call home in the beginning. But look at the sketches. I think he saw some awful shit that fucked him up."

Ryan sorted through another stack. "Check this out." He held out a photo of Noah with a group of young kids in grubby clothes, carting assault rifles. The grief was almost palpable. "Seeing awful shit doesn't make you... doesn't make a person do *this*. I wonder if he was trying to fix it. Maybe he was trying to create a super soldier or something, tap into the power of the feral."

Bodie sighed heavily. "Now that sounds like something Noah would do. He was more the save-the-world sort, which he couldn't do from here."

"Didn't go the way he intended," Lana whispered.

Ryan asked, "Think your cousin Rain has the stuff to isolate the chemicals in here?"

Bodie shook his head. "Maybe. I'll give her a call, but it would take time."

Astrid nodded. "And she'll be busy cooking up those explosives. Even if she had the time... would it change anything?" She reached across the box and wordlessly laced her fingers with Bodie's.

A knot wrenched his guts until his vision darkened, his head swimming until he felt he may pass out. He hated the answer before they'd even said it.

Astrid breathed in deeply before speaking. "Whatever pain drove him to do it, our responsibility is to end it before others are changed or killed. Even if Rain could break this down and see what's here, we don't have the time. It could take years, if it's even possible. If there's a way to turn someone feral, maybe there's a way to make an antidote. Someday."

Bodie nodded, his eyes clouding with searing hot tears. "Noah wouldn't want to live this way. This violence is not what he intended."

OVER AND OVER FOR days, they'd reviewed and revised and solidified. Everyone knew their role. There was no room for error. The plan was solid.

Astrid's brain hurt. Her soul hurt. Something about the piles of explosives, crushing so many in a matter of seconds—if they were successful—didn't settle well.

But it was her job. She knew there was no other choice.

Bodie had called Rain, going over everything they'd found, what they suspected was in the serum. Squashing any sliver of hope they'd had for an antidote, Rain didn't think it was possible. Even if they could somehow attempt the experiment, if they could even capture ferals to test it out on, plus the bizarre ethics of the whole thing, they might actually make things worse, potentially serious enough to make the ferals even more powerful. Or make them die slow and painful deaths. Or bring them back but have them end up eternally deranged beyond recovery, or comatose or in some awful state worse than death.

They were out of time, and there was no room for error.

Staring out the window, she watched as the waxing moon faded, and the sun hinted at its impending arrival.

"Hey," Bodie said as he came up behind her, wrapping his arms around her middle. He kissed her temple and held her close.

"Hey."

"Ready?"

"As I ever will be."

"Come on, I can hear the others up and moving. I smell Grammy putting bacon on the griddle."

"I don't smell anything."

"It's still raw. I have enough wolf in me that raw meat smells amazing."

"You're weird."

"I know. I wouldn't actually eat it in this form."

"Random question." She turned in his arms and grinned up at him. "What happens if you eat a rabbit as the wolf but shift back while you're still digesting? Would you get sick?"

"I've shifted back mid-chew. Trust me, it's revolting, and I'll never make that mistake again."

She chuckled and nuzzled into his neck. "I'm grabbing a shower before breakfast."

"No making out under the waterfall this time?"

"I've always wanted to do it in a tent."

"Not as romantic, but I can help you with that." He winked and dragged her toward the shower.

Down in the kitchen, the eclectic collection of dining chairs was crammed around the table. As much friends as they were a demon-fighting team, the six, plus Bodie and Molly, chowed down on the rancher's meal with gusto. As usual, Bennett and Ryan found any excuse to jab at each other, but in a lighthearted way. This time, Ryan tried to snag a piece of sausage from Bennett's plate, while Bodie took advantage of the distraction and stole a piece of Ryan's bacon. While they messed with each other, Bodie stole a piece of bacon from each of them. Vann sat back in the corner, quiet, but his eyes were twinkling with amusement. Lana and Quinn were whispering something to each other, giggling over some inside joke. Astrid sat back and watched the interactions, letting the moment wash over her.

Molly regaled them with tales of her fighting days. "1896. Four hungry vampires on the prowl in Chicago. My clever husband, Thomas, God rest his soul, not a werewolf, mind you. Anyway, he and I were there on vacation, attending the theatre that night. As was the style, I wore a satin gown. He wore a stiff jacket and carried his useless walking stick. Those vampires thought we looked like a tasty treat. Certain they would die of astonishment at their mistake, I shifted into the wolf." By that point, Molly was laughing so hard already, tears streamed down her cheeks. The rest of the table was laughing right along with her, even though she had yet to reach the punchline. Collecting herself, she said, "But my wolf head was stuck in the narrow neck of the impractical getup. Thomas was jabbing at the vampires with the walking stick to defend us both, but his movements were so restricted by the stupid coat."

Astrid nearly choked on her toast, enjoying Molly's self-effacing humor. "How did you get out of it?"

"Eventually, I just shifted back to the woman, grabbed his cane, snapped it in half so we could each have a weapon while he ditched the jacket, and we fought them in our formalwear. That's the last time I ever wore a high neckline, that's for darn sure. I never was any good at demure, anyway."

Despite enjoying a superficially carefree breakfast with the rest, Bodie wolfed down his breakfast and disappeared while the others savored their last home-cooked meal for the foreseeable future. Astrid knew he'd be restless. He would have preferred to be on the road by dawn. In full Bodie style, he didn't make demands or rush others along. He just got the job done and waited patiently.

When she got outside, he had the Hilux loaded with their gear.

"Why did we take the quad before when we could have taken this?"

"How else could I have had my hands on you the whole drive?" His lower lip was pulled between his teeth as he grinned at her. He hooked his fingers in her belt loops, pulling her up against him.

"It's like running as the wolf. You like the thrill of it. The wind in your face."

"Got me." He leaned in and brushed his lips over hers. Losing herself in his touch, the electricity zinging down to her toes, she lingered.

A throat cleared meaningfully behind them. Raulf was standing a few feet away, grinning like a proud papa. "Okay, okay. Let's get a move on."

Astrid was still astonished at his complete turnaround. He'd been so hateful toward demon hunters on their first meeting, but you wouldn't know it now for all the positive vibes he sent her way. Perhaps this was how he never turned feral. For all his bark and bluster, he was all heart.

As much as she hated how he pushed Bodie to become alpha, she knew he prioritized the wellbeing of his pack, but worked damn hard to make his children happy. Maybe not in the order she would have preferred, but he tried. He'd be a decent alpha, yes, but he didn't come close to the calm, decisive, and effective leadership style that Bodie naturally employed. Although it broke Astrid's heart to think about it, he was already easing into the role.

Angus pulled up in a well-equipped Ford pickup, albeit with quite a few more miles and mud caked on it. "Alright. Let's get this show on the road," he rumbled from under his thick beard.

Bodie held the driver's door open for Astrid. Astrid stood on her toes and gave him a hearty thank-you kiss before she climbed inside. Rolling down the window, she leaned out to visit while the others tossed their stuff in the back.

Quinn came outside and saw Astrid behind the wheel. She nudged Bodie as she walked by. "Aw, you're so thoughtful."

Raulf was frowning, looking from Bodie to the pristine new truck to Astrid in the driver's seat. "I couldn't figure out why you let her drive the quad at first, but it's just a quad, and it was pretty obvious you were hoping to get laid. But your truck? You won't let the rest of us even think about driving it. She's already sleeping with you. What gives?"

Patting Raulf on the shoulder, Quinn headed for the backseat. "He's a hopeless romantic."

Bodie shrugged. "I don't want her to barf all over the interior. I just detailed it."

Tsking, Lana poked him in the abdomen on the way by. "You can always give the girl a puke bag. You just like her."

"That is true." He grinned.

Bennett walked outside and saw the truck. "Aw, man. That is a thing of beauty." He turned to Vann who stood beside him, his chin dropped in a matching gawk.

Bodie headed toward the passenger door as Astrid settled behind the wheel. "What can I say? She likes nice things."

Quinn and Ryan piled into the backseat. Nash and Raulf tossed their gear into the back of Bodie's truck, stripped down, tossed their clothes in with their gear, and changed into wolf form. Rain drove up in her truck, heavily loaded with very, very well-packed explosives for the rough trail. Vann, Lana, and Bennett tossed their stuff into the back of Lana's new truck and climbed in. Lilith and Stevie had ridden over with Angus. Stevie hopped out and climbed in with Rain, presumably so she had company on the trail.

Flipping on the engine, Astrid grinned over at Bodie. He settled into the passenger seat and cranked up *Alpine Universe* on the stereo, nodding toward the trail. Reaching across, he rested his hand on Astrid's thigh, the heat of his touch, the goofy attitudes of the bizarre caravan, the invigorating music, all filling her with a sense of optimism she hadn't let herself explore in weeks.

Spirits remained high despite the long, rough drive. It did take quite a bit longer in the trucks, as some of the recent rains had washed out the trail in several places. They drove through the night and most of the following day. Despite sitting for so long, the crew was wiped out by the time they reached the waterfall.

The wolves all took off, clearly craving the liberating run. Astrid watched as they disappeared into the wilderness, feeling that optimism slipping away as she considered how miserable Bodie would be in the city. Her house in Seattle would be suffocating. Wolf sightings in Centennial Park would create some crazy urban myths. Maybe if they moved to Fremont, no one would notice?

She tossed away the rambling images. Running a hand through her hair, she attempted to revive it after the long drive. No, Bodie needed miles of untouched land.

She started a fire while the others saw to fixing dinner, setting up tents. Tonight, they could enjoy each other's company and pretend to relax. After, they'd be too close to the ferals for fires and yummy food and exploring.

Knowing they had a big crowd, she stacked the firepit to the top. As the embers stoked into flames, Quinn moved next to Astrid and warmed her hands. Although the day had been humid, the setting sun brought a biting evening chill. "We haven't done enough missions like this lately. Kind of nice, getting out like this together."

Astrid nodded. "I'm not sure we've ever done a mission like this. But I know what you mean. It was nice to hang out at Bennett's a few weeks ago, just being normal. We should do fun stuff more often."

Wrapping her hands around her middle, Quinn smiled. "This baby is going to need her aunts and uncles around." She stopped and chuckled, leaning her shoulder against Astrid's. "Okay, so her mother is the one that will need you guys around. How about once this is done, we all take a well-deserved vacation? I'm thinking Hawaii."

"Or Europe."

Lana came up behind them and wrapped her arms around them both. "I've never been outside of Western North America. Let's do it."

Glowing orange over the escarpment surrounding the waterfall's lake, the sun announced its departure. Bodie leaped over the edge and shifted midair into the man with a whoop and splashed into the crystal-clear water. The other werewolves slipped into the water much more placidly.

Astrid couldn't help but grin. He was so much the opposite of what she would have imagined for herself. Not even in her wildest dreams. But that's life, she supposed.

The crew settled in for the evening. Tents were up, hot meals served on aluminum camping plates, and they all circled around the crackling fire. Bennett downed the last of his cheeseburger and looked up at the stars. "Anyone know any good campfire stories?"

"No ghost stories. We have enough to worry about," Lana pleaded, her voice muffled as she pulled her sweatshirt over her head.

Vann leaned back on his hands. "I believe you promised us a bedtime story." He raised an eyebrow at Bodie.

Snorting with amusement, Bodie shrugged. "I guess I did. Dad? You have good bedtime stories."

"You've heard them all."

"They haven't."

"You're the anthropologist." Raulf's amused tone was filled with pride and challenge.

"You still tell them better."

"Not as well as I used to. I'm not even allowed to sing Jessie to sleep. Just the other night, I started singing *You Are My Sunshine*, and she put her hand over my mouth and said, 'Shh, Dad, don't sing.'"

Bodie laughed out loud. "Little smartass."

Astrid leaned against him, staring into the flames that licked over the firewood.

All eyes turned to Bodie. Even his pack, that knew their history so well. And this was why Raulf wasn't wrong. Bodie was a gifted leader. Not in an overbearing way, but a subtle charisma.

He sighed and linked hands with Astrid. "Okay, okay. So, from what I've learned, demon hunters came from Deandra, the lover of the demon king. Thousands of years ago, they inadvertently unleashed a mass of demons into our realm. To protect humanity, she took a human lover and begat the first demon hunter." He winked at Astrid as he said "begat."

Bodie turned to Ryan. "But you're the demon king's son."

Ryan nodded. "That's right. He asked my mother to bear his child so I could knock up Quinn to save the world from his sister and send his lover back to him."

Pursing his lips in understanding, Bodie smiled. "Our story isn't quite so Greek, but equally mythical. We descend from a demon shifter, one of the few to have existed, even in the demon realm. Hrolfr. Like many of the demons that come here, he sought the quiet life. After settling in our realm, as with every epic tale, he fell in love with a human woman, and, of course, she became pregnant with his child.

"Now, he wasn't a shifter in a good way. His isolation was self-induced because he couldn't control the shifts. According to legend, he was forced into the shift with each full moon. Something about the lunar energy triggered something within him, a surge that empowered his inner beast to take over. From my research, this is where the original tales for werewolves come into play. But Hrolfr, he didn't shift into a wolf, but a rageful beast."

"Feral?" Lana asked.

He shook his head, staring up at the gleaming moon. Astrid could listen to him tell stories every night, his voice rumbling, melodic. He told the tale with heart. "Into a vicious demon, probably his true form from the demon realm. Not human, not wolf, just rage personified. Ever the fool, as in every classic love story, he selfishly hid his true self from his lover and would leave her each full moon. One day, shortly after discovering she carried his child, she grew suspicious and thought he was meeting another woman. Jealous, she sought him out. When she found him... it turned out as terribly as you can imagine. As the beast, he couldn't control his actions and nearly killed her.

"When the sun rose, and he shifted back, he found her bleeding and brokenhearted, inches from death. To save her from a literal broken heart, he replaced her heart with that of a local gray wolf. When their child was born, he had the ability to shift like his father. Thanks to his even-tempered mother and his wolf heart, he could shift at will between human and wolf. But, again, no story would be complete without a tortured hero. The son had to maintain constant control, or he would change to a feral state in between man, wolf, and monster, and destroy those he loved, no matter phase of the moon."

Astrid melted into his side. "Hrolfr must have felt terrible, nearly taking his lover's life. Their unborn child would have died as well."

Bennett nudged the glowing embers of the fire with a stick he'd been whittling. "Sounds pretty Greek to me."

Hands over her belly, Quinn looked into the fire on Astrid's other side. "What happened to Hrolfr and his human lover, after their child was born?"

"Here is where the story really gets good. In contrast to so many tragedies, they had a reasonable conversation and learned to live with each other for the next few hundred years, and they died peacefully after a long and happy life together." Bodie grinned at this boring end to the tale.

Snuggling into his side, Astrid felt a sleepy content fill her veins. She dragged Bodie to bed and made slow, quiet love to him in the serene glow of the tent.

THROUGH THE FILTERED MOONLIGHT, Bodie nuzzled his face in Astrid's hair, inhaling her soothing scent. She sighed in her sleep, unconsciously burrowing into him. Mummy bags really didn't zip well together or make good blankets. When all this was over, he was investing in a double mummy bag, if they made that sort of thing.

An unobtrusive rustling outside the tent stirred his eyes to open. Sniffing, he noted Raulf was getting a fire started. Once they'd eaten and loaded up, they'd start the final push. Had he been thinking, he could have come up with a trailer and wolf harness to haul some of the heavy explosives through the wilderness more efficiently.

He rubbed the sleep from his eyes. Something to think about for next time.

Good god, he hoped there wasn't a next time.

At least, not as far as an army of ferals was involved. Astrid did this sort of thing on a regular basis. Demons, monsters, paranormal baddies of all kinds.

Would he be content, never patrolling more than his small circle of the world for the rest of his days? With living under the same roof for the next three hundred years? Yeah, it was a great roof, but three hundred years... while the woman he loved was risking her existence on a regular basis, saving the world, without him?

Gripping his fist in his hair, he forced his breaths in and out. Shit. What a mess he'd gotten himself into.

Barely a month ago, he'd craved freedom because he lacked it. It's not like he wanted to leave and never come back. He loved his family and this would always be his home. His pack. He could tell them all to shove off, that he had his own life to live. But what if he'd been away when all this went down?

Turning his head, he watched as Astrid smiled softly in her sleep. Did that woman even have nightmares? Despite her claim that she was "an anxious mess," she always seemed to find the calm, understated optimism.

Clenching like a vice over his heart, yet flying free for the truth of it, he had fallen hard and fast into fairytale love. Who would have thought a fierce, studious demon hunter would have captured him so fully?

Utterly, completely exhausted from impossible indecision, he pulled on a pair of pants and a flannel shirt. Without bumping Astrid, raising the zipper of the tent quietly to avoid waking anyone else, he slipped out into the misty morning.

Just over the horizon, the sun hinted that it was almost here. Raulf had a pretty decent fire going already. Quiet, with the same mindfulness Bodie had shown, Raulf pulled out breakfast supplies from the cooler.

So only Raulf could hear, Bodie said, "Mornin'."

With a crinkly eyed smile, one of the few features that hinted at Raulf's age, his father nodded back. "Mornin'. Sleep okay?"

Bodie snorted. "As expected."

"Yeah, me too." Raulf set out the frying pan and laid out strips of bacon. Bodie had planned on oatmeal or something simple, but Raulf had packed well. Raulf shook his head as if he surprised even himself. "Gotta say, you were right about calling in the demon hunters."

"Damn right."

"No really. I was wrong. They're a lethal team, but affable."

"We still stand little chance of winning this fight. Even with their help."

"The stakes are a lot higher for you now than they were a few weeks ago."

Rubbing his hand over the back of his neck, Bodie felt the prickles of chills erupting over his skin. "How so?"

"Come on, Bodie. It's not just the pack. It's Noah. It's her." He gestured to the tent. "I..." Raulf started to trail off, but cleared his throat and flipped the pink bacon again. "Noah's already dead. We need to end his suffering. But if things turn south, and it's down to Astrid or the pack?"

"Dad, don't—"

"I'm just making sure you're prepared—"

Teeth bared, Bodie seethed, "That's not the kind of thing you can prepare for. Noah's dead, that beast that is killing everyone isn't *him*. I get that. Our pack is my life. Astrid is now, too, in whatever form that takes. There is no choice. Things get bad, I'll do what I have to."

A noisy swallow was muffled in Raulf's throat. "You and me both, kid. I... Our pack is resilient. Even if none of us makes it out of this, the pack will go on. Look, when this is done—"

Exiting the lake as the wolf, Nash shook his fur dry. Raulf bit his cheek at the interruption. From the far end of the clearing, Quinn and Ryan climbed out of their tent.

Bodie had the entire battle mapped out in his mind. Losses, wounded, sacrifices. No one was coming out of this whole, even those who survived.

Yeah. Nightmares. That was a fucking understatement.

16

SO THIS MUST BE what vampires feel like on a cloudy day. The late morning sun blazed above, its fiery rays prickling at her skin. Astrid adjusted her pack as they prepared to leave Camp Two, as she had titled it. Deep in the forest, they had stayed the night just outside the Smell-Zone, as Lana had titled it. Without clever names for landmarks, roles, and strategies, their expeditions could easily become overwhelmingly intense, not to mention confusing.

The thirteen warriors gathered in a small clearing in the subalpine forest. Rustling through their packs, each loaded up only the necessary supplies for the final push.

Bennett strapped his shield and sword to his back, securing his duffel filled with explosives. He glanced around at the unusual squad. "Anyone see that movie, *The Thirteenth Warrior*? With Antonio Banderas?"

Angus chortled in his gruff voice. "Most of these kids are a few years too young. Good movie though. Let's just hope this isn't *300*." Still smiling under his full beard, he shifted into a wolf, pure black with white-tipped ears.

At her side, Bodie stood and watched the team and the werewolves gearing up for the fight. He rested his hands on his hips. "Like Leonidas' army, it doesn't matter if we live or die. I'm aiming for us all to make it out of this, but we don't always get what we want. We're here to stop them. To protect the people in their path. To protect our pack. Demon hunters, this is what you do, and you're the best of the best. Thank you for answering our call. Werewolves, we've always policed our own. This is no different. We've got a solid plan. We're going to win because we care. Because we trust each other. Most of all? Because losing isn't an option. Let's move out."

"Damn right," Lana whooped. Checking each other's gear one final time, the troops chatted as they hiked out.

Turning to Bodie, Astrid cradled his jaw in her hands and pressed her lips to his. "Well said."

Wrapping his hands around her waist, Bodie deepened the kiss. Resting his forehead against hers, he said, "Don't forget, you owe me a date when this is done." He flashed her a wolfy wink and shifted.

Astrid hooked her swords into the sheaths along her legs and adjusted her explosives bag on her back. Fitted with his wolf backpack, Bodie nudged up against her, sneaking his nose under her hand. With a smiling eye-roll, Astrid scratched behind his ears. Good thing she didn't have a dog at home, or things could get competitive if he ever came to visit. Oh boy, another bizarre concern she'd never anticipated.

Bodie trotted along at her side as they hiked to the feral base. His lips would turn up in a low snarl when he caught the occasional drift of feral scent. The trek was fortunately uneventful. Or, more likely, that their arrival was expected, and the ferals were planning an ambush of their own.

Groups of two and three divided off as they neared the final hill. Astrid and Bodie angled north, so they could enter the compound behind the main house, while the others went straight over the hill or swung wide to enter from the south. Where they'd normally crack a few jokes and jabs, the tone was more sedate, and no more than waves and casual salutes were passed.

All was eerily quiet as the sun lowered on the horizon.

The forest thinned as the compound came into view. Bodie visibly grimaced as the wind blew their direction and the feral stench hit them like a ton of bricks. In the distance, she could just see Ryan and Quinn reaching their target.

Dusty, littered with the detritus of decaying leaves, the path ahead was clear of feral activity. Astrid advanced, Bodie close behind.

The lumbering footsteps of a nearby feral crunched in an awkward rhythm as they reached the shadow of the dilapidated ranch house.

The fingertips of her right hand danced over the silk cord that wrapped the hilt of her sword. Backing against the wall, she controlled her breathing and slowed her pulse so the creature wouldn't detect her. A few feet away, Bodie camouflaged himself in an overgrown shrub.

Grotesquely odorous even at fifteen feet away, it plodded past the corner of the building, sniffing at the disturbance in the heavy summer air. The mangy thing stilled, but seemed unimpressed and continued on his way.

Astrid bit her cheek, measuring each subtle twitch of its bulky muscles as it continued on its route. She wouldn't be scented easily, but the werewolves might wonder why a pack of wild wolves was encroaching on their territory. Normal wolves probably wouldn't be so foolish.

Stopping mid-step, the feral snuffled again rapidly, his nose following the air. After a cluster of sneezes, he bared his teeth and whipped his head around, scanning. Tapping the overgrown claws of his furry feet against the gravel path, he kicked dirt behind him and plodded toward the shrub Bodie was in.

It had been a good plan, hiding in the strongly scented flowers, but the feral nose was too sensitive.

Deep in the shrub, Astrid watched as Bodie lowered on his front paws, ready to pounce. After flashing him a cheeky grin, she pushed off from the wall. She scanned the sightlines, as she crept sideways, closing in behind it.

Fluid, graceful yet furious, she drew her swords and embedded one into his back. As his mouth opened to howl, she kept him pinned with one blade and spun and sliced the other across his neck.

He dropped to the ground in front of her, and the blood from his wounds soiled the dust at her feet.

Bodie trotted out of the shrub and scanned either side of the decrepit building. Coast clear, he started to dig a hole at the weathered foundation.

Once the hole reached the base of the foundation, she removed one of Rain's packages from her bag and tucked it deep into the hole, pushing it under the edge of the foundation. They did the same in key locations around the house, luckily avoiding any further feral attention.

Across the property, she caught a glimpse of Rain and Vann finishing their placements at the mine. She readied the makeshift detonator that Rain had engineered from some odds and ends she'd found on her shopping trip. Astrid and Bodie hiked upslope and out of the blast range. In a cluster of bear grass, they sat tight and watched the strangely tranquil ranch for the next few hours as darkness coated the valley.

When the first hint of moon formed in the sky, Bodie inhaled deeply. His body tensed then relaxed, his attention acutely focused on the compound. A chilling howl echoed across the property. Again, and once more. That was the signal.

Four, three, two... she pressed the button on the transmitter, knowing others were doing the same. Within a few seconds, thundering explosions erupted across the property. The aging house, the barn across the property, the old foreman's house, all blasted debris into the air, the ground shaking beneath them. Flames engulfed what remained of the crumbling wooden structures, smoke billowing to the sky.

What about the mine? Shit. Without the mine, the odds were markedly *not* in their favor. Come on, this is not the detonator to fail.

Before she could start scrambling for a backup plan, a single explosion collapsed the door to the mine.

That was it?

Holy shit, her heart stopped.

Bigger than the rest, the earth exploded. Bellowing across the ground, resetting her pulse at the magnitude of it, rocks and smoke blasted straight up from the mine. Flames licked out from the entry before it collapsed into a freaking hole in the ground where the mine once was. The surrounding hills rumbled. Loose gravel and debris tumbled downslope. What the hell had Rain packed that with?

Well, that ought to do it. She exhaled and let the tension roll off her shoulders. Rain's plan to load the mine with the hottest-burning explosives to fuse the stone inside had paid off. Nicely done.

Howls, furious, pained, desperate, ricocheted across the narrow valley. Their haunting voices seemed to draw the moon closer as night closed in around them. Three ferals pushed out of a crushed shack in the center of the property.

Drawing her swords, Astrid moved down the hill, Bodie at her side. With ease, following the instincts that ticked in her brain with each threat, tapping into the skills honed from endless training, she didn't hesitate. The others converged on the valley around her.

Her gaze didn't leave her target.

As a unit, her teammates did the same, dividing the battlefield.

A pair of ferals leapt toward her. Rolling her shoulders, she stalked toward them.

Swinging her swords in a fluid *port de bras*, she sliced through the abdomen of one and the neck of its partner. With effortless movements, she slayed two of the mindless beasts in a few efficient moves. At her side, Bodie eviscerated the next with his claws. He tackled another. She drove her sword through its chest.

Three dozen more limped from the rubble of the main house.

More, bloody and partly dismembered, crawled out of the remains of the mine.

Tearing into them, tackling, dispatching one after another, they worked their way across the property.

Between waves of them, Astrid swiftly scanned to assess the scene. No mercy, no lingering, Bodie was lethal. A flutter of pride echoed in Astrid's chest as she watched him fight with no holds barred. A goof-off and sweetheart with her, yet a steadfast brawler and badass to protect those he loved.

The ferals were pissed off. Well, that was a bit of an understatement. They snarled and snapped, foaming at the mouth. Slashing with the desperation of those that knew the war was lost. There were dozens of them, but Rain's explosives had been effective. Those that had survived were half defeated before they even joined the fight.

As the wolves and hunters pounded the remaining ferals, Astrid felt a sense of relief wash over her. This wasn't nearly as terrible as they had anticipated.

Smoke billowed out from the crumbled structures across the property. Dozens of ferals lay slain on the ground.

Sinking, heavy in her chest, she calculated.

Something was missing. As seamless as the plan had gone, as organized as the ferals had been in their attacks compared to others she'd fought before... she began to understand.

There was no sign of the feral they'd seen leading the pack before, in the camo pants and shredded jacket. Noah. If they were lucky, he'd died painlessly in the blast.

She'd never been that lucky.

The others held their guard, equally uneasy. Faces grim with doubt, they stalked to the middle of the grounds to reconvene.

IN THE DISTANCE, A ghostly howl struck the air, the sound waves rippling the air for miles.

Thundering growls, the heavy stomping feet of massive ferals and blood-curdling howls radiated from the opposite hillside. The violent chorus told Bodie everything he needed to know. His fur stood on end, his claws digging into the gravel as he prepared for the onslaught.

Another fucking trap. He'd known it wouldn't be easy. Still, sitting in the middle of it wasn't good for the psyche.

Four dozen ferals came bounding down the north slope as a unit. Their clothes were tattered, fur matted, but they all wore the remains of military fatigues. Twice the bulk of the dozens they had already taken out, these were massive. At least double Bodie's size, minimum, he had little doubt they were the result of Noah's experiments.

Noah hadn't seemed that massive when he'd seen him leading the pack. Where was he?

In a united line, hunters and wolves stood together, weapons drawn. Bodie's lips pulled back, a rumbling from deep in his throat sounded his fury. He hunched down, his shoulders tense, ready to pounce.

Cool as a cat, Bennett pulled out his remote detonator from his cargo pocket. In what couldn't have been more than five seconds, yet felt like a lifetime, he waited.

Bodie was tempted to rip the thing from his hands and press the damn button, but he trusted.

The pack covered another hundred yards. Their heavy sprint shook the ground beneath them.

Mouth forming a slow smile, Bennett pushed the button.

A series of explosions echoed around the property. Clusters of bodies were blasted into the air, crashing back to the earth as limp, shredded corpses. Others were knocked off course, hobbling at a much slower pace as they struggled to resume their course.

Quinn triggered another detonator, another handful of blasts, and another handful of ferals were dead or dismembered.

Fewer in number, but still too many, they continued on, fanning out into the valley. The numbers were much more manageable, but they were still grossly outnumbered.

The rest was a big fucking blur. With blind rage, Bodie dove into the fray.

Too late to retreat. The consequences too dire to not go all-in. The fight would be decided tonight. One way or another.

Spitting out the foul flesh of an unnatural feral, he pushed back the bile, the fear that they wouldn't survive this.

He had no doubt that the ones they'd wiped the floor with, those that had swiftly perished in the mine and the house, were no more than a big fucking diversion.

Tearing into the flank of the nearest, he didn't pause to see if his attack had been effective. Disable, then go back to finish them off later.

He hurled onto the back of the next, he ripped into her throat and was vaulting to another before her body hit the ground. Behind him, she flipped back to her feet.

As he turned, she barreled into his hip. At the impact, he skidded across the graveled field. Snarling, he sprinted back after her. As she reached for him, he dove to the ground, dodging her blow. He rose to his feet and shifted to the man.

With pure satisfaction, he grinned as she recoiled in surprise, leaving her open as he snapped her feral neck.

A mud-caked fist lashed at him. The wind of the blow brushed past him as he leapt out of the way.

Grabbing its wrist, he pulled the feral in and planted a blunt uppercut. His fist met jaw, the crunch of the impact reverberated into his shoulder. These guys were massive, most exceeding seven feet tall.

He pivoted and checked the battlefield. A dozen ferals were bleeding but kept swinging. Maybe ten were dead on the ground, if that. Fuck these assholes were tough.

Vann had a gnarly gash on his arm but kept on swinging. Quinn had blood trailing from her lip but didn't slow, always protecting the little one inside her. Raulf was having a field day, snapping and tackling, chipping away at the feral pack. He'd always hinted some old war stories, but Bodie hadn't realized...

On her elbows, Lana dragged herself off the field. She took cover under a dense shrub, pulling out a med kit to patch up her wounds before rejoining the fight.

Knocking down the next, Bodie shifted to the wolf and ripped out its trachea and scanned the area for Astrid.

Nash was down. Bodie sprinted to his cousin, then changed to the man and dropped to his knees beside him.

Chest rising and falling, Nash breathed slow and steady.

A feral pounced at them, claws slashing as he went for the tackle. Rolling out of its way, Bodie shifted to the wolf. Diving, he dodged its snapping jaw and tore into its side, then nipped a chunk out of its skull.

Free for the moment, he shifted back to the man and scooped up Nash. He ducked behind the shrub and laid Nash with Lana. "Can you—"

Right eye already swollen, she managed a wink. "I got him."

"Thanks." He rose to his feet and scanned the battlefield. No sign of Astrid. Anywhere. Where was she? He shifted to the wolf.

Something was wrong. He caught a trace of her subtle scent as he sniffed the air.

Following the lead, he bucked ferals as he charged straight through the middle of the fray.

Spinning, she sliced through another. Man, these guys were huge. And tough. Unnatural.

Astrid dropped to her knees to dodge a fist shaped like a fucking brick. Fluidly, she popped back up to her feet and sliced across its side.

Ready to attack with her other sword, but a clawed hand grabbed her from behind. Her arm snapped as it twisted behind her.

Rotating, she let the shoulder dislocate to free herself and jabbed her other sword into his middle.

Anticipating her attack, the wily one dodged her blow and knocked the sword from her grip. He yanked on her dislocated arm, then spun her and grabbed hold of her hair. Wow, he was strong, but he was half the size of the others. Normal sized, for a feral.

Astrid struggled to see him better, but the mangy beast clutched tighter at her hair. The pull on her scalp was excruciating as she was dragged from the battlefield. She tucked her remaining sword into its sheath. She grabbed her dislocated shoulder and tried to set it.

Nothing. Goddamn that hurt.

Tugging again, she felt the crunching release as it locked back into the socket. It still throbbed, but no more than her head.

Tossing her against the base of a thick-trunked apple tree, the beast growled to someone else, "Got her."

From behind the tree, another feral stepped into view. He stood at least a foot taller than the rest and twice as thick, even bigger than any in the army she'd been dragged from. "Good. He notice yet?"

The one that held her grunted and shook his head.

Astrid knew she couldn't take them both. If she could run back toward the fight, she could get help.

Daring to look up, she studied the two ferals that stood over her. The larger wore camo pants that were frayed from being stretched so tight. She finally got a good look at the one that had dragged her across the field.

Finding her studying him, he grabbed her by the shirt and pulled her to her feet. Nose in her face, he growled, "Mmm, you do smell tasty."

Her feet dangled in the air. She glanced down and saw the remains of a nametag on the uniform. *Connery.* "Noah." One knee-jerk away from sending him to the ground, she suppressed the instinct to take him out.

Snarling, he bared his teeth at her. "Not anymore."

She knew he wasn't Noah anymore, but she had to try. So only he would hear, she said, "It can be okay. We can make an antidote, I'm sure."

He winced, but tossed her against the tree with a furious roar.

"Bodie knows you were trying to make things better. Please."

The big guy stepped closer and rammed his fist into her face. In the flash before impact, she saw his name on his uniform. Simmons. The werewolf from the picture.

The metallic taste of blood flooded her mouth. Closing her teeth together, she grimaced, exquisitely aware of the fracture in her cheekbone.

Across the field, the fight raged on. From the mass of swords and claws, she caught a glimpse of the slick gray of Bodie's fur. Bodie sprinted toward her, leaping over feral carcasses, slipping past those that tried to slow him.

No, she tried to send him away. From danger. From heartache. From the trap intended for *him*.

A satisfied growl gurgled over her head. The big guy stalked toward Bodie.

Putting on the brakes, kicking up a dusty wake, Bodie stopped a few feet from the colossus.

With claws nearly a foot long, gleamingly clean, Simmons' gruff voice rumbled with laughter. He was faster than he looked and swung at Bodie.

Bodie slid under the colossus to dodge the blow. One well-placed hit from those massive claws, and he'd be sliced in half.

Charging, Bodie tore into its inner thigh and dove through his legs.

Again and again, the monster swung, but Bodie dodged with a quick shift to the man or a nip as the wolf.

A cloud of dust billowed in the gray night as Raulf came tearing across the field. Raulf launched for the colossus and landed on its back. He ripped a gash into his neck.

Noah's held her pinned against the tree. Astrid grabbed his hand and swung her legs, locking onto his waist. She twisted and knocked him to the ground. He wrenched from her grip and paused, his sky-blue eyes, pure Connery, bore into hers as he tried to anticipate her next move.

She risked glancing away to check on Bodie. A trail of blood oozed from the Simmons' side. Bodie dove again for the same wound. Alternating, Raulf and Bodie distracted and attacked.

Astrid drew her remaining sword from the sheath and stood ready. "It doesn't have to be this way."

Noah snarled, his lips pulled back. "And what, demon hunters are going to save us all?"

"Together with werewolves? Yes."

Noah moved quick as lightning, leaping at her.

She swung, but her blade did little more than skim his side.

His claw sliced along her ankle.

Furious, she hissed, "Why here? Why come after the pack?"

"Home," he growled, a fierce plea coated with rage. His eyes closed for a brief moment, and she nearly cried for the fleeting progress.

When his eyes opened, he sneered and launched at her. She sliced a gash across his shin.

"Your family loves you. Please, Noah. Fight it. For them. For Bodie. For the little sister you've never even met."

Before he could respond, or attack her again, she heard a pained yelp.

Flipping her head, her tightly woven braid loosened from the swift movement.

Still as the wolf, Bodie flew through the air. Crashing into the ground with an audible thump, his human body lay crumpled in the tall grass.

She swallowed the flaming fury that boiled under her sternum and gripped the corded hilt of her sword as she sprinted, calculating her attack in the few seconds she had to spare.

Raulf snarled, dangling from the monster's outstretched arm, inviting the killing blow.

In a murky, mangy blur, Noah roared and sprinted at the colossus. His blue eyes, so achingly similar to Bodie's, glowed with fury in the gray light of the clouded moon. Tearing at the monster, Noah punched, sliced, gouged with unbreakable feral claws and razor-sharp teeth.

Astrid ran to Bodie, taking advantage of the help, in whatever form it came. His chest rose and fell. He was alive. Bruised, bleeding from his forehead, but he'd be okay.

Noah crunched into the colossus' arm. It yowled and dropped Raulf to the ground.

Furious, his focus clear on his target, Noah pummeled the monster.

Raulf rose to his feet, his knee bent awkwardly, yet he limped back into the fight. Snarling, Noah bashed his foot against Raulf's sternum, sending him flying... away from the fight.

Her team, the other wolves, were making headway in the distance, but the fight was far from over. With controlled, measured breaths, Astrid studied the monster. Noah's buddy from the photos. He'd been the ultimate experiment to create the ideal warrior, but she and her team had yet to find a monster without a weakness.

With Noah distracting him, she came in from behind. She leapt onto his back and drove her sword into the Simmons' neck.

Shaking like a rabid dog, he knocked her off. Landing on the hard ground, her head cracked against the rocky ground. Fuck, he was tough. Her sword remained buried in his neck like an awkward piercing.

Noah launched at him again, snarling and snapping with a focused determination she hadn't seen from a feral. His fur was matted with blood, his own and hers and Simmons', yet he kept diving back into the fray.

She leaped to her feet, launched herself into the air, and vaulted onto the monster's back again. Gripping her blade that was still embedded into the side of the colossus' shoulder, she struggled to remove the blade.

It wouldn't budge. His skin seemed to have healed around it.

Keeping hold like riding a breakneck bull, she didn't let the creature throw her again. From the other side, Noah launched at him again and again.

Still, the monster stood.

In the distance, she saw Bodie pushing up from the ground, his limbs shuddering, giving out on him again and again, yet he pushed on, finally rising to his feet.

Limping closer, he gained momentum, his lips pulled back in furious vengeance.

As she struggled to keep hold, rooting around with her blade in the hopes she could hit something vital, the monster caught Noah by the neck. Squeezing tight until Noah's eyes rolled back, lifeless in his feral body, the monster shook him like a dead rabbit and chucked him across the valley.

Reaching back, the monster grabbed for Astrid.

Anticipating is move, she let go of the blade and tried to dive off. Too late, he caught her by her bleeding ankle in midair.

17

His legs throbbed, bruised to the bone. His arms were heavy at his sides as he fought to wake his broken body. When the fucking colossal feral had chucked him across the valley, Bodie thought he was a goner.

The battle in the valley pressed on. Blood, dust, cracking steel and skulls.

Taking no notice of the sharp gravel under his feet, he forced his body faster. Astrid rode the monster like a resolute cowgirl, her bruised jaw clenched unyielding in determination. She wasn't alone.

Noah? Noah fought *with* her. A weary shimmer of hope fluttered in his chest.

As quickly as the feeling had flickered, it was snuffed out as he watched the monster shake the life out of his feral brother and toss him aside like a used tissue. Raulf's wolf body lie crumpled on the other side of the colossus.

Rage pummeled through him, vengeance pushing him faster. Sprinting across the field, he focused to bring the shift, carefully, so he wouldn't aggravate his injuries.

Before he could complete the change, his heart shattered under his ribs as Astrid was plucked from the air. Swinging her over his head like a lasso, the beast hurled her across the valley. She landed limp and lifeless a few feet from Noah.

Searing hatred, fear, fury pumped through him, red hot steel filling his veins as he watched his family, the woman he loved, all defeated, teetering on the edge between life and death.

Wolf and human pulled at him from both sides. He felt a familiar dominance grasping for control. Prickling over his skin progressed to icy stabbing as his hair thickened into fur. Bulging, aching in his arms, legs, shoulders... everywhere, he cried out as his bones stretched and his fingers morphed into gnarly claws. His face transformed.

Howling in a voice not his own, he looked up at the sky. As if responding to his plea, the full moon pushed away the clouds that blocked it, claiming control of the night. Bigger, brighter than ever, the moon seemed to glow just for him.

Invincible, alive, fucking furious, he challenged the monster that had taken out three of the people he loved in a matter of minutes. Three of the strongest warriors he knew. Wild violence pumped through his veins, hotter than the fury that made him what he was.

The massive mother fucker plodded toward him.

Swaggering, Bodie strode across the field. He bared his jagged teeth with righteous arrogance.

Twice his size, the monster was unimpressed.

In the distance, he could smell the fight was nearly over. Ferals covered the ground like litter, warriors snuffing out the last of them.

Vibrating through his foreign, feral body, Bodie's barrel chest rumbled with vicious laughter. Accelerating, he winked at the colossus asshole as he drew closer.

Tensile steel, thick with dynamic strength, he lunged at the monster.

Claws flying manically, tearing, he gouged the beast's skin.

Ripping, he pulled flesh from bone.

He hardly noticed the colossus bash his beefy fist into his ribs.

Spring-loaded, he bounced right back up when he was knocked down.

Nothing mattered but the fight. The power. The rush.

He kept going, but wrestled inside his own mind to remember why he was fighting. Like a mantra, he chanted in his head with each pummeling strike, *I am Boden Connery. I am fighting for my family. My pack. For the woman I love. For me.*

Coating his veins, his nerves, brutal aggression took over. Lashing out with his claws, he knew the beast anticipated the strike. Spinning, he bashed a closed fist into its gut and dug his claws deep into its opposite flank.

A radiant flash of pure grace sprinted toward them from the distance.

Astrid? She was... *alive*? Not just alive, but brilliantly furious.

Clinging to what humanity he had left, he focused on fighting for her. His family. His pack. His home.

Launching onto the creature's back again, she ignored her sword, wrapping her arms around the beast's chin instead. Wrenching back, she cried out, "Now, Bodie."

He leaped and embedded his claws into the beast's chest and sunk his teeth into its neck. Tearing, he felt the crunch of its trachea as he snapped its jaw and ripped until a gaping hole remained where its throat had been.

Teetering, the colossus spun on its lifeless feet. Astrid wrenched and twisted until its neck snapped.

Bounding off as it fell to its knees, Bodie and Astrid stood on either side of the lifeless beast as it collapsed on the dusty ground, shaking the ground under their feet. Dust billowed into the night, dark blood coating the gravel around its filthy carcass.

Fists clenching at his sides, Bodie's muscles were tense, unyielding. Head spinning, his blood foreign in his own veins, Bodie huffed in and out. The night air bristling through his fur, he sniffed at the blood on the air and was overcome with the urge to *run*...

Something held him here. *I am...* What was it he'd been saying?

Lilting, sweet as the shimmering moon, a voice penetrated the shell around him. "Bodie? Come back to me. Please?"

He closed his eyes, backing away as he tried to drown out the vibrance of the voice, the unwelcome emotion it stirred.

Again and again, she said, "I'm not leaving you. Don't you dare leave me, Bodie."

Stumbling, he growled as he tried to shake the doubt from his brain.

In the distance, he heard another voice. Turning his head, he saw a man approaching... his... Dad? "Bodie, it's going to be okay. We're here for you."

Whipping his head around to dodge another fucking sap, he took off.

Footsteps pounded in the dirt behind him. The woman launched at him, linking her arms around his chest, her legs around his middle. He tried to shake her off, but she rotated around, tackling him onto his back. Pinning him to the ground, outrageously strong, her angelic blond hair fell around his face like a moonlit curtain.

"Dammit, Bodie, I said I'm not leaving you," she roared. "Please don't make me chain you up in the damn library and give you milk bones if you're good."

Twitching at his sides, he struggled to move his arms, but either her freakish strength or his own resistance kept him still.

She continued on, a teary laugh passing her lips. "And I'm not having rough sex with you in this state to bring you back. You're rather revolting at the moment."

His heart beat rhythmically in his chest. He blinked again and again to shake the vision.

"Dammit, Bodie. I love you so much. I'll do whatever it takes to make this work, but I need a little more effort from you."

Tension eased throughout his body. Tingling rushed over his skin like static electricity.

Voice filled with gravel, he growled, "Astrid?"

Laughing, crying, she kept him pinned to the ground. "Yes. Yes, it's me. As I told you when we first met, you don't scare me."

A new heat inundated his veins, joy, thrill, love. His teeth and claws receded. His fur faded away.

He ached from head to toe, but he was back. Reaching up, he wiped the tear from her bruised cheek. Cradling her face, he leaned up and pressed his miraculously human mouth to her soft, watermelon-pink lips. Lingering, he let her warmth, her love seep into him. "Thanks for bringing me back," he murmured, trailing his finger gently along the contour of her jaw.

"Always." Rising to her feet, she sniffled away a sob and reached to help him up.

Grinning, pulling his bottom lip into his teeth. He took her hand and stood tall. Breath steadier, body aching, battered and bruised, he leaned into her to find his balance.

In a blinding rush, Raulf nearly knocked him over, wrapping his arms around him. "Goddammit, Bodie, you scared the hell out of me." Rolling his eyes, Raulf said, "When you said you'd do whatever it takes, I didn't think *that's* what you intended."

Rubbing a hand over the back of his neck, Bodie sighed. "Me neither. I can't say I meant to, but I didn't fight it. When I saw you down, then Astrid get tossed across the field, and—"

Noah.

He took off toward his brother's body. Astrid kept pace, Raulf hobbling behind them on his shattered knee.

As if in a permanent grimace, Noah's feral body lie motionless in a rare patch of wildflowers. Bodie dropped to his side. Astrid stood behind him.

Raulf slumped to the ground at Noah's other side and uttered, "Oh god, Noah, I'm so sorry."

Bodie shook his head. "Dad, don't do that to yourself. He... even as the feral, he pulled himself back. He remembered."

The other werewolves formed a circle around them. Nash was moving pretty slow, but he joined the pack. They were all bruised, no doubt more than a few broken bones between them, but they all rallied to pay their respects. The soothing glow of the moon filled the area with a sense of life, despite so much death.

Limping to join them, Vann stood back, arms folded and expression heavy. Lana leaned against his side. Vann wrapped his arm around her. Bennett saluted in a warrior's farewell. Ryan knelt near Raulf and offered silent condolences. Quinn knelt at his side and brushed a lock of hair out of Noah's face, running her fingers over his almost innocent-appearing furry face.

Noah's hand twitched. His teeth and claws receded. His fur faded. His bones and muscles shifted back to human. Bodie felt his breath catch in his throat, a glimmer of hope.

Now looking like the man who had left all those years ago, Noah's chest rose and fell over the course of a long, shallow breath. The circle around him seemed to hold their breath as Noah took another faint inspiration, and then another.

Hardly recognizing his own voice for the uncertainty it carried, Bodie asked, "Noah? You in there?"

Face contorting in a pained grimace, Noah clenched his eyes tightly closed. His head subtly shook *no*.

Bodie motioned for the crowd to give him space. Astrid immediately followed his meaning and looked toward the bodies from the battle. "Come on."

Behind him, the werewolves gathered their belongings and got dressed, gathered firewood. The warriors piled the feral bodies for a burial pyre.

Supporting his injured leg, Raulf rose to his feet, shifting his weight. Bodie didn't know what to tell him. Raulf and Noah hadn't exactly shared positive words when they last met. Finally, Raulf cleared his throat and limped back a few steps. "I'll, just... I'll be nearby."

"Noah?"

After an eternity, Noah's eyes blinked open. Brilliantly blue, they shined under the light of the moon. Voice full of gravel, Noah asked, "Why. The fuck. Am I. Alive?"

Bodie's heart shattered for his waylaid brother. "I don't know. I'm so sorry. I know you were trying to make it all okay." It just turned out... so, beyond terribly wrong.

Noah chewed his cheek, his body tensing. "Always the fucking optimist, Bodie. I should be dead. I... I can't..."

Bodie sat back on his heels and glanced around. "Didn't exactly turn out how you intended, no. But you survived. You're going to have to live with that."

"Simmons?" Noah jerked up and scanned the valley.

"The big guy?"

"Yeah."

"Dead."

"Good." Sitting up, Noah pulled his legs in and wrapped his arms around his knees. "That guy was fucking crazy. Made me look like the sensible one—don't get me wrong, this whole thing started from *my* idea."

"The serum?"

Noah nodded slowly, face contorted in a grieving grimace as he looked over the dregs of the battle. "We had a pretty logical formula. My idea, so I tried it first. Didn't fucking work." He shook his head and kept looking over the carnage. "It was supposed to allow us to control the feral state, move in and out at will, and function with a clear head." Clenching his hand in his hair, Noah glared into the distance. "As I slipped into the feral, I realized too late that Simmons had messed with the formula. I should have smelled it, I don't know, but I wanted it to work so fucking bad. But then... I couldn't calm down enough to pull out of it. It was like all the grief from that last deployment morphed into a ruthless violence."

Bodie watched the others cleaning up the mess his brother had made. Noah was never going to get over it. And as much as the pack loved him, they'd never trust him again.

Expression still caught in a grimace like his head was pounding with the world's worst migraine, Noah held his palms over his temples. "Simmons made a special recipe for himself, took the serum we'd made and added a whole bunch of shit to it. Testosterone and growth hormones, norepinephrine, MDMA, whatever shit he could get ahold of... as if ferals aren't wild enough. Fuck, he was so angry about our last deployment."

"People go through bad shit in war. They don't turn into... *that*."

"We got creamed, lost our entire squad. Bunch of people died before we even got there. This fucked canyon, full of demons. Couldn't even see them, but we could smell them. Straight from the other side, but they had power."

"That's why you wanted to create an army."

Noah inhaled heavily, nodding. "We weren't going to beat those things as humans, soldiers, or wolves. The idea grew too big, too fast. Fucking eh, we used that serum on ordinary humans to amass our army. We had a contact in a virology lab that was working on gene editing and was disgruntled enough to join us."

"You were feral. You weren't exactly thinking clearly." Bodie held on to all the memories of his larger-than-life big brother. When Noah had carried him all the way home after he'd broken his arm. When he'd lovingly laughed at his awkwardness of his first shift. When he'd told him that he was leaving, but would come back for him one day. "Look, you don't have to tell me all this now. We've got time, now. Let's get you home."

Clenching his jaw, Noah shook his head. "I remember *every-thing*. I was in control, but I wasn't. It was like one long incoherent drug trip." He stared into the distance, his eyes red as he fought back the nightmares that would haunt him for the rest of his life. "There was this part of me that missed you guys so damn much, I needed to come home." He laughed ironically, his voice still full of gravel. "Simmons fucking loved that. I'd told him I hated that you would be stuck taking on the role of alpha because of *me*, but that you were such a natural leader, it was for the best. He got hung up on that and was set on making you one of us."

"You may not have pulled out of it in time, but in the end, you found your way home."

Noah snorted, shaking his head as he took in the remains of the battlefield, the cleanup operation as the team and werewolves took care of the bodies. "It had been coming back for a while. The serum worked, in a way. When I saw you clearing the road that day, with the demon hunter. Seeing you all grown up and happy, something clicked. But pulling out of it was like putting together a million-piece puzzle with my eyes closed while drunk."

Hope still fluttered in Bodie's chest at his brother's life, his humanity, but he knew there was nothing he could do to make it okay. He rose to his feet and extended his hand. Noah accepted the help and pulled himself up. "That's why you led me on that damn wild goose chase that day by the river. Not to change me or test me, but to reach me."

"Yeah, but I couldn't maintain control long enough to stop to talk. Then thanks to that stupid feral that followed me, I nearly made you change to the feral state all on your own, so I kept my distance after. Then it fucking faded again, and, until I saw Simmons tearing you and Dad apart, I found that glimpse of clarity again." Rubbing a hand over the back of his neck, Noah looked around. "I can't go home."

"I know." Sinking like lead in his belly, Bodie knew before Noah even said it. Living with what he'd done... Noah might be right. His death would have been a blessing. Bodie had a hard time not dancing for joy that his brother was alive, but his heart broke for him.

Noah forced a smile. "You did good today. You're going to be a hell of an alpha. Question is, do you want it?"

"I don't know. Maybe. Yeah." He watched the others clearing the field. "Where will you go?"

"Don't know. Nowhere humans are, anyway."

"Look, wherever you go, you'd better call home now and again. Got it?"

Noah grimaced in confusion but shook his head with an air of amusement. "Know what? I will this time. Apparently, you need someone to keep you out of trouble. Come on man, banging the hot demon hunter in the middle of a thunderstorm?"

Bodie caught Astrid's eye. She passed him a sad smile, as if she felt his heart breaking from across the field. He winked at her, letting her know he'd be okay. "Wait, you, uh, you weren't watching, were you?"

"Hell no. Caught the beginning and got my ass out of there. Feral or no, there are some things you just don't want to watch your brother do." He tapped Bodie on the shoulder with an open fist.

Noah looked around again, as the gruesome piles of feral bodies were set on fire. Breath coming fast, he squinted, his dark eyelashes dampening. "Love you, Bodie." Noah pulled Bodie in for a brotherly hug that felt like the goodbye it was intended to be.

Before Bodie could answer, Noah jogged across the field. He grabbed Raulf and gave him a long goodbye hug as well. He stopped to talk for a minute, then hugged their father one last time.

Shifting to the wolf, Noah took off into the moonlit north.

Wandering to Bodie's side, Astrid slipped her hand in his.

18

THERE WAS NO REASON to rush, except Astrid had asked it of them.

Lana dashed down the stairs and out the front door, overloaded with her massive backpack. Astrid watched as Vann stood in the bed of Lana's new truck and caught the flying pack Lana tossed to him. He stuffed it next to the others.

Stopping at her side, Bennett asked, "Want me to get your bag loaded up?" His voice was melty with sympathy.

She swallowed the impatient snap that he could throw it in the damn river. Wow, she had a hell of a temper today. Nodding instead, she followed him out the front door.

Bodie had been quiet last night. They'd all been quiet during the hike back, crashing out at Camp Two for a few hours rest, then skipping the waterfall and heading straight for the trucks and back to the ranch.

After they'd all gone to bed last night, Bodie had stayed up late to talk to Molly about Noah. She hadn't seen Molly yet to thank her for, well, everything.

Astrid had fallen asleep alone. A few hours before dawn, she'd watched Bodie undress in the glow of the moon, then slide in with her. They'd made quiet love and fallen asleep in each other's arms.

She'd felt it then, like she felt it now. Goodbye. She hated goodbyes.

By morning, he was gone again. Off being the alpha he was born to be, going from door to door, updating the pack on the state of things.

Her team was loaded up and ready to go. Bennett hopped on top of their gear for the ride. They'd saved her the driver's seat. Her family loved her.

As she piled in, she felt Quinn squeeze her shoulder from behind. No words were needed. She swallowed the hot lump of... everything, and drove away.

The flight home was mercifully uneventful. She was too miserable to even get airsick, which was neither a blessing nor a curse. The taxi from the airfield was equally dull.

Even when she got home, she felt little relief like she usually experienced on returning home after a long mission. As the taxi pulled away, she stood in the driveway and stared at her modern house.

It had been love at first sight. This house was everything she had been waiting for, from the natural-finished wood with steel beams, the floor-to-ceiling windows overlooking Elliott Bay, to the pots on the front porch she'd filled with cheery flowers. Unlocking the oversized front door, she dropped her luggage in the entry.

The afternoon sun warmed the wooden floors, yet she still felt cold. Plodding to the main bedroom, she opened the curtains to see the golden caps of water and the carefree adventurers enjoying the sunny summer afternoon.

Slipping off her cargos and tank top, she stepped into the walk-in shower. Hot water rushed at her from all sides.

Her parents had never talked about, well, anything, but certainly not the joys and sorrows of demon hunting. Her father never spoke of the grief of killing monsters that might have stood a chance at peace. Nor did he speak of the relief of the team making it out alive. Nor of the crushing pain of having your broken cheekbone repair itself over the course of a day.

Drying herself off with a plush towel, she crossed into her closet and grabbed the nearest pair of yoga pants and her softest tank top. In the kitchen, she popped open a bottle of chardonnay and poured a full glass. Carrying it out to the deck, she curled up on her cushioned outdoor sofa to watch the end of a sunny summer day.

"What the hell are you still doing here?" Grammy jabbed at Bodie with her cane.

After telling his mom about Noah, making stops around the ranch to update the pack, Bodie had come home to find solace, to grieve, to live... with Astrid.

But she'd left him. What the hell? Not even a goodbye? What happened to making it work no matter what?

"Me? Where else would I be?"

"Going after your girl. Don't tell me our next alpha is as dumb as a feral." She ambled to the coffee pot and poured him a travel mug. Filled to the brim. Astrid or one of her team must have restarted the pot when they left.

"Come on. She's got her own life. And it doesn't involve quiet evenings in the middle of nowhere."

The front door opened and slammed shut. Raulf stormed in. "What are you still doing here?"

"Where do you think I should be?"

"Didn't I raise you right at all?" Raulf dropped onto a dining chair across from Bodie. His limp proved he was far from healed, but he kept walking on it.

Bodie shook his head, spinning his lidded travel mug on the table. "My life is here. Hers is... not."

Grammy slid a coffee across the table for Raulf, poured herself one, and parked at the table next to Raulf.

Raulf cleared his throat. "We've been talking, and—"

"Wait, when have you two been talking? This morning?"

With a knowing shrug, Grammy nodded. "We had a conference call while you were walking back, kicking dirt and throwing stones on your way back from Eliza's after you made your rounds this morning."

"A... a conference call?"

Grammy grinned in her chair. "Video chat. We all agreed, we want you to be alpha, but we also love you and want you to be happy. Besides, what good is a mopey leader? We took a vote. We are no longer a monarchy, but a democracy. And we all want you to be alpha. And we all like Astrid."

"I think we've established—"

"Quiet. You're not alpha yet. Let me finish," Grammy snapped.

He would have been put off by the rare reprimand, but she was still smiling at him.

Raulf was looking remarkably pleased as well, leaned back in his chair and smiling over his coffee.

She said, "We're all ready to join the modern world. Today's conference call was good practice."

Raulf jumped in and said, "We're putting in an airstrip in the far field. Thought we'd pick up a snowplow and de-icing stuff while we're at it. I'm not sure how any of all that works yet, but we'll figure it out. Now, before you get all excited, thinking we're doing all this for you, think again. We've all had a bit of a wake-up call. Your mother and a lot of the others are hoping to start traveling more. I'm set in my ways, but I could use a bit of culture. Noah didn't want to stay here. You're restless, too. Rain almost didn't come back, and Morrison's not coming back anytime soon. Maybe we don't need to isolate as much."

Bodie could hardly breathe for the optimism that thundered under his ribs. "I guess I'm confused. I'm to be alpha, become a pilot, and—"

"And go propose to that girl," Grammy said. "You'll make a hell of a demon hunter."

"She already has a team. And I don't know how I'll be able to do *all* of that."

"You're a smart guy. You'll figure it out. Raulf and I will back you up when you can't be here. You know, like vice-alphas. Astrid loves it here. You and she can divide your time between here and, well, wherever. Fifty-fifty."

Raulf rubbed a hand over the back of his neck. "That is, if this is what you want. It's your decision."

Leaning back in his chair, Bodie bit his lip. "You mean, I get to boss you two around? Hell, yeah."

Grammy rolled her eyes.

"Kidding. Sort of." He looked out the window at the serene valley. Home.

Grammy slid a piece of paper across the table. Signed by the entire team, except for Astrid, was her address in Seattle, including a few threats to his life if he doesn't go after her. And his flight information to SeaTac. Presumptuous bunch.

Unable to contain the sappy smile, he let it all sink in. His family, his pack, loved him so damn much they found a way for him to live his life. Not that they'd let him off the hook, but, well hell, he would do anything for the pack.

HOLY SHIT, SHE LIVED well. Maybe this was a bad idea. Bodie felt that damn sinking sensation again as he looked up at the modern, very expensive looking Northwest home. The moment he'd gotten home and realized she'd left... well, that had been a damn terrible moment. But he'd wanted her to choose. So he'd given her space.

She'd chosen wrong.

He closed his eyes, still reeling from the bizarre intervention from Grammy and his dad.

Astrid's grand, modern house cast a long shadow across the driveway. Okay, no problem.

His ranch house, with its outdated style and lack of basic amenities, far from the liveliness of society, wouldn't appeal to a woman who lived in this urban oasis. If that was the right term for it. Honestly, he had no idea what that meant, but it suited.

She had the prettiest flowers adorning her front steps. He grinned, picturing her enjoying her solitude as she watched the world turn. Shit, he should have brought flowers.

He nearly turned back. No, might as well let her accept him for who he was, or... not.

Dashing up to the front door, he rang the bell.

No answer. She was no doubt watching from the fancy security camera and ignoring him.

He knocked.

No answer.

Peering in the window at the side of the door, he could see through to the deck. There she was, damp hair glinting in the sun, watching others play in the golden glow of the summer evening.

He dropped his presumptuously overstuffed backpack on the front porch. Moving around the side of the house, Bodie blazed a trail through the floral shrubs. The deck was high off the ground. He jumped up and grabbed the bottom of the rail to pull himself up.

As he hopped over the rail, her eyes widened, but she otherwise masked her surprise. She set down her glass of wine and pulled her feet onto the couch. Watching him, she made no indication as to whether or not she was happy to see him.

Crossing his arms over his chest, he leaned against the railing. "Didn't think you were the type to run away scared."

Her lush lips teasing a smile, she countered, "And I didn't think you were the type to travel across two states to reprimand someone."

He rubbed his hand over the back of his neck. "About that. It's not so far away. I didn't want you going to bed tonight, thinking you'd..." Shit, this was hard. "Thinking you'd gotten out of our date."

"I'll order takeout, we can have a quick fling, then you can go back home to live your life, and I'll live mine." She turned her nose up in a marked snootiness.

Okay, so this wasn't going at all how he'd planned. She was supposed to leap into his arms and declare her undying love for him and apologize for making him doubt it. Well, maybe not. But something a bit more welcoming.

Crossing the deck, he dropped onto the couch next to her.

She scooted her feet away.

"Astrid, this... I should have said something before you left. I guess a terribly infantile part of me wanted to see what you'd do."

Her hot pink toenails wiggled, but she held back, not quite touching him. He didn't push.

"Honestly? I'm glad you left so I could chase you down. So I could show you that I'll go anywhere for you. So I could sit out in this gorgeous evening with you to enjoy the sunset while we watch the humans you were born to protect. So I could tell you how much I love you, too, and that I want to spend the rest of my life with you, however you'll have me."

This time, Astrid took her bottom lip in her teeth. "You did hear me say it."

"Hell yeah. And, look, we can have rough sex anytime you want. Not just when I need you to save me from myself."

She chuckled, the lyrical quality of it danced over his skin. Wrapping his hands behind her knees, he pulled her legs around his waist and tugged her against him. Cradling her cheeks in his hands, already healed, he pressed his lips to hers. Soft and warm against his, the spice of wine on her lips, she melted into him.

He pulled back just enough. "Your, uh, your team left me a note. Sort of invited me to be 'Seven,' apparently to save Quinn and Ryan from arguing over the name. If you don't mind having a smelly werewolf on your team."

Her mouth curved up at the sides, the joy in it illuminating her brighter than the sun. "I like your stink," she said. Her eyebrows drew concerned. "What about your pack? They need an alpha. I know it's not your dream, but you are the one they look to. You're a gifted leader. Not demanding but decisive. Understanding and thoughtful. If you want it, we'll make it work. Whatever it takes."

"They voted me in via conference call. With Grammy and Raulf as my vice-alphas, so I can live my life, with you. If you don't mind splitting your time between here and the ranch? They're putting in an airstrip. My mom is already planning a shopping trip in Paris."

Astrid trailed her hand along his jaw. "You've got it all figured out, don't you? Dr. Alpha and Demon Hunter."

"Don't forget Spectacular Lover." He grinned and waggled his eyebrows. "Gotta say, there will be tough times, where we're torn between the pack and the team. And, well, we'll either prioritize or divide and conquer. For now, we may need to spend a few weeks here where no one can bother us, at least while I find a contractor to remodel the kitchen."

"Don't overhaul too much, I love that kitchen."

His phone buzzed in his back pocket. Who was the cockblock now?

Six numbers popped up in a group text. It read, *Well?*

Astrid grabbed her phone from the couch behind her. "I got this." *Looks like we're stuck with a smelly werewolf for 7. Careful though, he's a bit of an alpha.*

Bodie wasn't sure who responded, as he didn't recognize any of the numbers, but it read, *Oh darn, guess we'll have to find a real name for the baby.*

Another message popped up with an eye-roll. Then a thumbs up. Another popped up with confetti. Another with a kissy face.

He texted back, *Glad to join. Now shut the hell up so I can propose.*

Before he could shut off the phone, he saw another text, *Ooo, watch out for the bossy alpha.*

Chuckling, he snatched Astrid's phone and tossed their phones onto the table.

He plucked her up off the couch. Her legs wrapped around his waist. Giggling in his arms, she pressed her watermelon-pink lips to his neck as he carried her into the house.

The End

Carrie Thorne is the author of kick-ass romance novels, specializing in white-hot chemistry, healthy relationships, and a mix of action and dreamily falling in love. Whether it's a sinuous flow down a lazy river or evil bad dudes hot on heels, Carrie's stories will draw you in and ruin your sleep. Happily ever afters are for everyone, and kindness is everything.

She's also an introvert who loves people, travel, fitness, video games, food, and is a true Pacific Northwesterner who lives for rain and outdoors and trees and mountains and ocean, and... she's a total dork. At home, she's lucky to have two creative and confident kids, a witty veteran husband she fell at-first-sight for, and a tiny pup snuggled at her side. In addition to writing romance, Carrie has been a nurse practitioner, a Martian and Earthling geologist, a banker, and she is usually elbow-deep in a DIY project in which she bit off more than she could chew.

Where is she now? Depends on the weather. Cozied up by the fire with a steaming mug of black coffee, or stretched out on the hammock with a frothy IPA in the shade of her forest. Either way, she's working on the next great love story to conquer your TBR list.

www.CarrieThorne.com

www.ingramcontent.com/pod-product-compliance
Lightning Source LLC
Chambersburg PA
CBHW021117110726
47900CB00007B/2227